THE

INVASION

R.J. HILL

The Invasion
Copyright © 2021 R.J. Hill
All rights reserved.

www.rjhillauthor.com

ISBN: 978-0-578-84726-9

Images: 123rf.com/VictorZastolskiy, /LiuZishan

EMERGING
INK SOLUTIONS
Kara Scrivener, Editor
www.emergingink.com

For Conner and Rowan

PROLOGUE

He desperately hoped to see his Earth again before he was killed. But now, after decades of travel and being just one standard lunar distance from his target, he was consumed with terror and remorse.

He had wanted to abandon this mission countless times before, but the eternal freezing cosmos around him had made him a prisoner in this massive steel and alloy coffin. Besides, it was too late now.

The countdown had begun – all sights were set on the blue planet, and there was no going back.

PART ONE

"Whoever fights with monsters should look to it that he himself does not become a monster. When you gaze long into the abyss, the abyss also gazes into you."

Nietzsche

CHAPTER ONE

Day One: 1545 Hours

Donovan McCallister had always felt comfortable speaking in front of an audience, but as he glanced over his notes, he noticed his hands were sweaty and trembling. He nervously shifted his weight from one foot to the other. Standing in an expensive and form-fitting Hugo Boss suit to the left of the stage, Donovan was out of the lights and watchful gazes of the hundred or so people seated in the uncomfortable metal chairs before him.

He was an average five-foot-eleven, had a pronounced chin covered in a perpetual five o'clock shadow that hid a thin-rooted smile line, and eyebrows everyone would swear were professionally done. He had razor-sharp, blue eyes obscured by rimless square glasses that he would call his "readers" but that he wore more often than not. A boyish mop of salt-and-pepper hair he had trained to the right of his face never obeyed, no matter his styling. If Donovan could spend time on his muscle and skin tone, he would be what most women would call a very handsome man. Unfortunately, decades of working in labs and under harsh fluorescent lighting had softened his rugged looks and paled his complexion.

The promotion, among many things, meant no more T-shirts and Levi's to work. He had known taking the position of Director of Development at Imperium Energy Corporation, or IEC, would come with a heavy workload, but what he hadn't realized was that it primarily meant constant meetings, boring conference calls, and endless speeches. But by no means did he ever think he would be giving a presentation like this. He was a hands-in-the-dirt kind of guy and hated the sight of podiums, stages, or investors.

Wetting his suddenly dry lips, Donovan took out his silk pocket square emblazoned with the IEC insignia and dabbed the perspiration from his forehead. The pocket square had been in a gift basket from Eli Govern, the CEO of IEC. It was undoubtedly a formality, but the 2025 La Rioja Alta included was possibly the best bottle of wine he had ever had. It would have been nice to celebrate with a family of his own, but Donovan's ambitions left little time for dating, much less children. Yet Donny, as his few friends at the security gates would call him, still felt compunction for being promoted over the 25 on the list who were more qualified than him, but it was as he had always been told – never look a gift horse in the mouth.

He had gotten into this business purely for the science 20 years ago, and now, with the additional zeros in his paychecks, he wondered if he had sold out. Donovan was an MIT graduate with near-genius intellect. He had tried time and time again to convince himself that he was still a scientist, but the higher up the corporate ladder he went, the further away the field work became. Nevertheless, he had devoted his life's work to this company and was there for the long haul.

He could tell by the swell of commotion and the new set of black suits shuffling around that the vice president had finally arrived and the presentation was set to begin. Donovan choked down final sips from his Fiji water bottle and cleared his throat. He was accustomed to speaking to investors and shareholders about prospectuses and profit margins, but never about something with such profundity to the most powerful men in America.

Cathy Fawkins, Director of Public Relations, a tall, slender woman with the face of a vulture, walked to the podium, her pants suit perfectly fitting to her every stride. Her short, black hair curled at her shoulders to accentuate a long, featureless neck. She brandished no jewelry or makeup. The slight swell of her small breasts under her Anne Klein executive suit jacket was the only hint of sexuality she exuded.

Cathy was succinct, brief, and humorless; that's probably why the higher ups loved her. She talked for a boring five minutes with the obligatory thank yous, mundane corporate vision statements, and the obsequious 'who made it possible' flattery. She ended by introducing Donovan to no applause and no buzz of chatter. These were stoic military and government officials; adulation was not in their M.O.

Donovan glided to the podium, eyes trained on his feet, determined not to misstep. He set his notes down and looked at the sea of military uniforms and expensive suits with stern faces. The room was movie-theater dark, long, narrow, and dead quiet. Gray soundproof pads – which seemed wholly unnecessary – adorned textured, tan walls. The air was stuffy and dense, the kind expected in a basement which hadn't felt fresh air in a decade. Being several floors beneath ground level had a way of making the recycled air seem thick and heavy.

He believed he was still in the Navy building he had originally entered, but with all the corridors and elevators he had been led through, he actually had no clue where he was currently located. He had the feeling they wanted it that way. The offices of EIC were in the same city, not far from where he was standing now. He was used to doing these kinds of talks from there. The fact that they had sent him to the depths of this building was quite disconcerting. What Donovan McCalister was about to unveil to the leaders of the free world would have implications that could last millennia.

"Mr. Vice President," Donovan began in a strong, confident voice, "distinguished military personnel, and members of the board, thank you very much for attending this afternoon's presentation."

The bare room seemed vast with space and stillness. Bright lights directed at the podium made it so Donovan could only see the reflection of eye glasses and the flash of fancy badges from his vantage. A large, balding man with spectacles glued high to his nose and a pudgy face cleared his throat in the back of the room, breaking the heavy silence. Donovan recognized through the darkness that it was Jeffery Jordan, the United States Secretary of Energy.

Jesus Christ, Donovan thought to himself. *Everyone's here.*

"As you all know, for the last decade, the United States of America has been the world leader in using nuclear resources for all its energy and military needs. And," Donovan pushed his glasses back on his nose, "Imperium Energy Corporation has been the company setting the standard on all U.S. nuclear energy wants. Our development of state-of-the-art enriching techniques 15 years ago cut the cost of the enrichment of uranium-235 by two-thirds. This, in turn, led to a boom in uranium mining and processing. This boom, of course, led to a substantial increase in nuclear reactor development. Consequently, we experienced an immense increase in energy production."

Although Donovan had not been in his position for very long, he had this part of the speech memorized. They were the go-to corporate talking points when speaking to any government officials or prospective investors. Although the mouthy explanations had become rather banal to Donovan, the technology was actually quite miraculous. It had literally revolutionized the field of nuclear energy production. And it was thanks to Donovan and his team that this technology even existed in the first place.

"Six years ago, because of developments made by IEC, the last non-nuclear power plant was shut down – for good," Donovan said, peering over his glasses with pride. This, to Donovan's surprise, received applause from the crowd he had begun to believe was completely emotionless and indifferent. "With the introduction of the U.S. Department of Defense's newest Titan-class nuclear destroyer, the entire military is now completely free of fossil fuels and powered entirely by nuclear energy. The nuclear consumption rate in the U.S. alone has sextupled in the last 20 years and we've been able to keep up by capitalizing on a few new mines in Niger. But to maintain that kind of production, we were forced to dredge into our stores for nuclear material."

With this, Donovan pulled out a small, black remote control from the podium's inner shelf and clicked to life the projector along the ceiling. With a faint hum from above their heads, an image of the world came to focus on the screen to the right of Donovan.

"Here is where the world received its uranium in 2020, roughly 25 years ago."

Donovan, still brandishing the remote, held it down at arm's length. He peered down the bridge of his nose under the frame of his glasses and subtly squinted to find his focus on the small device. He was only 42, but had certain idiosyncrasies of a man in his sixties. He thumbed the button he was looking for so a fulgent, green laser cut through the stuffy air. He began pointing with the device to the various red dots that were illuminated on the projected map.

"The mines in these six countries – Canada, Kazakhstan, Australia, Niger, Russia, and Namibia – were supplying an estimated 2,000 tons of uranium worldwide. Today, those same mines are being utilized, but for a world consumption of 45,000 tons. That's roughly a 2,500 percent increase in just two decades. And, as our honored guests in the military will concur, we have been at the brink of nuclear war for the last 18 months, a consequence of discovering that these mines were all but tapped out. Uranium became an endangered commodity. This, as we know, sent half the world into a serious economic downturn. We had gone nuclear, but Mother Nature only supplied us with so much ore. The second cold war with North Korea jumpstarted the world's superpowers on a nuclear-warhead-building frenzy, thus depleting the uranium supply even further."

Donovan clicked to the next slide and a set of data-crowded charts appeared overhead. This part of the presentation Donovan had actually contributed to and thoroughly enjoyed. Although to the layman's ears it was full of scientific jargon and mathematical theoretical computations, for Donovan this was his life's work.

For the next ten minutes, Donovan described in detail the revolutionary technologies he had helped develop for uranium enrichment that had completely upended previously established practices. It was a technology that had made IEC the largest and wealthiest energy company on the planet and, as Donovan liked to think, had brought a majority of the planet out of poverty and into modernity.

"And with that," Donovan concluded, dramatically

pulling the glasses from his face and placing them on the podium, "I will tell you why you are here."

There was a small commotion and creaking of chairs as the powerful and important men and women in the audience shifted in anticipation. Another slide transitioned onto the screen. A map of the northern half of Arizona and southern half of Colorado illuminated on the white canvas to Donovan's right. The map was featureless except for a large highlighted area that encircled the border of the two states.

"Approximately 60 years ago in the 1980s," Donovan continued, excitement creeping into his voice, "what are known as 'collapse-breccia pipes' or just 'breccia pipes,' were found here."

The area he pointed to was large, the size of Connecticut, and straddled the border of the two western states. The map was a satellite-transit map that showed the natural topography as well as roads and towns. Cedar City, Colorado, Flagstaff, Arizona, The Grand Canyon, and Zion National Park were the only cities and natural features displayed on the map.

"Mining operations were established soon after, and a fair amount of enrichable material was pulled from the ground. The veins of material, primarily in northern Arizona, were deep, at about 3,000 feet, and were relatively modest, at approximately 300 feet across. By 2010, it was assumed that it had been mined dry, and we went searching for better, more prosperous mines. However, 18 months ago we discovered something astonishing. IEC mine developers went back to the mine sites with the suspicion there was more to be found. Their suspicions were correct. A UMP, or unmanned mining probe, drilled down past the 3,000-foot mark, and this is what we found..."

The next slide overlaid a red misshapen oval atop the yellow one, encompassing an area essentially three times larger than the highlighted space.

"What we have here, here in the red circle which, by the

way, has been verified by both lab results and field tests, is
a network of untapped uranium pipes the size the world
has never seen, the size we didn't even know could
possibly exist. Our most conservative estimates are
upwards of 200 million tons. We have already extracted
most of it and are currently transporting it here to
classified, well-protected underground storage facilities
just outside of the city."

Instantly a buzz of voices and energy filled the
room as heads turned to look at each other; several
mouths remained agape. High-ranking men in blue and
olive military uniforms, left breasts adorned with countless
ribbons and medals, began conversing with each other.
Both hands gripping the edges of the podium, Donovan
paused. He took a half-step back and scanned the
audience to let the gravity of the information they had just
received digest for a moment. He moistened his lips with
the tip of his tongue and continued.

"The ramifications for a discovery of this
magnitude will impact both the economy and the military
profoundly. Very soon we will be the sole manufacturer
and supplier of nuclear energy and nuclear weapons
worldwide, becoming once and for all, the world's greatest
and only nuclear provider for energy and milit –"

"This is a goddamn matter of national security!"
interrupted a short, muscular man with a tight crop of
blond hair and fierce black eyes as he sprang from his
chair.

Although Donovan didn't recognize him, the stars
on his shoulders and the mere fact that he was in
attendance verified that he must be an important figure.

"Why wasn't the pentagon notified of this?" the
major general barked. "Do you have *any* goddamn idea

what Russia or the DPRK would do if they knew we had this? Half the goddamn Earth will ally up against us!"

With this, a man who had been standing off in the corner of the room hidden in the shadows, raced to the podium. Ted Mahone, a featureless individual except for a wide, toothy grin he brandished no matter the circumstances, bounced into the picture. He was the Chief Operations Officer of IEC, a position he loved for the power in a company he loved for the money. He made it to the podium in three long strides, the entire time his movie-star smile displayed in the direction of the vice president.

"Thank you, Donny," Ted sang in a hearty deep tenor, relinquishing Donovan of his speaking duties. Ted charismatically put a large hand at Donovan's side and gave him a nudge, pushing him from the podium. Donovan, before he even knew what was happening, was being escorted off the stage by a 20-something-year-old pretty blonde who was unable to hide her contrite embarrassment.

Lindsey Burnside had been working for IEC for three years and already showed signs of burnout. She was average-sized for a girl, just over five-seven, but the expensive black heels she invariably wore tipped her toward the side of too tall. She had a pretty face with or without the concealer she painted on that was just a shade too dark to match her complexion and blond hair that, despite being in a neat bun, seemed to escape in aberrant wisps around her cheeks. Her full bosom pushed its way past her stylish, two-button black jacket, emphasizing her prominent visual attribute.

She had known that it was her looks and flirtations that had initially gotten her the job, but it was her grit that had gotten her to this coveted position. It turned out she loved the corporate world and had a knack for it. She was as cunning and cutthroat as the next guy but worked twice as hard. And best of all, Ted Mahone loved her. She followed Mr. Mahone's every order, even the ones that seemed a little out of the ordinary – like the one he had given tonight.

Several hours earlier, Lindsey had been called into his temporary office in the massive military building. Mr. Mahone always wore a conniving look, but she was dubious of the expression today.

"Hey you, come on in," he half-flirted, half-ordered.

She told herself she hated when he talked to her like that, but deep down she was attracted to her boss. The power, the influence, the charm – he was her senior by two decades, but had all the aspects of a man to admire. Unfortunately, his eyes were, like always, focused on her chest, a reaction from men she had known since puberty. It still, however, brought up a terrible feeling and worse a disturbing memory.

Lindsey grew up in a small apartment in Chicago with her dad. Her mom had left the sprouting family early on, seeking a career and fortune out west where "people are more like-minded to me," as she would so often say in one of their countless vicious arguments. The Lincoln Park area of Chicago was, continuing through the 2030s, an affluent and highly sought-after neighborhood. However, between the election of the last president and the regulations established by the newly-elected mayor of the city, it quickly turned into a new center of drug use, poverty, and squalor.

She often heard her dad late at night after he had finished the last six pack of homewreckers, talking to one of his friends. His friends now stayed over later and later, and drank more and more beer. She would hear her dad say how unbelievable it was that, for the first time in history, women were allowed to leave men with sole custody of children. "There's equality for ya, fucking up today's youth," he would say. But Felix had actually fought hard in court for Lindsey's custody and believed that he could raise a daughter that would be pure in not only nature, but in faith.

Unfortunately, the artificial intelligence market boom had turned bust and sent the economy into a harsh downturn. That had shifted Felix's focus away from his little daughter and into survival mode, leaving Lindsey to her own devices – a young teen in a big city.

She had developed breasts extraordinarily early and had thus learned early on how to distract men. At first, she thought it was just a silly, innocuous feature. To Lindsey, it was just another kooky way of getting boys' attention and recognition. But the "silliness" of her new, large bosom had, almost as quickly as it had grown in, made her life susceptible to trouble.

It had gotten to the point of dangerous one night in late October when she was 15. Her dad's friend Amheel, a work buddy they had known for only a couple months, overstayed his welcome one night and had one too many beers. As the night dragged on, Amheel and Lindsey's father started yelling at the TV, making their way with ease through the 30-pack. She always ended up staying up late with her old man when he had friends over, partly because the apartment was so small and partly because they always got drunk and loud. Normally she didn't mind it and laughed at their drunkenness. But that night was different.

Lindsey always refused the drinks her dad's friends and her dad would offer, but that Tuesday night she decided to choke one down. The buzz that hit her was quick and strong, and Ahmeel's obvious glances began to bother her less. *Fuck it, another creepy pervert*, she told herself. But as the hours and beers ticked by,

Amheel's eyes grew droopier and glossier and the glances turned to stares. Ahmeel became more interested in Lindsey just as her dad became more interested in going to bed.

Her father finally tapped out for the evening, telling Ahmeel to make himself at home and crash on the couch if he needed to. Eventually, it was only Lindsey and him in the small kitchen. Too many minutes ticked by with only the two of them up, so, politely as she could, she excused herself. Lindsey remembered saying goodnight to her dad's intoxicated friend and trying to edge past him to the door to the hallway.

She remembered his hand grabbing the top of her arm as he playfully asked where she was going. She, as tolerating as she could be, pulled her arm from his grasp and told him she thought it was time for the party to end. His immediate response was a hiss whispered through a toothy grin. "The party's just getting started." The alcohol was so strong on his breath she thought her buzz would return.

Lindsey told him that it was late, that it was her bedtime, and that her dad wouldn't like her being up so late on a weeknight. Amheel, not seeming to care about this blatant reference to her father and host of the home, grabbed Lindsey by the buttocks and squeezed hard. His eyes fixed on her breasts, he started with his vulgar compliments. Too frozen with fear and discomfort, she didn't move. His hand had begun to make its way up her shirt before her dad finally reappeared.

It took all of two seconds for her dad's *friend* to have his teeth rearranged in a way that would never look the same.

After the incident, Lindsey stood shaken and

disturbed, weeping into her father's arms as the police dragged the pervert away. It was there, in her father's embrace, that she learned valuable lessons of being formidable and tough and to never cede any ground to anyone, no matter male or female. It was there that her father told her that sometimes it was okay – no, sometimes it was *good* – to use physical force if something truly bad was being done to her or anyone she loved. It was there that she learned lessons that would follow her throughout her life. Lessons that would make her a fighter and a survivor. Lessons that brought her into her role in the IEC energy corporation.

Mr. Mahone, oblivious of her sinking thoughts continued. "Big meeting today... huge announcements and probably the highest profile audience to date. Listen, I need you to do something that will seem kinda odd, but you must do it if the need arises. Are you okay with that?" he asked, steepling his fingers as he leaned back in his drab, creaking metal chair.

He told Lindsey that during the presentation, the second any military or important government personnel asked a tough question or posed a comment for the stammering Donovan, she was to hurry to the stage, grab Donovan as politely as she could, and bring him to the reception room. No questions asked.

Donovan followed the young woman offstage. Only when she briefly relinquished his arm was he able to find the surprisingly youthful face of a woman grinning at him. He froze not knowing how to respond to her shocking beauty or to her persistent authority. He had never experienced anything like this in all his years at the company and floundered for a moment between anger, embarrassment, and bewilderment. Could a woman that looked half his age really be leading him off the stage like an ill-prepared talent show contestant bombing his act?

This was possibly the biggest talk of his career and with the tug of a sleeve, he had allowed himself and his attention to be redirected.

He glanced back at Ted who had the remote in hand and had already turned off the projector, ending everything Donovan was there to talk about. As the young woman continued to usher Donovan away – more like, drag away – Donovan had a moment to scan the audience without the fierce glare of spotlights to see, for the first time, who was in attendance.

In a room that held roughly 100, he saw mostly military uniforms. Come to think of it, he recognized only a couple faces of people from the energy industry. He had worked at IEC for a long time and had shaken hands and drank champagne with all the who's-who of the energy and nuclear community. He was even on a first-name basis with some of the guy's wives and children, and could remember at least a half dozen vacations with fellow energy sector families. But in this small sea of suits and faces, he recognized almost none. He knew the Energy Secretary, a handful of lobbyists, and a couple of guys he worked with at IEC, but other than that, it was all military and government people. Them, and armed security – lots of armed security.

It wasn't until he passed through a huge, steel blast door that Donovan finally woke from his lumbering trance to realize that she had led him several hundred yards. The door looked out of place in the office building corridor. It was six-by-four-feet wide and was not the same drab tan as the rest. This was cold, black steel reinforced with imposing bank-like safe locks. Was this to keep people in or out, he wondered.

The mighty portal looked as if it could withstand a massive explosion. At this realization Donovan stopped in his tracks. He grabbed the woman by the arm, with a little more force than he meant to, and blurted, "Uh ma'am. What's going on? I was halfway through my –"

"Fantastic presentation, Mr. McCalister!" the cheerful woman exclaimed, cutting him off. "I was told to bring you to the B-1 board room for the reception when you were done."

"Yeah, okay great... thanks... but I wasn't finished with my pr –" Donovan replied, obvious irritation in his voice.

"Looks like fun! Champaign, catering, and all –"

Donovan frowned. "Well, thank you. That does sound like fun and all, but I really think I need to be going back. I know there is a Q-and-A session that I need to be part of."

"No, no, that's all we required of you tonight. Thanks again so much fo –"

"Listen, what the hell is going on?" Donovan demanded. "Why are you taking me away from that room? What exactly is going on here?"

The woman pulled her arm free of Donovan's grasp with a look that could be described only as hurt. Her cheery smile faded and the face of a girl her age broke the surface, annoyed and pestilent. "Mr. Mahone just told me when he gives a *sign*," she air-quoted with her fingers, "to get you and escort you to the B-1 room for the reception, no matter where you were in the presentation. He told me the second he gets up to walk to the podium, I am, as politely as possible, to get you off the stage. No questions asked, he said. I have no idea why." She slouched, but the look on her face hardened. She may have been young, but this woman was obviously strong.

Donovan stood in the narrow hallway, staring at the polished linoleum floor. The square tiles were so highly glossed they reflected the nonstop buzzing of the fluorescent lightbulb tubes overhead. The hallway seemed endless, stark, and forgettable, as most government building corridors were. He was lost, perplexed by the events that had just unfolded. He stood there for several moments with the young woman in flummoxed silence. He had truly assumed he had attained a position of power and importance, and to have him hurried off the stage like a misbehaving child... He couldn't understand. Why in the world would Ted have him removed –

An earth-shattering boom broke his concentration. That's when it all started.

CHAPTER TWO

Day One: 0819 Hours

Sam Hunt's relief was running late again and nothing pissed him off more than less-than-punctual people, especially when their negligence chewed into his vacation time. Sam had heavy, dark bags under his eyes; the third cup of coffee he was working on didn't seem to make a dent in his grogginess. It had been another busy one at the station that night and he was in no mood to put up with other people's bullshit.

Leaning on the large, commercial steel kitchen counter, he stared at the ticking hands of the clock and then shook his head, an impetuous glare carved into his eyes. He drummed his fingers on the shiny surface, watching the specks of food and dust bounce around. Normally he would get a cloth and wipe it, but he was sick of this place and didn't give a shit. In just a couple of minutes – if that bastard showed up – this place would be someone else's problem, someone else's mess. He hadn't even bothered putting his uniform on that morning and was in his cargo pants, a worn, brown "fill-the-boot" shirt, and black tennis shoes.

Sam had a solid six-two muscular frame where decades of lifting weights showed through his cotton shirt. Intense, steel-gray eyes were tucked in deep sockets adorned with crow's feet which added years to his lagging boyish looks. Sam was only 36, but years of late nights and not taking care of his body made him look significantly older. He sported a crop of buzzed, dark-brown hair that was gray in places. His nose flattened on the bridge where it had been broken more than once in his younger more rambunctious days. He had a sleeve of tattoos that covered his left arm and several more that he could cover with a collared shirt. Besides the initial intimidating appearance of the man, he was fairly good-looking and usually bore a smile, except for days like today when some asshole was making him late for his family trip.

When his relief *finally* sauntered through the station door, Sam dramatically brought up his wrist, tapped his Luminox wristwatch, and strode past him straight out the door without a word.

"Good morning to you too, Sammy boy," his relief had the audacity to mutter. Sam answered very clearly with a middle finger aimed straight to the sky.

Although he was certain that this had been his life's calling, there were days when he just wanted to go-the-hell home. He had been a firefighter for nearly 15 years and a paramedic for half of those. And although with the newest in building materials and codes, house fires were a rarity, people found newer and more imaginative ways of dying or mortally wounding themselves.

There had been a 25-year booming economy and the quality of citizens' lives had substantially increased over the past half-century. The average lifespan was nearly 100 years and cancers and chronic diseases were a thing of the past, but people were interesting animals and found ways to die all the same. It seemed to Sam that people's respect or love for life was, for whatever reason, waning. People were killing each other and themselves at higher rates than anyone could recall in the last quarter-century.

Sam often thought to himself that Nietzsche was

right. When people only have to occupy their time with sleeping, eating cakes, and the continuation of the species, they will burn it all down just for something interesting to happen.

It had been a long night of 911 calls and this vacation couldn't come soon enough. San Diego had been a family destination every year since his kids were born. As of late, the trips out there were not so much for leisure, but to visit his ailing and increasingly-needy mother. Regardless, it remained his favorite city to visit and, to ice the cake, his older brother, whom he had always looked up to, was meeting up with them there. He could not wait to see his ugly mug.

Sam climbed into the charcoal-gray 2043 Chevy Magnum, a vehicle that appeared like an aught's Suburban-looking monstrosity but with smoother edges and modern design. New to him, it was nothing like his 25-year-old Silverado three-quarter ton, gas-burning truck. Sure, this new thing had touch-screen navigation, incredible self-driving capabilities, a heads-up windshield display of MPH, road maps, and interactive music channels, and anything else you could possibly want to download, but it was no Silverado. The silent and powerful vehicle was completely electric, able to cruise a solid 800 miles on a single charge, and fast as hell.

But if he was being perfectly honest, he missed the growling hum of the archaic gas-guzzler. He sat at the wheel and closed his eyes. He did his customary deep sigh as he exhaled the last two days of work out of his system and made the drive home to the people he adored more than anything in the world.

They were already packed up and waiting in the driveway when Sam arrived home some 30 minutes later. He pulled into the driveway, keeping to the right to hug the garden wall like always. His house was a 19-mile drive from where he worked, quite a long commute in this town, but he absolutely loved the suburban feel of the neighborhood; it was worth living a little further out of town. The houses were crowded together, each one vaguely reminiscent of the last. Shimmering solar panel shingles and siding made him feel as if he were living in a futuristic space colony, but the green oaks and fiery red cherry trees that lined the street put him at ease. The fact that his kids could walk safely through the streets to the park made it all worth it.

As he pulled in, his wife Maggie appeared, standing on top of the three-foot block wall that contained their front garden to give him a tired, but loving look. Years of motherhood and graceful aging had turned her runner's body soft and made her tomboy face slightly wrinkled, but Sam still saw her as stunning.

She had crisp, natural red hair with a hint of gray that laid gently over her collar bones. Her prominent cheekbones and large, round eyes fit perfectly into the deepening lines that had begun to crease around her delicate face. Full eyebrows and sensually long eyelashes that the years had never seemed able to tame were what made her so attractive.

Two kids had made her marathon-running days a thing of the past, but years of marriage made such trivialities like that the last thing a husband worried about. The floral, yellow sundress she wore picked up just enough of the breeze to reveal the fading blue ankle tattoo atop her smooth, olive skin.

But it was what was on the block between her bare feet that Sam knew would make the long drive both excruciatingly silent and long. A three-quarters-empty bottle of Jim Beam sat on exhibit on the wall between her legs, evidence of his slow slip into the darkness that he had flirted with too many times before.

"Hey babe, we all ready to go?" Sam said softly, feigning ignorance.

"Really Sam, almost a whole bottle of bourbon in one night?" Maggie whispered with disdain so the kids couldn't hear her. "I knew you were drunk but, really?"

"Baby, I —"

"I don't wanna talk about this now. The kids are dying to see you. They're all packed and ready to go. Just, please promise me you won't be drinking that heavy on this trip," she pleaded.

"I promise," Sam replied, walking up the steps and grabbing her around the waist. He kissed her hard and passionately, sealing the promise with the touch of their lips.

Their kids Zachary and Liam, 14 and 9 respectively, had taken the initiative of packing the car and were squirming with excitement. They were good kids and better brothers. They were best friends, and although Zachary was perfecting his rebellious side, he wouldn't let his younger brother start that epoch yet out of pure love and respect for his parents. The neighborhood was teeming with kids their age, but most of the time the boys wouldn't leave the house unless they were together.

The two boys and their mom had packed themselves in tight with a week's worth of food, bedding, toys, and all the beach gear a family of four could possibly need. Sam knew full-well that the ten-hour drive would be painfully mundane with a cloud of palpable tension suspended between Maggie and himself. They had had another fight only a couple weeks before on account of his drinking again. Sam had an acute talent to be able to start a fight with his wife before any big family foray. But he was hellbent on making this trip a good one. He knew even if it was the last thing he did, he would make this family whole again.

Once Maggie changed into jeans and a shirt and hurried back out to the car, Sam started the muted electric engine and plotted his course on the windshield map for San Diego. He took a second to take his wife's knee into his hand and give her a playful wink, a gesture he had done for the entirety of their relationship, a cursory "I'm sorry" and "I love you" wrapped up in one motion. She smiled back, her eyes frescoed with a look of true love, a look that made him wince with disbelief at his luck in finding a woman like her. He touched another button on the windshield, switching the rear-view camera to train on the back seat so he could take in the love he had for his two boys. And with that, he left his driveway in his suburban neighborhood and headed west to the most devastating week of their lives.

As they drove through the neighborhood, Sam found a small button on the steering wheel which prompted a menu on the windshield; "phone directory" flashed. "Call Brosky," he ordered into the microphone hidden somewhere in the dash. A picture of his brother appeared on the screen in the upper left corner of the windshield. Several rings went by before an answer.

"Hey, fucker!" his charming older brother Paul exclaimed over the car's eight-speaker audio system; the boys chuckled in the back seat.

"Kids are in on this, bro," Sam replied, rolling his eyes to the unhappy glance his wife gave.

"Oh fu – I mean, *shoot*! My bad. Hey, little losers!"

"Hi Uncle Paul!" the two of them cheered back in unison, their admiration of him obvious in their voices.

Paul Hunt was a stud of a man. Shorter than Sam but twice the musculature, he was a force to be reckoned with. He had joined the military right out of high school and had made it easily through boot camp. He had enrolled as fast as he could for the Special Forces to "actually be tested for once," he would gloat. He was covered with tattoos and donned a beard that made him look both charismatic and insane.

After his ten years in the military, he had gone to work as private security in Saudi Arabia after the war. He always joked that since the U.S. had been in the regional quagmire for 50 years, he might as well make a career of it. He loved serving and he loved adventure; he was a military man through and through.

Paul had many demons that followed him throughout his life. The ones that haunted him the most at night were those he wouldn't talk about, and were the reason he preferred the company of a bottle of Maker's Mark over just about anyone or anything. They were also why he loved his nephews so damn much, and why he felt such a deep need to protect the two young men.

During his first tour in Iran, Paul had been on patrol duty with a squad of local legendary hard-asses. At first, he had loved the reputation and the respect the squad of eight had garnered from the rest of the battalion. They had acquired a sort of celebrity notoriety for the shit they did over their four months of the deployment. The Hateful Eight, what they had become known as at the base and on the streets, had become his new identity. It was a name that sounded fucking cool to the new guys fresh off the plane; to most of the fellas that had been there for any amount of time however, they knew that the name meant only one thing: merciless assholes.

Most of his operations had been pretty standard for a war zone and hadn't bothered him too much. It had only really hit him hard one day in late May when the heat was unlivable and the sun seemed to refuse to go down. The squad had received orders to find and take (dead or alive) one especially evil haji supposedly holed up in the basement of a local, half-blown-to-hell elementary school. The mission had started off according to plan. But in no time, it went to hell and became the genesis of his PTSD.

The Hateful Eight had made entrance to the building with precise shots to exact locations and had made it to the strategic position flawlessly. There had been only three shots fired – into the brains of ratty-looking sentries holding turn-of-the-century AR-15s.

The squad, with years of practice and perfection under their belts, knew exactly how to raid a building like this with near zero casualties. But this mission had gone the opposite direction.

Paul had been on point for this particular raid and had waited for the breaching charge or master key, as they call it, to do its job. With a squeeze of the detonator, the door was blown clean off its rusted, metal-hinged frame, and burst inward with a deafening explosion and subsequent heat and percussion. Paul entered first, clearing the short stairway down to the school basement-turned-subterranean-military-fortification.

The first things he encountered at the bottom of the stairway were the muzzles of two machine gun barrels that, for some reason, did not fire on him. Without hesitation, Paul aimed at the figures holding the weapons and fired a burst into each combatant. The threat was quickly neutralized, but the damage had been done, and had been life-changing. The two figures holding the machine guns had been two young children around ten years of age. Paul, upon realizing what had just transpired, fell to his knees in disbelief.

The squad had filed in behind, flown past him, and finished the mission quickly. Paul remained on his knees, silent and wide-eyed. He was never able to rid himself of those ghosts.

Afterward, Paul had made it up the private security ladder quickly and was on a short list of men who were requested by name for high-profile security jobs. He hadn't been given much info about the specific assignment, but he had read through the encrypted email which stated that he was to be highly armed for some kind of meeting between the government and a big energy company. He had gotten used to clandestine meetings with powerful people and foreign dignitaries, but this one – which was to take place on a San Diego naval base – seemed considerably more important than most. There had been rumors that the vice president of the United States would even be in attendance.

"So, we will be in town in about seven to eight," Sam continued, ignoring his brother's language. "When are you gonna be done with whatever secret-agent mission they have you on now?"

"Yeah, I'll be doing detail all day starting here in like an hour, but Wednesday, let's meet up and go visit our dear mother," Paul sarcastically mused.

"What the fuck do they have you doing this time?" Sam scoffed. At this, Maggie turned to him with an incredulous look of disgust on her face. Sam mouthed, "Sorry" to her, realizing he had cursed in front of the boys.

"Whoa whoa, I thought you had kids in the car," Paul chided mockingly.

"Yeah, tomorrow sounds good, man. Be safe."

"See you creeps tomorrow!" Paul roused the boys and hung up the phone before they could reply.

"Just promise me you guys won't go out all night again,"

pleaded Maggie. "That was horrible the last time you two got together."

"Baby, that was my dad's funeral. That was a one-time-thing. Of course, it won't be like that again," Sam replied with a hint of guilt. How many times had he said the same thing before?

Three years ago was the last time the brothers had been together. They had gone to San Diego to lay their father to rest. John Hunt, a man who had worked as a cop for over 30 years, had plain and simple drank himself to death. He was a good man and was loved dearly by his two sons and close family. He, like so many, had his list of vices and drinking was right there at the top. The celebration of life was short with only a handful of people in attendance.

John had been a friendly enough guy, but he had burned so many bridges over the years that most people he considered good friends had written him off completely. This had been heartbreaking and depressing for Paul and Sam to witness, and both of them had taken silent vows to not follow in their father's footsteps. But that night after the celebration, Sam and Paul tied one on that left them both hungover for days. It left Maggie and the kids essentially alone and was one of the worst San Diego trips in their recent memory.

After the death of their father, spending time with their mom had become more of a chore than a delight. The family over the years had grown distant in values and interests, and the only person who didn't seem to notice, or possibly didn't seem to care, was their mother. This had made conversations arduous and awkward. Plus, there had always been a rift between Rebecca and Sam. This had made their trips to San Diego not a time to vacation and play, but to see an ailing woman, whom they all viewed more and more as an outsider.

Paul and their mother seemed to always be on the same team for which Sam was grateful. Paul was truly a champ when it came to taking care of her and being her proponent. Sam hated that his relationship with his mother, whom he deeply loved, had grown so strained and shallow. But she was a wonderful grandmother to his children and they loved her very much, and for that Sam loved her.

———————————————————

Having Sam and Paul together always worried Maggie, but what could she say? They were brothers and they loved each other. She knew that at some point they would go out to the bars and end up stumbling back home, waking the boys. Paul had never been her favorite person, but she knew he loved Sam, and more importantly, he loved his two nephews with all his heart.

Paul and Sam had had their disagreements like any siblings, but they were also a great team and bolstered each other when needed. Their father had often joked that the two of them would survive the apocalypse as long as they were together. Of course, their father had never thought such a half-joking quip would be tested.

CHAPTER THREE

Day One: 1622 Hours

At first there were several faint percussions, as if a high-powered rifle were being fired in the distance, but at perfectly timed two-second intervals. Then, just moments later, there they were again. Initially, it didn't register in Donovan's brain that anything out of the ordinary was happening. They were, in fact, on a military base located downtown of a major metropolitan area. Donovan suspected this kind of noise was part of the daily circumstance.

Then again.

BOOM BOOM BOOM.

Still replaying the last several minutes of his speech inside that darkened room, Donovan ignored the distant noise. Scouring his mind, he remained unable to justify what had just happened. He pictured himself over and over again giving his presentation, then being plucked off the stage like an insolent child. It didn't make sense and he found it deeply troubling.

When he finally opened his eyes and mind to the present moment, he fully tuned in to the inordinate distant sounds. The first set of three blasts he stored away in the primal part of his brain and paid it no heed, but the third set now garnered his full attention. He quickly ran down the list of possible explanations for such deep, percussive booms. Was it a trick of the brain or were the walls actually rumbling with the sounds?

As a scientist, he was particularly fond of Occam's razor, the principle that the simplest solution was the most likely answer, and his rational brain took control. They were in a big city on a navy base. Of course, there would be some background pops, bangs, and vibrations. But the daily rumblings of metropolitan and military city life usually weren't accompanied with a deep trembling of the walls, floors, and ceilings, and they definitely weren't timed so perfectly and methodically. This was a huge building; it would take something enormous to rumble it the way it did. Something enormous, or incredibly powerful.

937 Harbor Drive was a large military waterfront building just 100 yards from the ocean. The building had started to show its age and talks of demolition and rebuild were more than just rumors, but it remained the home to Navy Region Southwest. The office provided logistics, business services to fleets, and industrial command to the Navy and Coast Guard. It was an eight-story tall building with several more clandestine levels buried under the structure and nearby roads. The top floors boasted a spectacular view of the USS *Midway*, a World War II aircraft carrier that had been berthed there for over 50 years. The aging carrier looked diminutive and obsolete juxtaposed to the other modern pieces of naval military warfare stationed along the San Diego waters.

Although the furtive subterranean levels were bomb-proof, the above-ground structure was not and shook as if made of plaster and wood. The sensation and noise brought Donovan back to the Nevada White Sands missile range, where nuclear weapons had first been tested over 100 years ago and where he had been three years prior.

No longer pristine desert, the region had become more of a wasteland, crowded with a century of nuclear debris and fallout. He had been new to the DoD development sector of the company at the time and his boss had thought it would be inspiring to see where all their hard work and billions of dollars of research and development funds were going. They had been there to oversee a new weapon EIC had developed using newly-enriched Uranium and a detonating device that caused an explosion twice that of any other developed to that day. They had watched from inside a bunker ten miles away with lead-insulated walls and thick, steel blast doors. The blinding flash and heat were awesome. But it was the accompanying visceral shockwaves that had rattled Donovan to his core – and that he now experienced at 937 Harbor Drive.

Lindsey's head shot up, as if she were prey spotting a predator in her periphery, and focused blankly on the sound thrumming through the walls. Donovan's eyes refused to blink and began to water. He noticed that with each burst, vibrations tickled his toes and feet through his polished black BOSS loafers. Puffs of dust jolted from the brackets holding the fluorescents in place. He and Lindsey met each other's eyes.

A thick silence hung in the air for a full minute. A terrifying realization that this was more than big-city traffic or offshore military exercises raced through Donovan's mind. His naive intellect was too apprehensive to give the thought of a foreign attack the respect it deserved. The vibrations and percussions abruptly ended and the two of them stood motionless in the empty corridor staring at each other.

"What... What was that?" Donovan said under his breath, eyes searching her face.

"I have no clue," Lindsey whispered unsteadily. "An earthquake?"

"No. I think they were timed out too perfectly; had to be man-made."

Lindsey didn't acknowledge his logic. She just stared, panic filling her eyes.

Donovan finally trained his focus on the buzzing fluorescent light tubes over their heads. The countless rows of lights now hung in a fog of dust just liberated from the rattling brackets. He glanced down the other end of the hallway, eyes still affixed on the lights which were undulating in brightness, almost impossible to notice at first but becoming more pronounced each second.

Lindsey followed his gaze. "What the fuck is going on?" she mused worriedly, breaking the silence.

"I haven't a goddamn clue, but maybe we should get the hell outa here."

After a full minute had passed, a low, electrical buzz began to radiate from every surface of the hallway around them, making the hair on their arms stand on end. It was as if they were standing too close to high-voltage electrical wires and were feeling the current through their bones and flesh. The fluorescent lights from one end of the corridor to the other flickered soft yellow before surging to blinding white and forcing Donovan and the young woman to squint and mask their eyes with their hands.

POP. POP. POP.

One by one, the lights down the isolated hallway blew out so that glass rained to the floor. Donovan, acting on pure instinct, pulled Lindsey to the wall, hoping to avoid the falling debris. As the electrical buzz increased in intensity and volume, the two were forced to cover their ears – which had little effect. With one final pop, the last of the three-foot-long, gas-filled light bulbs shattered. Lindsey let out a scream as she squatted in place and held her ears. They were alone in the empty hallway, littered in glass, eyes reaching for something to focus on as they adjusted to the all-consuming darkness. The buzzing grew to a terrifying halt with a crack.

Lindsey cried out, "Where are you?" Donovan felt her cold hands on him before he could reach out to her. Her delicate fingers groped the arm of his suit coat and clutched at him. Donovan kept perfectly still, straining to hear beyond the walls. The buzzing had stopped, but the feeling of electrical charge still hung in the air.

There were several moments of tense quiet, then another series of ear-splitting booms knocked Donovan to the ground. Everything quaked with such ferocity around them he was sure the building was coming down. The noise itself was enough to disorient to utter confusion. It was as if they were inches away from a massive thunderstorm that could only exist in nightmares. Terrified, they grasped for each other, hugging the floor as light fixtures crashed down and plaster broke from the walls to topple around them.

This is it. We are going to die down here, thought Donovan. *We're going to die; we're going to die.*

The terrible rumbling and destruction around them stopped as quickly as it had begun. The building still shook with amazing intensity, but the cacophony was over. Although Donovan still anticipated the building to come down on them, killing them right then and there, he remained amazed to be alive. Whatever had just struck San Diego was going to change their lives forever. But in that moment, all he could do was sit in the dust and glass and hold Lindsey in the utter silence and darkness.

CHAPTER FOUR

Day One: 1612 Hours

Maggie found herself dozing to the mundane drone of Sam's latest horror-thriller "book on tape," as they were colloquially called, projecting from the speakers in her headrest. The voice actor had a deep, calm baritone voice that was both soporific and creepy. They were just past Pine Valley, about 45 miles outside of San Diego with only an hour left.

The drive was as uncomfortable as Maggie had set out to make it. There were several hours where she wouldn't engage with Sam at all, an awkward theatric of half-show and half-real disappointment to really let her anger with him sink in. The kids were sound asleep and she loved taking advantage of the unbearable silence to punish him. The tried-and-true silent treatment.

The fact was, yes, she was upset with her husband and wanted to make a point, but she still loved him so much that it had become a forced gesture. She, through those harder times when the whole marriage had been in question, still loved Sam unequivocally. The two of them had made up, as they had so many times before with no words but with tender touches and loving glances that only a long-married couple could use as a remedy.

They had met at Silver Valley High School when they were several years younger than what the state deemed old enough to be an adult. They had happened to be seated next to each other in social justice class, him with the last name Hunt, and hers with Hulley. Although Maggie thought he was cute, she had become immediately annoyed by the jokester and quickly wrote him off, putting him in that worst of categories – the class clown. But right from the get go, there was a chemistry that even to this day Maggie would say she couldn't understand. Sam always boasted that his attraction to the cute redhead next to him was instantaneous, not least because of the constant bright-colored G-strings that popped out every time she leaned forward in her seat.

They had started off as just two strangers who sat next to each other in a boring class for at least the first month. Only the friendly "hey" teenagers who are forced to say when in such close proximity was the repartee that the two held onto for the majority of that time together. But they had grown closer over the languishing semester. And the formal singular "heys" had turned into interesting conversations, harmless flirtations, and, in Maggie's case, side-stitching laughs.

For the entirety of their short time sitting next to each other, she had viewed Sam as a goof until one day, a week from the end of the semester, he had shown his true stripes. That fateful day, as the class' final was being passed out, Maggie was getting hell from one of the class jerks who was teasing her for being a redhead. It was an insult she had heard before from other people all semester, but it had really started to get to her. She knew Sam could tell by the look on her face that the bully's words were really cutting deep that day; Maggie couldn't hide her misty eyes.

"Hey red fishface, I got sumin' to ask," the harrier quipped.

Maggie glared at him, but it was Sam who leapt to her defense, kicking his chair over and shouting, "Dude, fuck you, Dillan! Leave her alone and just shut-the-fuck-up!" Sam was red with anger.

At first taken aback by Sam's explosive response, Dillan had no choice but to try to retain his "honor" and confront Sam. The entire class went quiet and the stares of the students and the teacher were locked on the two boys.

The two stood face-to-face for less than two seconds before Dillan threw a weak clout that grazed Sam's left ear. Sam responded with a well-focused punch, connecting squarely with Dillan's nose to instantly break it; blood splattered down the front of the bully's shirt.

Gaping, Maggie stared at Sam, both alarmed and utterly smitten. Not long after that they were in the back seat of Sam's father's truck after the school's formal dance, knowing that they were meant to be for eternity.

All was quiet for the last leg of the trip as the self-driving vehicle passed through rolling green bluffs and soft rock faces onto the meandering concrete river of southern California's I-8. Sam had been asleep for many hours, making up for his lost rest on whatever emergency calls he always ended up on before family trips. His whimpers and grunts were dead giveaways of his flashback-plagued nightmares. Maggie had grown accustomed to seeing him in this state while dreaming. She felt a deep sorrow for the man she loved and knew there were some evil demons that even she couldn't soothe. She turned her gaze to the road and lost herself in her own thoughts before slipping into a doze.

The autopilot of the vehicle was infallible. That was one of the main selling points for the big car companies these days, that "no single accident happened under our AP software," the commercials bragged. One could set out at ten at night, sleep the entirety of the drive, and wake up refreshed and rested at their destination without a hint of apprehension. In fact, when Maggie next woke, she was surprised to realize that the sleeping family had made it so far without a pee break or stopping for food. The streaming cartoons into the 24-inch TV inlaid in the back of the two front seats was the perfect answer to restless boys on long drives, but they had been out for at least two hours and she cherished the silence.

As nice and luxurious as it was, the technology and artificial intelligence had always weirded her out. The advent of the newest AI automatic-driving technology had cut the amount of highway accident deaths by more than three-quarters in the last decade, but as her husband knew only too well, people still found ways to create death and destruction, either by malevolence or accident. And, although Maggie trusted the technology enough to get some shut eye, her rest was always a shallow, thin sleep.

Maggie stirred awake from the bumps and rattle of the aging and dilapidated California freeway. Rubbing her eyes, she glanced back at her two sleeping children who wore warm smiles of naiveté and youth. She loved being a mother; it was what gave her life meaning. She had an innate knack for care.

She was raised by her father in a loving Catholic family with two younger siblings. Her father was an admirable man who worked from sunup to sundown at a solar plant to provide for his children. He had instilled a deep love of family and God in her. Her mother had died in childbirth of her youngest sister Bella, something that was unheard of with modern medical developments. Maggie had taken on the role of maternal presence in the household. She was quite a bit older than her siblings and, even at 13, she had found that taking care of other people was what she did best.

Maggie glanced at her sleeping husband to find his face contorted in a desperate and pained way. She reached for the smooth glass panel of the dashboard and turned off the deep baritone voice. Sam often gloated about the number of books he read each year, but she always retorted saying that listening to an hour a day of a stranger reading aloud didn't count.

With another press of her finger, she reengaged manual drive, taking control as the passenger. The steering wheel slid away from Sam to lock in front of Maggie. She adjusted her slumped posture and then explored the frequency bar of the radio, scanning from cheery trumpets and driving beats of Spanish music channels to faint static. She found the station she was looking for after several moments of searching – KOGO AM 600, San Diego's news. A chipper voice exuberantly pleading listeners to come to his car lot to check out the newest "Gorgeous 2047 Ford Electro, with all the bells and whistles you could ever imagine!" filled the car, making the children stir but not wake.

After several more commercials, KOGO finally sang its opening jingle and went straight to city traffic. Maggie tuned this out to daydream about one of the first trips they had taken when the boys were young, and the joy of frolicking on the beach as a growing family.

"The I-8 interchange to the 15 is heavily jammed and, if heading downtown, we suggest going a little further to the 805," the tinny voice of the newscaster said as if speaking directly to her. She had just seen the sign for the 805. Perhaps she should make a quick exit.

"And if heading to the beaches, we sugges –"

Distant bursts of thunder made the car rattle. The radio burned out with an electrical hiss and the glowing components of the dash faded. Their car lost power and slowed with the rest of the once-organized traffic around them.

BOOM BOOM BOOM.

Maggie nervously shook Sam's knee to wake him. Something was terribly wrong. A second before her world was engulfed in light, Maggie swore she saw something massive flying directly over the highway. A violent jerk forced her eyes away from the sky as a burst of light and sound overwhelmed her senses.

The sudden explosion from all around the vehicle sent the heavy SUV skyward in a dizzying spin. A deep, visceral electric buzz shook her to her core, cutting through the chaos and cacophony of the moment. Her brain tried to remain conscious as she strained her neck to see if her husband and kids were okay. Then all went black.

CHAPTER FIVE

Day One: 1704 Hours

Sam came to consciousness, blinking the confusion of the last 40 minutes away. Thick dust and smoke hung like morning fog as he lay on the cold cement of the highway, coughing up blood from somewhere in his body. His first breaths were like drawing thick sandstorm air – course and slicing. Pain radiated throughout his body as he raised his head and brushed off the dust and concrete fragments. A small pool of blood had collected on the cold pavement around him. The stack of overpasses, that just moments ago had been sprawling in front of them, was now a heap of twisted steel, jagged concrete, and ravaged vehicles. Aside from the infrequent screams and groans, it was deathly quiet. No horns, no car alarms, no radios – it was as if everything were dead.

Realizing that his car and family were nowhere in sight, Sam looked around, panic swelling in his gut. Head on a swivel, he searched for their vehicle. Behind him was a demolished overpass, a twisted collection of rebar, cement, and steel atop crushed cars. He and his family had missed being a part of that calamity by mere seconds.

Once he struggled to his feet, he realized he was trapped between two massive piles of overpass rubble. The space between the two heaps of gnarled debris was about 150 feet. It had been another typical bumper-to-bumper day on the I-8 in southern California which meant that at least 50 cars were trapped in the narrow space between the massive pile of downed on and off-ramp bridges with countless more crushed underneath. Survivors clamored out of vehicles, hands on their heads and hips, faces contorted in pain, incredulity, and grief, expressions Sam had seen in history books of those caught at ground zero of the collapse of the mighty Twin Towers back at the turn of the century.

Spurred by the survivors' disheveled bewilderment and dazed hurt, Sam continued his search for his family, audibly praying that they hadn't been caught by the overpass destruction up ahead. How could they have? They had all been together! Sam took a few uneasy steps, brushing off the remaining debris from his body, and then took another moment to collect his bearings.

As he stumbled toward the closer of the two fields of destruction, he studied the remains hanging far overhead. This was no mere accident. Up in the air, approximately 75 feet to his left, the edge of the fallen overpass came to a straight edge, as if it had been cut precisely with a laser. From ramp to ramp, an exact 100-foot section had been sliced out of the overpass and allowed to collapse on the highway below.

A cursory glance at the other six on-ramps suspended on massive pillars told the same story, 100-foot sections seemingly cut out with smooth, finished ends. *This is impossible,* he thought. *What the fuck could do that?*

His head was fucking killing him. A quick dab of his fingers to his brow confirmed that he was injured. In fact, he sported a rather nasty laceration which oozed blood along the side of his face; the ringing in his ears was deafening. But he ignored the pain, ignored disorientation. He had just survived some catastrophic, earthquake-like event and to his knowledge, his entire family was lost to the carnage.

How had he gotten separated from them? Last he remembered, they were ensconced and dozing in the car. In a dazed panic, he started running toward the smoldering mountain of pulverized bridge and automobiles, screaming his wife and children's names in sobering desperation. Where the hell were they?

He made his way to a mound of cement and steel piled 30 feet high, following a screeching woman's frantic cries for help. Rebar and twisted metal littered the highway like ubiquitous pine needles under a canopy of trees. Taking care as to where he placed his hands, he clambered over rubble to a green, brand-new vehicle layered with dust and wreckage. The car lay upside-down on its crushed roof. The screams were coming from the rear of the vehicle just out of view from where he stood. Cautiously he circled the demolished car. Since fossil fuels had not been used in road vehicles for nearly a decade, the fears of fuel leaking and igniting were essentially zero, but high-voltage batteries held dangers of their own.

As he turned the corner, he saw a sight that he had seen many times before in his long career, but still made him taste bile in the back of his mouth. A pale woman who looked to be in her early-twenties languished, torso half-hanging, out a crumpled window; her wet cheek brushed the dusty highway. Blood covered her and the car. If not for her screams, Sam would have thought her already dead.

Limping, he edged closer to her. The woman's right arm and leg were twisted in broken lengths of pillowy pink flesh and bone. He noticed a pearl-white, inch-and-a-half-round bone jutting out of her sleeve. The rest of her arm was mangled and looked to only be attached by sinuous tissue and skin.

Her once blue jumper was now tattered and covered with blood and her golden hair was strewn hopelessly in matted blood and filth. His instincts as a firefighter took hold and he knelt beside the ailing woman, hoping to render any care he could. Her screams of pain and imminent death rattled him. As carefully as possible, he turned her over.

"*Oh my God*," she shrieked. "Please, oh my God, help!"

"I gotcha, I gotcha. I'm here, I'm here," Sam uttered. "Listen, I'm going to have to try to get you the rest of the way out of this car, okay?

"Oh, Jesus no," she whispered as he watched the life slowly drain from her face.

"I'm here," was the only thing Sam could think to say. She responded with a look of terror, anguish, and finality.

Delicately, Sam moved the woman just half a foot to the left to untangle her from the steel and aluminum wreck. He searched the vehicle with a cursory glance, taking notice of the driver who was about 60. The man's skull had been crushed well into his hairline and pieces of pink and red brain matter lay just off to the side of his ear. A black pool of blood collected on the ceiling of the car where the man's head lay twisted in an unnatural direction on his neck. The car had obviously been hurled through the air and had landed on the driver-side roof, killing him instantly. Sam looked back at the young woman now lying on the highway beside him, hoping his efforts would ease her suffering.

Unfortunately, by moving her, he had jarred a deep laceration into her leg, freeing bright red blood to spurt and cover Sam's cargo pants. Blood spewed from the cut artery with each pulse of the woman's weakening heart. He quickly threw his hands on the billowing cut, applying as much pressure as he could to stop the arterial hemorrhage. As soon as he covered the gaping hole, the woman stopped moving and all color vacated her pretty face; she grew ghostly white and hauntingly quiet. Her dead eyes continued to look at him and terror remained etched on her face as he held her lifeless body.

For a long moment, Sam knelt there in silence before slowly standing to take an uneasy step back and eye the scene before him, disbelief and defeat overtaking him. He had been around plenty of death in his career, but never when he was so ill-equipped and unprepared. He wiped what blood he could off his hands and face, glanced at the young woman, and then limped off, continuing to call out for his wife and children.

For the next five hours, he came across countless other survivors – and dead and near-dead victims – as he searched. The sun set and night fell on the scene. All the road lights were out, but a full moon and sea of stars gave more than enough light. With the electrical grid out and not a light for as far as the eye could see, it was the clearest night sky San Diego had seen in 100 years.

As he walked the edge of the collapsed overpass, he scanned every person he could to ensure it wasn't one of his children or his beloved wife. He knew though. Something in him told him that somehow they had managed to escape and were alive. But still, as he trundled the collapse area, he prayed to God that the next set of bodies he would come upon wouldn't be his families'. The not-knowing was torturous. Making several passes and investigating as thoroughly as he felt he could, he concluded they were not there.

Several people ran freely down the concrete interstate yelling and screaming in fear and agony, or searching for loved ones like Sam. The place was in complete chaos. A man in his early-thirties, blood running down the front of his T-shirt passed Sam shortly after twilight, his gaze distant. Having still been unable to get an answer from anyone, Sam grabbed the guy, nearly clotheslining him to the ground. "Hey, hey man, you know what the fuck happened?"

The man shifted his thousand-yard stare to Sam. "You didn't s-s-see? We were fucking attacked man. They finally f-f-fucking got us, man. I knew it was a m-m-matter of time. I called it, man —"

"What the hell are you talking about? Attacked? What did you fucking see?" Sam pleaded.

"Fucking spaceships or something, dude. Fucking aliens or some shit – they were flying everywhere." With this, the guy escaped Sam's grasp and resumed jogging mindlessly to nowhere to do nothing.

With panic setting back in full-bore, Sam began once again yelling as loud as his tired vocal cords could for his wife and children into the endless destruction. He was exhausted. He had barely slept the night before while running calls and his concussion was making staying awake more and more impossible. He couldn't rest until he found his family, but he was becoming delusional.

Soon he found himself sitting against a culvert. He fought sleep but his mind caught up with his body, and he knocked out.

CHAPTER SIX

Day One: 1830 Hours

Filthy and wet, Maggie sat slumped in a storm drain off the side of I-8, clutching her two sons. They were battered, bloody, exhausted, and dazed, but none of them had broken anything as far as she could tell; she thanked God for that. Her eyes were swollen red with the residue of sobbing and dirt as she stared into a vast concrete skeleton of endless rubble laid out before her.

Her two boys had finally stopped shaking and had fallen into a light sleep. She pulled her phone out for the fourth time, cursing under her breath again as it refused to come to life. She glanced at her smartwatch; it too boasted a black, dead screen. Everything was fried. The last few hours had been a true testament to their resolution to live. She replayed the events in her mind the best she could as her dirty and blood-matted eyelashes finally closed deep in thought.

She barely remembered the first part of the drive, a symptom she knew of a probable concussion. But as she sat in the dirty culvert, a light mist of water from a broken water main showering the three of them, more parts of the puzzle slowly began coming together.

She remembered the hypnotic drone of the audio book as she woke from her light nap to read SAN DIEGO printed bolded on the green, reflective sign. She remembered turning on the radio and seeing a big sign for the 805. So much of the last day had been a blur.

Maggie figured if she could retrace their steps in her mind, she could work out where Sam could be. Maybe she had forgotten some crucial part of the event. She closed her eyes hard, training her focus to the point where their lives had fractured.

She recalled the radio filling the silence before three faint booms reverberated in the distance – then the car died. The vehicle's electrical components glowed with an eerie, neon buzz as the car came to a rolling stop amidst hundreds of other commuters. Another set of explosive bursts, this time louder, more immediate, caused the car to quake.

Maggie remembered reaching out to Sam and shaking him, but… She tried to grasp what she had seen. From the corner of her eye, through the glass of the windshield, she had seen a terribly massive metallic object drifting over the highway.

A bright and powerful force had vaulted the vehicle into the air. Unearthly g-forces had pulled her from her seat as the car spiraled. Secured only by her seatbelt, she had glimpsed movement to her left as Sam was ejected through the windshield.

Trash, soda bottles, and phones rattled and tumbled through the cab, bouncing off windows, seats, and bodies. In the chaos of it all, she remembered spotting the cement hurling at them and thinking of nothing but her children, how perfect they were, and how much she loved them. Then black.

She had come to sometime later, confused and aching. Dangling by her seatbelt, the first thing she had noticed was the empty seat to her left. In a painful stupor, she had cleared blood and glass from her mouth and immediately began to yell for her two boys, and then for Sam. She released the seatbelt and fell to the roof of the car, landing hard on her head and neck. Gasping, she lay crunched for a long moment. The patter of running feet and yells of "Mom!" made her break into sobs of relief.

"Thank Jesus! Are you two okay?" she croaked, scrambling upright.

Zachary's voice was unnervingly calm. "Yeah, we're okay. Do you know where dad is? We can't find him?"

"No baby, he's not here. I don't know where..." She stopped herself. She pressed her eyelids to stop the tears, but now was not the time to tell them how the laws of physics had jerked their father through the window – and from their lives.

It seemed the two boys had gotten themselves out of the wreck as Maggie was still unconscious to go looking for their dad. The thought of the two alone on the highway in this mess was more than she could manage at the moment.

"Boys! You can't go running off like that without me!" she yelled as her voice broke and tears streamed down her face.

"We wuh looking fow Dad," Liam replied, his innocent toddler speech impediment still very much present.

He should have grown out of the toddler way of speaking years ago, but the speech therapist, along with being incredibly expensive, had grown too flirtatious with Sam when he was around. The woman's progressively revealing blouses had been the last straw.

Maggie would never admit to her husband that's why she had fired her, but it had started getting a bit out of hand when black lacy bras began peeking through silk shirts. She was sure that Sam would never act on anything and betray her in that way, but she was fired before the next session anyhow. She had felt incredibly guilty about it since they hadn't been able to find a replacement for the last six months and Liam's impediment was only getting worse. But two young boys did not need to see that kind of lasciviousness and the firing had saved them from a nasty divorce, at least, that is what she told herself.

She had wiped her tears with the end of her wet and filthy sleeve and hugged her two boys tighter than she had ever done before. Together, they ran to the edge of the highway, jumped the three-foot cement barrier, and hid in a culvert overgrown with grass and shrubs.

Maggie squinted against the setting sun. Why had Sam been thrown from the vehicle so violently? And what the hell was the thing that had flown over their car?

With another quick squeeze of her children, Maggie left them in the culvert and crawled to the cement barricade they had jumped, keeping her head down. Fearing what lay on the other side, she peered over the top, resting her hands on the edge of the jersey barrier.

The first thing that caught her eye was a red stream of liquid from the pile of cars and destruction, running the length of the highway to the culvert that had been their momentary refuge. It didn't take long for her to realize what the steam was and what darkened the water her sons sat down in. As the realization hit her, so did the smell and she gagged. Thick blood trailed from the mighty heap of debris, cars, and bodies that loomed in front of her. A nearby broken pipe added water to the river of horror to keep it from congealing.

Overtly disgusted, she turned to her two boys and yelled at them to get out of the stream and follow her. They followed suit, crawling on hands and knees, dirtying themselves further. She was amazed at their stalwart braveness; in that instant, both looked a decade older as they didn't even hint at their distress. They were so much like their father.

As she waited for the boys to join her, she studied the highway in search of another hideout. An empty van no more than 30 feet away at the edge of the road caught her attention. Its white sliding door was ajar, allowing her to see the blackness of a perfect hiding place within. After instructing the boys to stay put behind the barrier, she leapt over it and dropped onto the highway.

Staying as low as she could, she ran across what felt like a vast emptiness of highway to the abandoned vehicle. The outside was clean and dent-free; it looked fairly new. She knelt by the passenger's door and squinted inside.

Not only was the windshield caved in, but the interior was littered with glass fragments; a massive piece of blood-stained concrete had settled just to the side of the driver's seat. Then she saw blood – a lot of it. The seats and interior walls were adorned with it but she thankfully found no one. She crept around the front of the van, again on all fours, this time the pain of her scratched hands and knees causing her to wince as they were swollen and tender. She made it to the driver's side only to softly curse upon spotting the driver's corpse.

A 25-foot-long trail of thick, clotted blood revealed where the driver had finally collapsed face-down along the side of the road. A huge puddle of black blood was pooled around the person's right thigh. The concrete chunk had obviously fallen through the windshield and struck the driver's leg. The poor guy had only made it a couple dozen steps before the loss of blood had caused him to collapse, exsanguinating on the pavement.

Maggie averted her horrified gaze and, staying on hands and knees, made her way back to the other side of the van. She slid the door open and cautiously peered in. A small set of shelving holding an assortment of hand tools graced the inner wall of the van. Other than that, it was vacant.

She motioned her boys to join her and watched as they ran fully upright and unafraid. She told them not to look around and to get in the handyman's work truck. All she wanted to do was to get them inside to wait out this nightmare. Together, they cuddled in a corner of the van, eyes and ears electric with caution. Darkness overcame everything followed by the cold. She hoped to stay awake to keep guard over her kids, but all three found sleep almost immediately.

Maggie woke up just as the sun began to creep over the eastern hills. She wanted to get up and investigate the area more as the boys slept, but her movement stirred them awake. She told them to stay in the van until she returned, repeating several times not to leave the safety of the van no matter what. The boys agreed and Maggie cautiously slid open the door and set off in the opposite direction of where they had hidden the day before.

She reached the edge of the road, moving as stealthily as she could. She made it to the highway barrier and looked down from the small hill which the highway was located on.

A dense coastal fog hung in the air, obscuring many of the distant visuals, but Maggie could see the devastation. The highway stacks that had towered before them not 12 hours ago were crumpled and destroyed, piled like a concrete-and-rebar sandwich on the freeway.

Below her was the tan and orange Dave & Busters perched along I-8 where they had stopped shortly after Sam's father's funeral.

The day of the funeral had been one of the worst days of her life and she had hated that restaurant ever since. It had been Sam and Paul's idea to go to the *family* restaurant to lighten the mood after the funeral.

At first, she had thought it a great idea, a great way to get the kids' minds off of mourning. But not too long into the family excursion, she had noticed Sam was taking advantage of it. He always ordered a beer or two with dinner and she expected him to have a few more, considering the day's circumstances. But in Sam's fashion, he had taken it too far and had ended the three-hour family get-together stumbling drunk. He added 100 percent more attention to the kids when he got that way and, of course, they absolutely loved him for it, but in reality, he was just a hammered guy playing with the boys.

It hadn't started out too badly, like so many of their fights did, but this one had cut her more deeply than any other. As the night had wound down, she had noticed the kids were growing weary; Sam had remained oblivious, continuing to play some shoot-em-up game with Paul, beers in tow. She walked up to the loud machine and yelled over the gunshots and music that the children were ready to leave. Sam gave her a look and went on a drunken, nonsensical rant that drunk people do, telling her how she only wanted to ruin everyone's fun and that she should just leave because he and the kids have more fun without her around.

For some reason, Maggie held the place personally responsible for it all. But, logically speaking, that was most likely where Sam would end up – a close and recognizable meeting place they all knew. She had to give it a try.

Although she had seen no one on the now-vacant highway of destruction, Maggie was reticent and nervous about being vulnerable for that amount of open stretch if they were to try to make it to the restaurant. After several deep, calming breaths, she made the final decision that she would go get her two boys and they would make the run over the stretch of highway, down the embankment to the restaurant. She prayed the coast remained clear.

She was 30 yards from the van when she heard voices.

Keeping a low profile, she crept from one car to the next, searching the disaster zone for who was talking, all the while keeping a constant eye on the white van. As she reached a tiny, abandoned sports car, she noticed that the loud and belligerent voices were much closer than she had thought. Realizing that they were drawing nearer still, she hunkered down beside her cover, which was not an ideal hiding spot.

Just as she heard footsteps, a voice cried out, "Fuck y'all, wait up for me!" She peered out from the corner of her eye to see two teenage boys run past the sports car; they didn't notice her. Apparently the two weren't waiting for the third. She prayed their friend who was trailing behind would do the same – run past her oblivious.

"Ah shit," came an alarmingly close voice.

Maggie flinched as the last young man slowed to a stop not six feet behind her. Although he looked to be no more than 16 or 17, his eyes were like those of a starving animal's. He was short and skinny and wore clothes that were too baggy for his little frame. Tattoos covered his arms and hands and the number 858 in faded ink adorned his right cheek. He looked dirty, probably homeless, and no doubt a drug addict. His teeth were misshapen and black with rot.

"Watchu doing there, girl?" the young man said with the swagger and bravado of a kid pretending to be a thug.

"Just run along and find your friends, okay?" was all she could manage, more afraid than she cared to admit.

"I got bad news for you, bitch. You aint fucking talking to me like that. Ain't no one fucking around." The look in his eyes was bone-chillingly terrifying.

"Please just leave me alone. My husband is about to come back and..."

"Yeah-fuckin'-right." The youth dropped a bundle of shirts and jackets, every one of them decorated with the same big orange circle and white *Dave & Busters* lettering. They must have just pilfered them. The place was most likely still teeming with looters and thugs like this. She wouldn't expose her children to that. The restaurant was now out of the question for the three of them.

She forced herself to keep her gaze off the white van so as not to give way the boys' location. She prayed they weren't seeing any of this. But really, she so badly wanted her husband to show up at that exact moment.

"Listen, you little punk. Just go on. My husband is almost back and if he sees you, he will fucking kill you." She tried to hide her tremors of terror.

The young man took a step closer, biting his lip. She noticed his eyes glance over her body predatorily. "Lying little cunt," he scoffed. In two strides, he was on top of her. She smelled alcohol, body odor, and cigarettes, and became frozen with fear. She let out what she could of a scream, but his dirty hand shot to her mouth and pressed it closed with surprising strength. Another wretched smell invaded her nostrils.

"Shut the fuck up, bitch," he snarled, reaching for his belt.

She couldn't believe how strong he was or how petrified and weak she was, but the teenager had overpowered her in a matter of seconds. She glanced down to see his belt undone and his dirty fingers going for the button on his pants. Apoplectic with fear, she cried freely, silent tears tracking down her cheeks.

His disgusting hand still clamped over her mouth, she glanced down to see his other tattooed hand forcing his pants down. She drew away as he brought out the terrifying piece of himself and pinned it, erect, against her stomach.

She now started thrashing and fighting, but he moved his hand from her mouth to her throat and grasped impossibly hard on her windpipe. She tried to scream again, but not a sound escaped. His probing hand found the edge of her pants and, like a frantic parasite, began searching around, trying to get in. Unable to unbutton her pants, he forced his hand down her front. Despite her morbid reality, Maggie cringed at the thought of this disgusting teenage reprobate permanently contaminating her.

Please God, she prayed, clenching her eyes shut.

A hard crack like a bat hitting concrete broke her whimpers. Her eyes flew open and she felt a splash of warm, viscous liquid fly on her face. The man's grip loosened on her neck before the other one went limp in her pants. She grabbed the hand like a loathsome invading cockroach and ripped it from her clothing. Panting, she looked up to see Zachary standing over them, his mouth quivering and body shaking.

Maggie drew away to find the teen's skull bashed in. A basketball-sized piece of cement replete with hair and brain matter lay beside them. She broke into unrelenting sobs, holding onto the feet of her rescuer – of her son.

She forgot all conceived notions of mother and

son, protector and child, and sat there weeping at the feet of her boy. Zach collapsed into his mother, shaking and unable to speak or move. The two stayed in that position for several silent and horrified minutes, unprotected and exposed to anything coming their way.

CHAPTER SEVEN

Day One: 1654 Hours

Generator-driven backup emergency lights flickered for a moment as they tried to find life, but failed and died with a lazy flash and pop, decaying into a thin hum and eventual darkness.

A lingering, putrid smell of burned wires, drywall dust, and the faint sweet smell of Lindsey's perfume was the only sensation Donovan was truly aware of in the dark and silent corridor. His first reaction, being a man of science, was to take a couple of minutes to rationalize through their predicament and come up with a game plan. But his gut had brought him far in life and he readily aimed to obey that compelling inner feeling that they needed to get out of that building as quickly as possible. They were in the worst possible place to be trapped – underground surrounded by thousands of pounds of concrete, pipes, and steel infrastructure. He knew that with a lack of circulation, the air would eventually thicken and become dense with carbon monoxide.

Wearily, he forced his eyes open to be struck with absolute darkness. His throat forced a cough to clear the particles of dust and debris and his lungs delivered three painful and deep hacking barks. "Lindsey! Lindsey, are you okay?"

After a loud cough of her own, a few sobs escaped her. "Yeah… I'm-I'm okay… What the – what just happened?"

The two sat a moment on the question, but they knew the answer without having to respond.

"The whole freaking building just came down on us, huh?" she asked. Donovan felt her wipe at her face.

"Do you have any idea where we are?" he questioned.

"I think B-2 or 3 in… in the Navy building still? Shit, I don't know. This place is a maze. We could be anywhere." Her voice trembled. "I've only been here once before."

She had only been in this beehive of an underground office building once before years ago as an intern and hadn't busied her mind with the layout of her surroundings then. The hallways were stuffy and repetitive. Each corridor looked like the one before and there were scores of unmarked, gray doors. She knew how easy it was to get lost down here.

After a long moment, Donovan, still holding her tightly, stood. "We need to get our bearings."

The silence pressing in on them, they started blindly down the darkened hallway, moving cautiously as if they were walking on ice on a moonless night. Each step though soft and careful was loud enough to reverberate off the bare walls of the passageway.

"Let's try to get back to where we came from. I think I can get us back from there," Donovan mustered, trying to keep panic at bay. He found himself gripping her hand so tightly that he could actually feel the pressure in his own knuckles. He wasn't quite sure why he felt so protective of her and why, at every thump or sound, he instinctively reached for her. He had never really felt the primal urge to protect a woman before, especially a stranger, yet he couldn't bear to let her go for fear she would be beyond his defenses.

"What do you think happened up there?" Lindsey whispered.

"Well," Donovan replied, "To be honest with you, I think we were attacked; those electrical hums we heard were EMP blasts"

"EMP, like Electromag—"

"Magnetic Pulse, yeah," he intervened. "My guess is it was a HEMP, one of those high-altitude magnetic pulses. The explosions were far too faint to be nuclear explosions on the ground. If they were, we would be dead."

"You mean, you think those were nukes?" Lindsey quavered.

"No, I think they were something far more advanced."

Donovan had been a consultant for the DoD for several new nuclear weapons programs and knew from research that all nuclear explosions have a corresponding EMP, pulses that disable any and all electrical devices within a blast radius. Of course, many factors can change the effectiveness of such weapons, including the size of the warhead, altitude of detonation, and gamma ray output. The primary wave of these blasts caused an incredibly high surge of voltage to travel at 90 percent the speed of light, which took out electronics instantaneously. Even modern surge protectors were no match for so much energy. But such incredible power surges happened in nanoseconds.

The EMP they had experienced had been slow and increased gradually in intensity. It was something he had never seen before or had come across in his research, and he couldn't reason through it.

"The explosions, or whatever those were, came before the lights went out, not after. Wouldn't it be the other way around if they were bombs of some sort?" Lindsey asked, as she tripped over some rubble.

Donovan steadied her and then stood in thought for a long moment. He had watched several nuclear detonations and had felt waves of energy shake him to his core. But she was right; the piercing booms had come long after the shockwave. The EMP had been different than those other blasts and had instantaneously blown out anything with electrical components, including, much to his dismay, his Resco Instruments Patriot dive watch he had bought himself as an early Christmas present the year before.

This was nothing like his past experiences. This, as far as Donovan could tell, was no nuclear bomb or any EMP weapon the current United States Military had in its arsenal.

"What the hell is it then?" he growled in frustration.

"I dunno, but I wanna get the hell outta here."

They crept along at a snail's pace, each footstep as careful as the last. Their senses afire, every indentation and imperfection on the barren wall was crystal clear to their fingertips along the blackened, naked hallway. For what seemed like an eternity, they inched along.

All the while, Donovan couldn't shake the nagging feeling of dread in his gut. Why was it so damn quiet? Why couldn't they hear movement, talking, screaming, or debris shifting from other victims? They couldn't be all that far from them, especially those who had been seated in the audience. There had been some notable people within that auditorium. No doubt the meeting had been cloaked in secrecy and shielded by heavy security, but with all the notable people there, including the vice president, a response to an attack would no doubt be immediate and massive. Yet, in the deathly silence around, he could hear no signs of humanity.

The strangling darkness finally broke after another ten paces and a turn in the hallway when their eyes found something to glom onto. Ahead of them, a barely visible six-foot-high, half-inch wide opening emitted a red hue.

Like others, he had been in power outages before; the first thing he always noticed was that when one sense had no utility, his others compensated, increasing in sensitivity tenfold. He was reminded of the first apartment he had taken when he had first moved to San Diego as a recent graduate. It had been a small, dank, and aging box, fitting for a college student. His first paychecks would have been adequate for a nice condo in some flyover state, but on the coast, it barely fed him and put a roof over his head.

One lazy night around midnight, there had been a city-wide power shortage. This occurred when nuclear energy became scarce; he knew the "freak" accident brownouts were just the state government's rationing of power to supply the more critical areas of the city. *Socialism at work,* he would always think. Within a few moments of his eyes adjusting to empty blackness, his ears had taken over primary sensory duties. He first had noticed moans and pleasurable cries of the skinny crackheads who lived two doors down as they fucked animalistically. He had heard the conversations of the older, downtrodden Korean family next door clamoring for candles and flashlights to help the numerous family members see their way through the squalor. Just moments prior, he had been desensitized to such sounds; then he had heard his life in stereo.

Donovan clutched Lindsey's hand tighter as they sneaked along the wall, the faintly-glowing, vertical stripe growing closer and closer. The air was thick in his lungs and he could taste dust in the air – dust and something else far more pungent.

At the opening, Donovan noticed the glow from within, flicker. Particles of dust lazily drifted in the thin beam of light emanating from the thin crack as an alarmingly familiar sound reached his ears. The soft, but unmistakable pops and crackle of fire sent his heart to his throat. The air had become harder to breath and the smell of smoke was unmistakable. A mere foot from the opening, he noticed his hands were trembling and sweating again; he was terrified of what he may discover on the other side of that steel blast door that hung ajar. Squaring his shoulders, he tightened his grip on Lindsey's hand and then hit the door with all his might.

The door swung open with a protesting creak and Donovan peered in. The first thing to meet his gaze was the warm red-and-orange glow of flame.

"Jesus," he gaped under his breath.

Everything seemed to be on fire. The corridors through which they had gone down only minutes earlier were unrecognizable. He shut the heavy door and turned to Lindsey, unable to say anything else.

Obviously not satisfied with his response or otherwise too curious, Lindsey pushed past him and, using her hip, pushed the door open so that they both stood before the complete scene of destruction and conflagration. Donovan felt her take his hand once more.

"It's all, it's all... gone," she said despairingly, defeatedly.

"Well, we need to get the hell out of here before we end up dead and in ashes," he replied, struggling to maintain his own composure. The comment was more for him than her. They looked at each other, and with no words, agreed on the plan. They had to go in.

CHAPTER EIGHT

Day One: 1715 Hours

Lindsey and Donovan stood at the threshold of the blast door for a full minute in complete bewilderment and horror. The hallway through which Donovan had been dragged a mere 45 minutes earlier was gone. Their only source of light came from a fire that burned some 50 feet from them and cast the room in an austere infernal glow.

"There has to be an exit, a hole for the smoke and heat to go out, otherwise I don't think we would be able to see," Lindsey remarked.

"Or breathe," Donovan added. "I was just thinking the same thing. The heat would be untenable in here if there wasn't some exhaust vent, but it looks like the damn floor collapsed or something."

Just beyond the threshold of the door, the floor of the hallway was gone. Together they peered down at the black emptiness at their toes.

"There must have been at least two or three floors under that one," she said. "Looks like the floors collapsed at least 20 or 30 feet... Why didn't this one?"

"Well, I'm assuming this was made as some kind of bomb shelter, hence the huge door. I bet the ground below and above us is concrete, several feet thick."

A sound like a cough made them both turn in the direction of the empty pit.

"You heard that too?" whispered Lindsey.

Donovan glared down into the gloom. "Jesus, is someone alive down there?"

Another two hoarse coughs reverberated up the walls, quickly answering the question.

"Hello!" Lindsey yelled "Is anyone there? Are you alive?"

Donovan briefly thought about the silliness of her yelling, but instinct overtook him and he joined her. After a brief moment of further cries, they fell silent. A faint but unmistakable cough and grunt was the only response they received.

"God damn, there *is* someone down there!" Donovan affirmed. After a long moment of deep contemplation, he said with angst, "We gotta go down there; we gotta see if he's okay. I have no idea how someone could live through that, but we gotta see."

"Maybe there is a stairway down back there." Lindsey gestured toward the long, black hallway at their backs.

"Uh-uh, I doubt it. Doors like that are there for a reason – one safe way in, one safe way out. Plus, it's completely dark back there; it might take us all day to find our way."

"So, you're climbing down?" she stammered, making it clear she had no intention of doing so herself.

"Heh, so *I'm* going?"

"I sure as hell am not," Lindsey avowed with a playful scoff, the first semblance of normalcy she had in her voice since this began.

Donovan had never really thought of himself as a brave or heroic man, but the thought of someone down there struggling to live assured him he had no other choice. Something in him urged him to clamber down and investigate. "But how in the hell am I gonna get down there?"

He sat on the edge of the void, heart hammering and hands slick. He leaned over the edge of the concrete and searched the area directly beneath him for a foothold, ledge, or anything that would bear his weight. The air was growing thicker and more rancid, more deadly. He had to do this quickly to give them time to get the hell out of their buried coffin. He felt a small, warm hand on his shoulder.

"Be careful, okay?" Lindsey's voice was soft, caring.

He looked up at her, catching her eyes for a long-sustained moment. And for the first time, he thought to himself about how beautiful this woman was; a smile was all he could muster.

After a minute of shuffling and searching, he found a four-inch ledge of jagged concrete three feet down, took off his suit jacket, and went over.

The climb down was arduous and slow and he ended up cutting himself several times. One of his more serious injuries was a deep laceration along his thigh which he had received from an aberrant piece of sharp metal jutting out from the wall. He felt blood trickle down his leg and soak in the calf of his suit pants. The fabric clung tightly to his leg the rest of the way down.

He was lucky the collapsing floors had left several ledges and chunks of cement and metal that he could, without much trouble, brace upon. He tried to make mental notes of the good, and not-so-good, foot and hand holds for Lindsey's eventual climb down or his climb back up. When he reached the bottom, he was happy to learn that it was only about 15 feet down; only one floor had collapsed.

Although covered in rubble and uneven debris, the

floor he now stood on appeared to be intact. HVAC ducting and a web of electrical wires adorned the wreckage around him, but he was able to navigate without much difficulty with the light from the fire.

"You make it? You okay?" Lindsey yelled down.

"Yeah, yeah, I'm down. Stay up there. I'm not sure how stable it is down here."

"'Kay," was all she replied. He didn't know how much he trusted her response.

Donovan turned to study the ceiling which was being consumed by fire at an alarming rate. He knew they had to move fast.

Another bout of rough coughs erupted from nearby. "H-hello?" came a faint cry.

Donovan scoured the area, picking over the debris field hurriedly. "Yeah, I hear you! Keep talking!" There was one more cough and then silence. Donovan stopped at a heap of white ceiling tiles and ducting. "Say something! Say something to me!" When there was no response, he realized the survivor was probably going in and out of consciousness.

Behind him, Donovan heard a shuffling and saw Lindsey climbing down from the ledge with much more grace and ease than he had.

"Sounded like you needed help," she said with a coy smile. He nodded and they got to work.

As they began shuffling rubble around, a cough seeped out of the pile. Spurred by the immediacy of the man's coughing, Donovan and Lindsey began rolling rubbish away. Donovan finally saw a boot and black pants protruding from under a large piece of metal ducting. It was heavy and appeared as though it was buried deep in the person's upper leg.

They heard guttural moans and screams as they moved the ducting. Frantically, the two of them threw the rest of the ceiling tile and steel off the pile and freed the body. The cries abruptly stopped and Donovan feared the worst. *Oh God, we killed him.* He took a worried step back and surveyed the victim.

A large, bloodied and bruised man with a swollen face lay in the filth, his body decorated with various cuts and scrapes. Although deathly still, Donovan could make out the faint rise and fall of his chest. He noticed the man's right arm was flexed under his back in an unnatural position; it looked disconnected. The black, tactical suit he wore was filthy, mangled, and singed. A small pool of congealing blood under his right hip hinted at further injury. By all accounts, the man shouldn't have been alive, and yet he was.

Donovan knelt beside the muscular stranger and prodded his chest with two fingers. No response. He glanced back at Lindsey with a worried expression before shaking the survivor at first gently, and then with more force. The man's eyes slowly peeled open as he turned to face his rescuer looming over him. He drew in a deep, life-sustaining breath.

"Hey there, you alive?" Donovan asked, again realizing the foolishness of the question.

"Holy mother of fuck," were the only words the bloodied man managed to say no louder than a whisper before promptly passing out.

CHAPTER NINE

Day One: 1216 Hours

He hated these dicks. He hated the way they talked, the way they dressed, and most of all, the way they talked down to him. Paul was a man who wasn't used to being talked down to. The money was great, but it hardly made up for the bullshit that powerful suits and veneered smiles put him through when a job came his way. But anything was worth being back stateside.

Working odd jobs for the last three years after his retirement from the military had put good money in his pocket. Besides, he was thrilled to no longer be in a Middle Eastern sandy-ass oven of a hellhole. He had retired with a long list of medals and commendations, but a much longer one of non-judicial punishments.

Despite Paul's service dress uniform adorned with ribbons and medals, it had been made clear to him that the top brass was not a fan of his. In fact, his reception of any accolades gave his commanding officers pause. He was damn good at his job, but dogmatic and unafraid to speak his mind.

He had once refused to storm a school zone area occupied by a *handful* of insurgents because of shoddy intel. For that, he had almost been court-martialed and jailed for insubordination, but had gotten off with disciplinary action. But of course, he would have done it all over again. His main mission, above all else, was to keep his men safe, even if that meant not following orders and being sent to Leavenworth. He loathed the bullshit minutia of the armed services but *damn*, he loved his country.

Paul was everything a military-man-gone-private-security-warrior could be. With a hefty, six-foot-one build and wide shoulders, his musculature could be traced through his fatigues. His jawline had surely inspired the new line of advanced G.I. Joe figurines that had come out the previous year. And he shared his brother's intense, gray eyes. At one point while "back east," he had sported a tangled beard and thick, black hair to safeguard against the sun. Now though, all of that had been tamed and cut. To his chagrin, he remained clean-shaven so those he was hired to protect could better identify him.

Understandably, he exuded nothing but threat. He knew the aloofness and intensity his gaze gave off was intimidating, but he couldn't help it, not after spending so much time surrounded by warfare. Although he prominently showcased a variety of tattoos along his arms and knuckles, his most celebrated ink was the Special Forces skull and beret insignia emblazoned across his right forearm. He looked like a hardened killer, he knew, which was why he often flashed his cheerful, boyish smile at standoffish acquaintances. Sometimes he even revealed his high-registered laugh that could get an entire room of military men rolling.

The war in Iran had changed him not only physically, but mentally. The mental scarring he had received during his deployment was far more destructive than the shrapnel wounds he had incurred. He was colder than he used to be and joked less, but he was still all heart, and for as much as he bitched and moaned about his current employment, he loved to serve and would die in a heartbeat for the men and women he swore to protect.

He had found this particular job not three weeks earlier through a friend with whom he had served back east years ago. His friend, who also worked in private security or "pri-sec," as they called it, had referred to this security detail as the biggest government meeting in a decade. Naturally, Paul's interest had been piqued, figuring it was time to transition from war hero to James Bond anyway.

Paul had spent the last year making a comfortable six figures working security for a "United States Asset," a uranium mine in Kazakhstan. The world had been put on high-alert when North Korea had perfected its nuclear program in the mid-twenties and Kazakhstan, being a close neighbor of Russia, had subsequently finalized its ally-ship with the United States.

After the terrorist attack in New York nearly a half-century prior, the U.S.-Kazakhstan Energy Partnership had established a beneficial relationship which, 20 years later, became a strong alliance. The partnership was based entirely on the production, transportation, and consumption of nuclear material; as far as foreign policy was concerned, that's all that really mattered.

Although holding an M-18 assault weapon in a combat zone was where he felt most in his element, the thought of being a hired gun made him squirm with shame. He still got a rush from the intensity of it, but missed the brotherhood of the military.

From the little information he had received regarding the job from his pri-sec pal, he had gleaned that he was heading to San Diego to be a bodyguard for a handful of nerdy types from IEC Energy. He had gotten used to getting these kinds of gigs after his service. "Ole big guns upstairs," as he referred to God, had gifted Paul with an almost photographic memory which had proven damn useful for the private security companies doing dirty business overseas. After reviewing a folder of assets and security detail information for half an hour, Paul could recite everything from memory.

This specific skill had made him a legend in his unit in Iran. He had, in fact, been inserted into Delta and SEAL missions because of his photographic memory. He could see the blueprints of a building once and know exactly where to lead the team. His 'brothers' especially loved him because, after spotting a poster of the 25 most-dangerous terrorists, he could name each by appearance, hometown, and family relations.

Now he stood in the depths of an aging Navy building getting paid an exorbitant amount of money to run security for another waste-of-fucking-time who's-who meeting. He knew the company only because he had seen the name stamped with block lettering on the heavy ordinance and weapons he had used. He actually hadn't realized, until a cursory internet search, that they were a massive energy corporation responsible for most of U.S. nuclear energy.

He had gotten a short list of names, pictures, and bios of the people he was there to "keep secure" in a manilla EIC folder that read TOP SECRET on its front cover. The first one he had pulled out, which had turned out to be ten-pages thick, contained the picture of a nerdy-as-shit-looking fella named Donovan McCallister – 42, single, Director of Development at the San Diego Office of IEC's ten-billion-dollar research and development branch, five-foot-eleven, blue eyes, yada yada yada. Underneath his dissertation of information were other high-ranking officials as well as a brief description of the building and grounds where the clandestine meeting was to take place. One glance at the info and it was stored in his brain.

Paul hadn't been to San Diego since his old man's funeral. Although the city was a vacationer's paradise, since his father's passing, the ideal Californian city had lost its luster. He had gotten overly drunk at the wake and said things to family members that he regretted to this day. But, for the sake of an easy, couple-day security gig, he could muster through it. Besides, he had made plans to meet up with his little brother afterward. He couldn't wait to dote on his bro's kids.

After landing in San Diego, Paul had gone straight to his favorite watering hole in the city which, by luck, happened to be within a 15-minute walk of his new assignment. This had become more than a routine for him after departing an airplane; it had become a necessity. He found himself sitting on a barstool earlier and earlier as the months ticked by and, for the first time ever, thought about it before a job.

The bar was softly lit, dank, and too warm, like most dives seemed to be. Stale beer and recycled cleaning detergent hit his senses hard. He liked it there; there were no college kids trying to show how tough they were to their girlfriends by picking fights with every guy they saw when their liquid courage set it. It was where he would go to meet his dad when he was in town.

He ordered two beers like always and set one down next to him for his dad. In the complicated family that the two boys were raised in, Paul and his father remained extremely close and this ritual of buying his old man a beer kept the memory and love of his father with him. But he had a couple hours to kill before he was supposed to check in at the Navy building and ordered the first IPA he saw. Then he ordered several more.

Paul spent more time and money there than he had intended and finally made it to the naval base where the hot-shot meeting was to take place. He figured he would scope the place out first, find the best means of in and exfil and strategic locations, and locate defensible areas. Although these jobs were usually uneventful, surveying the surrounding area eased his nerves; plus, it made him feel more deserving of the huge paychecks he received for these inconsequential jobs.

He flashed his several top-level security clearance IDs at the front desk guards and set foot in a building that, in just a few short hours, would no longer exist. After scoping out the area, he hurried to their meeting spot as he realized he was about to be late. He was clean-shaven and presentable, but his head was cloudy. A hangover was imminent.

"Hey, hey, hey, look at this goon-fuck," goaded a voice from up ahead.

He found his long-time service buddy Jordan Brady smiling at him impishly. Jordan had been a SEAL in his past life and had been through some hellish deployments, so it was no surprise that he bore the look of someone who was regularly haunted by those ghosts. Paul knew he was a good soldier and knew that behind those young eyes, Jordan suffered. It was, however, great to see a familiar face.

"Aw, come here, you little shit. How are ya, buckaroo?" Paul exclaimed, giving Jordan a strong hug.

"Hey, fuck you, old man. How the fuck are you anyway? Where you been?"

"Pri-sec in the devil's playground, baby," Paul replied, glancing over the kid's shoulder. "Let's catch up later, Jordy. I'm late as fuck here and I gotta check this place out better."

"Yeah, yeah, all right. I'll see you in a few. Let's grab some cold daddies after this."

Paul threw him a smile and strode away. He liked

Jordan, but he *hated* small talk. Of course, it wasn't just his distaste for inconsequential conversation that had him skirting his friend; if anyone smelled alcohol on his breath, he would never be hired again.

The next few hours were mindless and monotonous. Paul was absolutely pissed at himself for buying those beers, but the buzz wore off and his head eventually cleared. The three sticks of gum he chewed hopefully masked any lingering smell.

The folks from EIC who had hired him arrived and he greeted each of them by their respective titles according to the manilla folder. He always gained trust by asking of the whereabouts of wives or children and other important people he had learned of from the secretive files.

His *assets* filed through the government building, down the maze of hallways and offices and into a black auditorium with him closely in tow.

He stood for 20 or so minutes in the back of the dark, narrow room, listening to the nerdy Donovan-guy talk about the future of America and some ass-load of uranium they had found.

Ever-watchful, if not also bored, Paul's attention was pricked when the afternoon program suddenly changed. In what seemed like the middle of the dark-haired science-boy's speech, an important-looking goon – Ted the COO whom Paul recognized from the folder – raced to the stage and a little blond woman yanked Donovan from the podium. According to the folder's synopsis, the guy was important and one hell of a cutthroat. But he had a look he didn't trust and a toothy grin which made Paul uneasy.

Paul watched, wondering what the fuck was going on as Donovan was stripped from the podium and escorted to the back door of the hall by the sexy blonde. He knew these big-dollar energy companies worked in weird ways, but it was the expression Donovan made as he was being torn from his position that made

Paul uncomfortable. The look in the scientist's eyes was a weird mix of confusion, anger, and worry. And Paul didn't like any of it.

As the COO took the mic, Paul watched the blonde and Donovan leave through the back door. The woman was not on Paul's list of important people tonight, but Donovan was.

Paul knew Jordan would be plenty capable of handling the rest of the presentation by himself. He caught Jordan's eye, who appeared just as confused and annoyed, and signaled with his head that he was going to go see where the two were off to. Jordan nodded in agreement.

Donovan was one of the names on the list of important people *he* was being paid to protect; it was his business. Paul sneaked to the back and out the door Donovan and the girl had exited a moment before. The blonde must have been moving at a clip because he spotted them several hundred yards down the connecting naked hallway. He could hear the girl's light but commanding voice carrying on and on as she escorted Donovan away.

Hugging the wall so as not to be noticed, Paul lost them through a massive, steel blast door. The door shut with a heavy clang, but the click of the solid locking mechanism didn't follow. Looking over his shoulder to make sure he was alone, he followed.

Distant booms reverberated somewhere and Paul paused in step, taking notice of his arm hair standing on end. A shriek buzzing overtook the earbud in his headset and he ripped it out as the hum became high-pitched and unbearable. Paul stood in nervous expectation. He had a sixth sense for looming calamity. His hand fell down to the holster on his hip which carried a 9mm Ruger depleted-tip gen-ten pistol, a reaction from pure muscle memory. His stomach twisted as he thought about how he had just lost one of the people he was being paid to protect and he broke into a jog after them.

He hadn't made it a few paces in before the hallway exploded into a conflagration of white light and shattering debris. Paul was thrown backwards 30 feet down the hallway, landing on his right shoulder. He cried out as he felt it tear from its socket. He lifted his head in time to see the entire hallway before him collapse into dust and flame as the floor crumpled into the basement levels below.

The emptiness racing toward him, Paul froze in nonplussed disbelief and waited. The last sensation he remembered was falling forever only to land onto his back. He opened his eyes briefly to see the ceiling rain down on him and was instantly knocked unconscious.

CHAPTER TEN

Day One: 1746 Hours

Lindsey and Donovan, after confirming the man was alive, pulled him from the rubble. As they drew the weary man from the debris, Donovan noticed the man's arm didn't feel quite right. It moved in ways an arm shouldn't move; it had to be broken or dislocated. Once the victim was clear of the rubble, Donovan was able to get a good look at him.

"Oh gosh, I know him. He's one of the security guys. I remember seeing him in the auditorium." Donovan couldn't hide his relief.

"Yeah, I think you're right. In fact, I *know* you're right." Lindsey pointed to the man's hip where a security badge and the black of a pistol grip showed. "The only people armed around here are troops and these private security guys."

"Yeah well… he looks pretty jacked up. Let's try to get him some help, or…" Donovan looked about in thought. "At least get him the hell out of here."

"Where do you think everyone else is?" Lindsey mused, following his gaze.

Donovan shot her a solemn look – they both knew everyone was either dead or buried. "All I know is it's a freaking miracle this guy's alive… That *we* are alive."

The large tattooed man let out a loud moan

followed by a dry, painful cough. His eyes were swollen shut but he managed to crack one open and train it on Donovan for a long moment. "Holy shit…" he said, finally looking around, taking in the scene around him. "Am I dead? 'Cause if this is heaven, I got some serious words from the big man."

The man's gaze turned back to them and Donovan could tell he recognized him. "What the fuck happened, Donny?" the man croaked

"You're security, right?" Donovan replied, eyeing the man in disbelief. His arm was dangling from its socket and hung limply at his side. With careful hands, Donovan and Lindsey helped the man to his feet and steadied him as he wavered there. Standing, it was disturbingly obvious his arm was fucked.

"I see why they pay you the big bucks," the man grunted sardonically. "But yeah, I'm Paul. I was hired as a bodyguard for you and the whole EIC entourage, excluding blondie here."

"Lindsey," Lindsey supplied with some irritation.

"Well, hi Lindsey…" Paul replied with the same intonation she had used. "So, who else have you seen? Who else survived and do we know who the fuck attacked us?"

Lindsey's voice was suddenly small. "So, you think we were attacked too?"

"Well, that wasn't no earthquake… I was working with a buddy, an ex-SEAL, on your detail. We should start by finding him and getting things lined out."

"This place is leveled, man. I think it would be best for all of us to get topside and work on possible rescue strategies from there," suggested Donovan. "I have a feeling this place is gonna get worse."

"Yeah," agreed Paul with a sigh, again looking around at the destruction. "That may be best." He looked down at his arm. "Well, fuck me. That ain't good."

Donovan started to offer some help – though he knew not

what – but stopped as Paul bent over and rested his right-hand on the ground. He stepped on his four fingers and, with a quick jerking movement, popped the joint back into place. The security guard let out a roar of pain and frustration then fell silent, panting. He was obviously dazed and shaken.

He fingered the deep laceration on his thigh, shaking his head like it was more of an annoyance than a serious injury. Donovan suspected he suffered from a concussion due to his wavering balance, but the man's fortitude and resilience gave Donovan and Lindsey a renewed sense of action, and they began to scout possible ways out of the collapsed hole.

As they clambered over debris, Paul worked his pistol free and then attempted to rack it with no luck. The fall had dented the slide so much the gun was as useful as a prop.

"So, like I was asking before – do we know what the fuck happened?" Paul asked, this time directing his question specifically at Lindsey.

They stopped and Lindsey and Donovan exchanged uneasy glances.

"Well," began Lindsey, "I don't know if you heard, but before anything happened, there was a series of far-off explosions. This was followed by what we believe was some kind of EMP detonation."

"We *were* fucking attacked then," Paul concluded matter-of-factly.

"As far as we can tell, yes," Donovan confirmed gravely.

"Was it the goddamn Koreans or the fucking Iranians?" the man exploded. "I swear to Jesus I have been saying this day was coming goddammit."

Donovan fidgeted under the stocky man's bellows. "Well, we have no clue, but we do know we have to get the hell out of here and find help." As he said this a burning piece of ceiling fell and landed just feet from him, still ablaze. He looked at them, his face illuminated by the simmering piece at their feet. "And we need to do it now."

The three of them spent the next 30 minutes frantically trying to find possible routes out of the cavernous ruin. Several more pieces had fallen from the fire above, missing them by mere feet. They were running out of time.

The small hint of red and orange light they had been relying on to navigate had grown to a fierce yellow thanks to the spreading fire overhead. The brighter light was appreciated, but the growing flames sent Lindsey and Donovan into panic mode as the heat gradually increased in the room.

Paul, keeping his cool as he was trained to do, searched the ceiling for a way out. They had thoroughly checked the floor they were on for doors or other means of egress, but had found nothing. Paul could see several openings in the mangled building above them – exhaust holes where smoke and superheated gases had been able to escape – but nothing that the three of them could possibly use. Scouring everything above his head, Paul finally found a large crack away from any impinging flame through which he could see faint, dying sunlight. *An exit.* He called the two over, giving orders to find a way up to it. Hopefully it would be big enough. It had to be.

After another long ten minutes of rising temperatures and anxiety, they identified the only possible route up and set off scaling the uneven walls. Donny led the way just as the sun began to stretch its last and softest rays on the desolate destruction.

Scraped, exhausted, and bloodied, they climbed the 25 feet out of the demolished building to rest on a concrete landing which must have, at one time, been part of the first-story flooring. There, they gazed at the true nature of that from which they had just emerged in the meager dusk sun.

What had once been a massive government shrine to military prowess now lay in a pile of smoldering destruction. Paul gaped in utter awe and reverence of the carnage. How had they survived?

The three of them stood on the precipice of the ruination for several minutes in silence. Paul noticed Donovan gripping Lindsey's hand tightly but didn't say anything. With a sigh, he turned to view San Diego harbor. Donovan made a sound as though he was going to say something, but stopped upon spotting what Paul was gaping at.

Every single U.S. military warship was in flames. Smoldering pieces drifted lazily on the waves and debris speckled the docks. The question of whether they had been attacked was answered instantly.

Oh god, Sam and the kids, Paul thought. After a moment of further musing, he said aloud, "Hey… thanks for the rescue, but uh, I gotta go. I-I have family I need to find."

Donovan and Lindsey gauged each other's responses before Lindsey said, "Well, we are coming with you."

"No no no, this is my own shit, *family* shit."

"Hey, we're here alone. We trust each other… sort of… right?" Lindsey argued. "I think we should stick together."

Paul considered her for a moment and then looked at Donovan. "What you thinking, Donny?"

"Let's find whoever you gotta find, then get some answers," the scientist declared. "But first, I don't know about you guys, but I've been up since about three this morning," Donny said. "I say we try to sleep for a couple hours. This has been the longest day of my entire life and I am in no shape to go wandering off in the dark."

"God yes, agreed," Lindsey cheered.

In a comic fashion, the two looked to Paul simultaneously to await his response.

"Yeah," groaned Paul. "We won't be able to do shit in this pitch black anyway. Only a couple hours, then we set off to look for them."

It didn't take long before they found a place to rest behind a pile of debris atop what looked like a loading dock. The pad there was covered and relatively clean. They had no blankets and nothing in their hungry bellies, but the three were asleep the second they lay their heads down to rest.

CHAPTER ELEVEN

Day Two: 0450 Hours

Sam fought to open his eyes which had been glued together by a thick layer of grime. Realty donning on him, he rose in utter panic, angry with himself for somehow passing out before finding them. Early morning sun painted the eastern sky orange. He took a moment to find his bearings, then came up with a game plan. He had seen it earlier, but hadn't registered its importance – Dave & Busters. Sam took off in the direction of the only landmark he recognized, the only place he knew his family would be drawn to during this time of chaos.

The massive, pentagonal restaurant was located about 100 yards north of the I-8. As Sam drew near, he slowed. From his location just off the highway, it appeared as though the whole back end of the building had been caught in the mighty collapse of the colossal highway overpass. Despite its partial destruction, something told him to go in.

He made it over the chain-link fence and walked to the front where the huge blue-and-orange eponymous sign that normally hung 20 feet above two sets of glass front doors had fallen from its perch to block much of the entrance. Sam approached cautiously. His training as a firefighter reminded him of the inner collapse risk and that a fire could easily break out at any moment.

He heard a rustle and stopped to watch as, to his surprise, three teenagers hastily clambered through the broken glass of the double doors, worried expressions on their faces.

"Hey hey hey, is there anyone else in there?" Sam probed. The first two ran by without as much as a glance in his direction. "*Hey!* Is there anyone still in there? Did you see a woman with two small boys?"

The last of the three teens, a scrawny homeless kid with a crappy prison tattoo on his cheek and a fading 858 below his right eye, paused in step. "I dunno man. I think some of the roof felled down. We just shot in to see what's leff. I'd get the fuck outta here if I was you though. Some mothafuckas in there." And before Sam could respond, the teen turned to chase after the other two, yelling, "Fuck y'all, wait for me!"

Knowing he had no other option, Sam turned to face the dark entrance and, after a moment's consideration, ducked through the broken door and went inside.

The sprinkler system had obviously been running for at least a half hour. An inch of water was free-standing on the carpeted floor. A musky, copper smell hit his nostrils as a mist dampened him. The building was dark save a handful of dull battery-run emergency lights. A series of aberrant sparks shot off from a splayed and angry wire overhead. The interior was vast.

The front area was littered with tables, some with meals still sitting on them thoroughly soaked with putrid water while the large gaming area occupied the back. The place, for the most part, looked deserted.

Maybe the teen had been right. From what he could make out, now that his eyes had adjusted to the darkness, it appeared as though the back-right corner of the building must have caved in where the overpass had fallen. The place was unusually quiet; people had fled in a hurry. He thought about yelling for his children and wife, but thought better.

As he carefully stepped through the water and debris, he passed a bar on his right and, for a brief second, pondered pouring himself a full glass of bourbon. The thought was fleeting, but powerful nonetheless. Just beyond the bar in what he assumed to be the kitchen, he heard an angry outburst from a man. Sam sneaked in further to investigate, hiding behind a huge Batman arcade game, lifeless and dark.

"The fuck you mean *you can't*? Open that motherfucker!"

Sam heard someone with a peevish and feeble voice respond to the yelling man, but was unable to make out the words.

"Imma give you one last chance to open the fuckin safe or my dude here will fuck you up."

The response this time was clouded by soft begging sobs.

BANG BANG.

Sam stood bolt upright and hastily made his way to a wall. "Fuck," he mumbled. "Oh fuck."

One of the first phenomena to take place in civil unrest, power outages, or otherwise unexpected urban incidents was looting and widespread anarchy. People, knowing the police would have more than their hands full with other duties, began to break into stores, homes, and restaurants to take anything they could. The looters in the back office were no different.

Voices high with adrenaline and confidence, the men in the other room grew more animated as they left the kitchen and entered the main room of the restaurant.

With the murderous looters a mere 15 feet away, there was no way Sam could make it to the front door or even to the exit 30 feet to his right. Heart hammering, he turned and slid under the booth nearby, bumping his leg on the table stand. Silverware jittered off the table into the sodden carpet with a dampened splash. The looters fell silent.

"The fuck was that?" one of the men said after a moment. "Sounded over there."

"Someone's fuckin in here, man," came the whispered reply.

"You better get the fuck outa here, yo!" called the first man to the vast room. "I'm not fucking around. I'll fuck you up!"

Sam held his breath; he knew they would hold nothing back and shoot him where he lay if they found him.

Their footsteps grew closer and Sam recoiled into the water under the table, his back pressed to the booth bench. They would need to look directly under the table to actually see him.

Footsteps moved the water next to the booth as the men neared. Sam spotted two sets of legs a foot from his cursory hiding place. Thank God the silverware was hidden under the murky water.

As one of the looters sighed, he lowered his hand which gripped a handgun that, although old, very much still worked. The long minute of silence was suddenly broken by a loud splash followed by a crash.

"What the *fuck*?"

"Holy fuck, that mothafucka aint dead!"

"Shoot that mothafucka!"

The two slogged through the water back to the kitchen, leaving Sam in complete and utter confusion. Momentarily, the entirety of the handgun's magazine – 14 rounds – was expelled. The audible thud of a body crumpling into water ensued. The two men, in the thrill of murdering one man twice, ran from the building.

Sam lay in the cold, rancid water under the table for what was no doubt 30 minutes. Part of him wanted to go check on the man who had just murdered, but he knew of course no one could survive that. Once he was certain the looters were gone, he stretched his legs out and sighed in relief. He was unsure of his next move. He felt as though some of his hope had been ruthlessly slaughtered in the kitchen with the looters' victim.

CHAPTER TWELVE

Day Two: 0224 Hours

Paul stirred awake, his few hours of shallow sleep cut far too short. He glanced at his Citizen kinetic eco-drive watch, glowing hands still ticking thanks its completely mechanical movements: 0224. He had only been asleep for a couple hours, but he felt a strong urge to wake the others and get moving. He resisted and decided the other two could probably do with a couple hours' more shut eye.

He started to move, but felt a weight on him. Lindsey the blonde was using his legs – well, his crotch – as a pillow. Donny lay beside her, his head in her lap. For a long moment, Paul gazed down at Lindsey, taking in her matted hair, thick with dirt, soot, and debris. Following a lock of her hair around her ear with his finger, he marveled at their circumstances with gravity. Just a day ago, he would have asked this young woman out for drinks and, more than likely, he would have woken up next to her the following morning with his head in a drumming fog.

But now he stared down at the small lock moving gently with each breath she took and felt nothing but empty sadness. He reflected on that last week or so with his ex, on what could have been. He thought about *her* thick, blond hair and about the many mornings with her sleeping on his chest as he breathed her in.

Paul stayed there with Lindsey on his lap for several moments, not wanting to get up and accept the devastated world around him. He took a second to think of all the simple things in his life that he had so speciously overlooked and had taken for granted. His ex, his parents, his brother's family which he loved as if it were his own. He wondered what those two boys would look like when they grew up, what they would be like. Would they admire him as the warrior uncle who was always playing with them and spoiling them? Or would they think of him as the heavy drinker that could never find himself a wife and family? So many thoughts and foresight into his own life raced through his brain in that short moment of utter stillness.

Most of Paul's experiences with woman had been in the form of drunken one-nighters or short spans of loveless and sex-filled dating. He had managed, with the help of online dating apps, to secure short trysts, most of which were just ways of eating up time when he was on leave. He found he pretty much had to wait to get back home to find any sort of physical attention during his deployments; he couldn't get himself to pay for a prostitute – the women back east had had half a century of hating Americans to pretty much wholly dispel the attraction to the foreigners.

Paul wanted what Sam had. He wanted the family, the wife, and the kids. He wanted to live in a four-bedroom three-bathroom house on the edge of town where he knew the neighbors by name and he could have snowball fights with neighborhood children. He had spent most of his professional life becoming the badass that he had always wanted to be, but now, he was less concerned with being a hot shot full of piss and vinegar and more worried about a legacy – a family.

He had always thought Sam had made a mistake getting married so young and starting a family and gave him plenty of shit about it, but now it was what Paul wanted most. Those dreams seemed farther and farther from his grasp as Paul couldn't seem to keep a damn girl for more than a month.

But several years back, he had caught his break and, although his philosophy was to take it day by day, after a couple dates with this girl, he had begun to think long term.

Her name was Shyann. Aside from her thick, dirty-blond hair and shapely body, she was a warm and welcoming presence in his life. She took care of him, respected him, and cooked for him – every quality of the dying breed of woman known as "housewife." Although they had warned him never to date a bar rat, he had started dating this one and fallen for her quickly.

In the early stages of their relationship, Paul had felt butterflies in his belly at the sight of her. After long – or short – absences, they would exuberantly, desperately, tear into each other until they could no longer move. It had been some of the happiest times of his life.

But they had slowly grown apart. His traveling around the world coupled with his inability to talk about his work because of the confidentiality disclaimers he signed drove a massive wedge between the two. Plus, he was a Hunt, which meant he was a booze hound. He was very capable of handling his liquor, a skill acquired in the military, but damaging to the relationship nevertheless. After a mere year of living together, Shyann had had enough and bid him farewell. The split had been rough on him and had only drawn him deeper into the bottle.

He thought about her, deep in a far-off daydream a million years and a million miles away. He wondered if she thought about him late at night like this. But none of that mattered now, none of that existed now in this fucking nightmare of an apocalypse.

As a soldier he was used to waking up mid-sleep and being able to act and fight and show courage; it never seemed to bother him. But now he was hesitant to get up and, although he wouldn't admit it even to himself, he was scared.

As his eyes slowly adjusted to the dark Californian skies, he took in the harrowing sight around him. Most of the naval base appeared to be leveled and burning, the empty black of night alight from buildings in conflagration. The ocean looked on fire. Nothing was left floating on the black water. His heart sank.

Still aware of the eerily vacant wharves and shipyard, Paul slow shifted his gaze to the sky. His fears were suddenly buttressed by a deep, electric hum which rattled his very core. Instantly, he was struck by the realization that this shit-show was no nightmare. For the first time in his life, he felt utterly helpless and, worst of all, irrevocably afraid.

He scuttled his body back into Lindsey's, eyes wide open, heart pumping, and mind racing. Between a battered body, a mild concussion, lack of sleep, and a deep fear he had never encountered before, Paul found himself unable to move. He had heard the phrase "frozen with fear" before and had thought it was a thing for pussies with no adrenaline control. But there he was, eyes fixed to the sky, too scared to move an inch or make a sound.

He lay perfectly still, Lindsey's warmth radiating through his coat, and watched as a dozen spacecraft flew overhead. Their silent and silver bodies were barely visible except for the blue-white electrical currents running along their lengths. The ships were long, wide, and impossibly big. The hull of every ship seemed to move, to crawl as if it were alive. But there was something familiar about them.

Although they gleamed metallic and seemed to be adorned with technology far more advanced than anything Paul had seen in his entire career working for the DoD, they reminded him somehow of U.S. Navy ships.

His eyes fixed on the largest of the mysterious craft which flew in the middle of the group; something about its bulging mass and long, wide hull reminded him of an aircraft carrier. The ship was flanked on either side by a slightly smaller but far more destructive-looking craft. Three ships half that size, slender and streamlined with short wings and a stubby front, led the formation. And behind, although hard to see from where he was, Paul could make out more ships of varying shapes and, Paul assumed, capabilities. Everything about it was familiar, hauntingly familiar. It looked exactly like a U.S. Navy carrier group.

He knew no good would come from freaking out. There was literally nothing he could do; there was nothing any of them could do. So, he just sat in awe – blood coursing with adrenaline, eyes disbelieving what they were seeing – and watched as a whole squadron of ships passed overhead.

They were gone as quickly as they had come, taking the distressing electrical hum with them.

Paul sat there wide-eyed with one terrible thought in his head.

We are fucked.

We are *so* fucked.

CHAPTER THIRTEEN

Day Two: 0558 Hours

The meandering trail of blood from the dead boy's head had finally reached the two of them before Maggie gained the courage and willpower to stand. It had been a full five minutes since she was attacked and subsequently saved by her pubescent son, but she had another, younger and more vulnerable one hiding not far from there. The dead kid's two buddies who had run past would no doubt come looking for their now silent friend.

Zachary's hand tight in hers, Maggie led him back to the van where they found Liam sitting in the back corner, his hands around his legs. He looked tired and scared. Zachary went in first to comfort him. As Maggie made to crawl in after her son, she felt the hairs on her arms and along the nape of her neck stand on end. Within seconds, another low vibration began to resonate in her eardrums, shaking a layer of dust off the sheet metal of the van. A sensation of déjà vu hit her and she recognized it was the same hum that she heard and felt right before their car had been blown sky-high. Heart thrumming, she scrambled into the van and heaved the door shut, taking care to leave it open just a sliver so she could see out.

Within seconds, a gray, metallic aircraft drifted into view, emanating a deep and undulating electrical hum that sounded like a subwoofer turned to maximum. Beside her Zachary and Liam covered their ears.

It was like nothing she had ever seen; all she knew for certain was that it was not of this world, it was not manmade.

It was about 200 feet in length with a front shield likened to that of a spider's head which was adorned with 12 to 15 black, oddly-shaped projections. Perhaps they were windows. Around the windows or sensors were spiny, metal rods that moved and twitched like the whiskers of a sniffing dog.

The apparent helm of the ship convened atop the front of the enormous feat of engineering before narrowing into a single ridge that formed the spine of the craft. Although Maggie understood it to be a machine, the surface of the ship moved and undulated as if it were covered in a skin of mercury or liquid metal. Arachnid-like pincers appendaged from the body in sets of three as the ship surged and swelled. A glowing, dancing string of white plasma energy adjoined the pincers.

Attached to the entomological anatomy were long, smooth wings that showcased varying sections of what appeared to be chrome steel and nonstop movement. The spacecraft's expansive cylindrical body pulsed with electrical currents which seemed to warp the siding of the ship as if it were bending the very fabric of the space.

The flying abomination did not linger as it rode the sky, but Maggie was able to take in every inch of the nightmare. Once the machine passed on, the hum in the air faded into nothing. Maggie collapsed back into the darkness of the van and pulled her kids to her chest. She knew they could sense her fear and feel her violent shaking, but she didn't know what to tell them, or even if she dared to.

This can't be real... goddamn aliens. Fucking aliens, is all she could think.

"Ma..." Zachary said, breaking her disquieting thoughts. "Ma... What was it? What did you see?"

"Mama," Liam whispered. "Mama, why would otha people do that? Why would they huwt us?"

"People?" Maggie said aloud. "No baby, people didn't... People couldn't have..." Her sentence trailed off. *People? Jesus, were the pilots of that ship people? Humans?* She pulled them in tighter. "We need to find your father."

Trembling and still in shock, the three held each other, unsure of what to do next. Maggie was low on strength and courage, but knew now was the time her boys needed her most. Weary not only from her violent encounter with the thug but from the mental gymnastics she had just undergone, she mustered strength and pushed her festering thoughts to the back of her mind.

She yearned for Sam's strong arms and confidence. He would know where to go and what to do. But he wasn't. They were alone in a white van surrounded by death and destruction on a desolate highway.

"Dads dead, huh?" Zachary breathed after a long while. Liam's head shot up, eyes as wide as basketballs, to his mother's face. "That's what you saw, isn't it? Dad's freaking dead and you saw him in the street and you don't wanna tell us, and now we're alone and we're gonna die too..."

"Jesus Zachary, no. Don't ever say that. Your father isn't dead. He just got lost and is probably out helping other people right now. You know that." Her response was frail and didn't convince anyone. She reached for Liam's hand to soothe him but his gaze had dropped to the floor. "He's alive and just... lost, that's all..."

Distant blasts broke the grave silence between

them and Maggie froze, heart in her throat. Despite dawn's glorious light peeking through the slightly ajar van door, the horrific sound of breaking glass, twisting metal, and high-pitched buzzing buttressed by the now all-too-familiar electric hum rattled them into terror. It took only a few seconds for Maggie to make out that the alarming sound was drawing closer – fast.

The blood drained from her face and she instantly knew what was taking place. Another one was coming, another wave, another attack – this second run would pulverize the roadway and kill whoever had survived the previous assault. She knew they needed to move, but she found herself frozen. As the noise swelled into a terrifying fervor, she could actually feel the whump of that electric hum in her chest.

"Zachary!" she screamed over the deafening cacophony. She already had a tight grip on Liam, but Zachary had pushed himself deeper into the van's corner thinking his father was gone.

Dust and debris rose around them, whirling and twirling like a dust tornado. She yanked both boys out of the van and ran, Zachary at her side and Liam scooped under her arm like an unruly duffle bag. Together they sprinted back to the culvert and leapt into the muddy and blood-soaked ditch.

Maggie turned back to see a ship much larger and streamlined than the first directly over the road, emitting a blinding, blue light that, when swept across the area, upturned everything in its path. The van they had been in just a moment before was flipped 50 feet while cars and pieces of asphalt flurried into the air with a mighty roar.

The craft was gone as quickly as it had shown up. Panting, emotionally and physically drained, and weak, they lay in the bloody water at the edge of the I-8. They couldn't catch a break, they couldn't win.

A large green sign that was, just moments ago, suspended over the freeway clattered to the ground to Maggie's right. It lodged itself in the soft mud but had several feet of white lettering still visible. SAN DIEGO ZOO EX…"

She read the sign over and over. Then it hit her like a cannonball. She sat bolt upright. "I know where your father is."

And with that, still holding both boys' hands, she got up and headed toward what she prayed was the right way.

CHAPTER FOURTEEN

Day Two: 0627 Hours

Unsure of what to do, Sam remained sitting in the inch-high cold, fetid water that had flooded Dave & Busters. Although the looters were gone, he was still terrified. He found himself trapped in a repeating nightmare that had stalked him since his childhood.

He was ten years old again and walking down Park Boulevard in his childhood neighborhood of Penn Station in San Diego. With each step, the sensation of impending doom and catastrophe swelled. Something was following him; he was sure of it.

He stepped up his pace to a jog, continuously looking over his shoulder for the invisible enemy. Finally, fear overtook him and he broke into a hard run. When he looked back this time, he saw it – a lion. With a heavy head of coarse, brown hair and eyes as black as coal, it chased after him, knocking aside cars and crashing into homes. Twenty feet in height, it was a monster and fully capable of eating him. The enormous incisors covered in blood assured him of that.

With a cry, Sam pushed on. Around the bend, his house came into sight. But he knew he wouldn't make it; the lion would catch him and tear him limb-from-limb. He could feel the lion's breath on the nape of his neck. Right as the cat had him in his massive, putrid jaw, Sam snapped awake.

That fucking lion again… It got bigger and more terrible

every time he thought of it. The lion had chased him since he had visited the zoo with his family as a five-year-old. He had wanted to visit the lion exhibit first as lions were his favorite, but what he had seen quickly fixed that.

Zoo staff had just thrown half a carcass of an antelope in the enclosure and Sam and his family had just walked up on the lion savagely tearing into bloody flesh.

He sighed. That stupid nightmare had been… A shadow of a thought occurred to him. When the idea materialized, he leapt up, smacking his head on the forgotten table above.

Crawling through the water, he gasped, "The zoo." The goddamn zoo.

The little house on the corner of Brookes Ave and Albert Street where Sam had been raised was about two blocks from Park Boulevard which, from there, was a five-minute walk to the San Diego Zoo entrance. It was a small 1,700 square-foot three-bedroom house with a beautiful garden and small front porch. It was a cozy home his parents had bought 40 years ago.

Although way out of their price range, Rebecca had inherited quite a sum from her father's passing and they had decided that buying a family home would be the best way to honor his memory. Plus, it had always been their dream to raise a family in that neighborhood. The schools were great, the city was beautiful, and they had one of San Diego's greatest treasures within walking distance. The home was so close to the zoo in fact, that that was how they gave directions to visitors planning to stop by the house. "You know where the zoo is? Just go two blocks this way…" The zoo became so much of the neighborhood and their lives that it quite literally became synonymous with home.

Besides the unbelievable pain that radiated throughout his entire body, that thought continuously coursed through his brain. He knew that heading in the direction of the sixth largest zoo on Earth would be the best chance he had of finding his wife and children. It was the landmark they had used for decades to navigate through the chaos of big-city traffic to find his parents' house. And somehow, he knew without a doubt, his wife would be thinking the same thing. That's where they would be. He *knew* they were alive; he could feel it.

Running through the streets of San Diego yelling their names and looking in every restaurant or building they had ever visited was just not an option, not with the attack that had happened earlier, not with what he had witnessed in Dave & Busters.

He had never felt so powerless.

Over the years, there had been many times when he had been absent because he had been on-duty at the firehouse. There had even been a 20-day stint of separation shortly after the terrorist attacks in Denver, Colorado. The Federal Emergency Management Agency had sent out a nationwide request for help to all agencies asking for paramedics, firemen, and anyone else willing to answer a call for help in a massive cleanup-and-rescue effort.

After a short but difficult conversation with his wife, Sam had received approval to go. Six hours later, his fire department had sent him over 700 miles to help treat wounded victims and assist in body recoveries. It was an experience he would never forget and never truly get over.

He had been away from his young family for longer than he thought he could handle. And he had recovered bodies of children no older than his own. The dedication to the job at hand and the service to his country made the sting of the distance of his loved ones easier to manage. Nevertheless, he had returned home a little off.

But these couple days were proving harder on him than those weeks four years ago; panic was not far from him.

He slowly and delicately crawled out from under the table. He had to get out of this vast, dank building. The smell of death and sewage filled his nostrils. With zero hesitation, he went in the direction that he had heard the thug's yells and gunshots. He knew it was futile; no one would survive a barrage of that many shots, but he had to check. In the faint red glow of the emergency lights, he quickly stumbled upon the victim of the wanton murder. There, in several inches of water, lay a kid.

Jesus Christ, Sam thought, looking down at the body.

A young man, no taller than five and a half feet by Sam's judgment, with a hollow eye socket and missing jaw lay dead in a pool of filthy water. A blood-spattered nametag on his chest with "Samuel" written on it was his only identity. Sam squirmed in disgust. Poor kid was most likely a dishwasher or a busboy, not a day over 17 by the looks of it.

"Jesus fucking Christ," Sam repeated, this time aloud.

Those assholes had thought this poor kid might know the whereabouts of a safe or where money might be kept. Sam doubted there was anything of the sort here, but his teen, this *kid,* lay in a pool of disgusting water with half his face missing because those punks wanted to get their hands on a couple bucks. A cursory glance down his body explained the earlier tirade of gunshots. There were a dozen black and brown penny-sized holes throughout the kid's torso. The realization of the anarchy that was taking hold in society was real. Time to move.

Sam clambered out of the broken door of the restaurant, squinting into the warm, orange morning sun hanging low in the thick ocean fog. He stayed there for several moments, squatting with his back on the warm siding of the building.

The Jacob Dekema Freeway that spanned 100 feet in the air had previously partially covered the parking lot for the restaurant. Now, it was a pile of rubble atop dozens of cars. Its edges were smooth and polished like cut marble meant for a countertop. Peering southwest from the entrance of the building, Sam could only discern collapsed sections of overpasses and bridges, all in the same hundred-foot sections. It was like a path had just been sawed through civilization. And it led directly toward his parents' home.

For several long moments, Sam listened to the distant but constant discord of people's screams, periodic gunshots, and an incessant growling of an electrical buzz.

It was almost over him before he even saw it.

CHAPTER FIFTEEN

Day Two: 0554 Hours

Lindsey was up before Donovan who remained motionless in her lap. After a few moments of bewilderment, she realized she had found a pillow on Paul's crotch. Not especially excited at this revelation, she gently drew away, not wanting to wake the security officer.

She had always been an early riser, even in her younger days with her dad. But ever since starting work at IEC, if she could sleep in until 5:00, that was a good night's sleep. She loved the routine and the fast pace, but her friends often remarked that she had swiftly aged a decade.

Her efforts not to wake Paul didn't matter; he was already awake. Actually, he appeared as though he had been awake all night as his face was taut with stress and his eyes were heavy. He didn't look at her as she sat up. His unwavering gaze remained on the sky overhead.

Unfazed, she glanced once more at Donovan who slept on, an arm outstretched and a hand on her lower leg. He had done so much to keep them alive and to stay with her. And still, as he slept, he had his hand on her as if in protection.

Making the executive decision to get everyone up and moving, Lindsey gently pulled away from Donovan and stood. Paul allotted her a mere glance before returning his stoic gaze to the sky.

Her body wanted to stretch, but her sore bones and muscles cried out in protest. The sun was barely waking; a faint glow from the waning moon and residual burning fires illuminated the area enough that she could make out some detail.

Donovan coughed, jerking himself awake, and Lindsey grinned. At this, even Paul labored to his feet. "Jesus fuck," Paul muttered.

"You can say that again," Donovan agreed.

"How'd you sleep? I know *you* were comfy," Paul teased with a flirty grin.

Lindsey rolled her eyes before looking back out at the destruction. "It's so much worse than it looked like yesterday. I mean, it legit looks like they took out the whole base."

"And they may have," Paul replied matter-of-factly.

"Huh, what do you mean? Why would you say that?" Donovan did not sound pleased. "There is no goddamn way."

"Listen," Paul instructed. "Do you hear that? It was like that all night..."

Lindsey glanced about. "Yeah okay, hear what?"

"Listen to how quiet it is…"

"Everything is burning around us," Lindsey replied.

"No that's not it... I mean, where are the jets, the fighters, the tanks? The goddamn *American* military? Why can't we hear them? Why haven't they tried to fight back? Where are the bombs and missiles?" Paul gestured to the smoldering mess around them. "I personally know the military might of the United States. It makes no sense why we're not fucking fighting back."

The three fell silent at this revelation.

Paul mused aloud, "Unless –"

"Unless they targeted all the military bases first," Lindsey concluded, exchanging looks with the two men.

"Ha, no way," Donovan snickered. "There is no fucking way that the *whole* U.S. military was destroyed beyond the means of a counterattack in half a day. Impossible… Right?"

"How else would you explain it, Donny?" Lindsey quipped.

"Look, there is no country on Earth that could do what these things did," Paul added.

Lindsey couldn't help but scoff in incredulity. "So, what are we talking about here? Aliens?"

Paul looked up at the sky. "Well, they sure as hell aren't from here."

Donovan laughed nervously. "We don't know anything yet. It could very well have been the Russians or Iranians or a —"

"It *wasn't them!*" choked Paul. After a moment of gathering himself, he looked at them. "I woke up last night and saw what the hell they were."

"What do you mean what *they* were?"

"I don't know. I woke up at like two-something and there was this buzzing sound, then dozens of these fucking huge ships floated just a couple hundred feet off the ground. They were going… way too slow for anything I have ever seen in the military."

"So?" Donovan prompted. "That doesn't really prove anythi —"

"Yes, it does. I've been with the DoD *for years*. I served overseas *for years*. I've held top-secret security clearance *for years*. And I have never seen what I saw last night. We don't stand a chance against these things."

"Okay, so we are really saying its aliens then?" Lindsey looked to Paul. When no one said anything, she murmured, "This is crazy."

They stood on the cement pad for half an hour debating what to do about food, sleep, and shelter. Discussions rose about where the mysterious invaders had come from, what they were, and what their purpose was for destroying San Diego.

Despite Donovan insisting that the attacks had originated from Russia or from the DRPK, Paul adamantly asserted that there was no way that weapons that advanced could have been kept a secret from the U.S. It was just impossible. Nevertheless, what they had were theories backed by anecdotal evidence. They needed to learn more.

Aside from the invaders' origins, they decided to travel to Paul's family house where he had grown up. From there, they would figure out their next steps.

Just as they began trudging through the naval port, a tremendous thundering pierced the air as a squadron of fighter jets appeared overhead.

"Fuck yeah!" Paul shouted heartily. "About *fucking* time!" The fighter bombers roared overhead and out of sight in less than a second. "A-45 Phoenixes," explained Paul somewhat breathlessly. "Get some, boys!"

Lindsey, eyes fixed on the sky, gave a short, elated laugh. "Thank God."

"About goddamn time!" Donovan yelled after the units.

Together, they ran the short distance around the building to gain a better view of what they hoped was the full-fledged wrath of an American counterattack. The deafening and sudden roar of another pack of jets rocketed over their heads, rattling the earth upon which they stood.

Ears stunned, Lindsey grinned after the squadron. Her elation waned just as quickly though as another aircraft accompanied by the all-too-familiar electric hum sailed overhead in pursuit.

The three of them watched in horror as it tailed a group of

three fighters who had separated over the bay. Seeing Paul break into a run, Lindsey followed. They made a short dash to a small ticket booth that, only days ago, had sold tickets to vacationers for jet boat rides. There, they nestled behind a plexiglass window and watched.

Several miles from shore, the three military aircraft swung around in a large circle as if to face their pursuer. A series of deep booms reverberated over the water as a brilliant beam of light emitted from the nose of the alien ship.

The A-45 Phoenixes dropped from the sky like flies that had been killed by a bug zapper. The distant roar of the aircraft collapsed into silence. Gaping, Lindsey, Paul, and Donovan watched as the pilots and their units tumbled from the sky. One ended up drifting downward like a kite that had escaped a wind current while the other two fell inland; great plumes of flame and smoke erupted around those. There were no missiles, projectiles, or contacts. Just three booms and the fighters had been rendered obsolete.

The other half of the squadron that had continued onward appeared now behind the alien craft, gaining on it with extraordinary speed. Two of the military jets launched missiles that made a cracking zip as they exploded forward. Lindsey was certain their opponent would be unable to defend itself against such a fast weapon.

An explosion of yellow-green electricity vented from the alien ship in all directions in a pulse of vitriolic energy. The missiles were intercepted and instantaneously nullified. They fell lifeless into the bay, exploding with hellacious booms upon contact with the water.

But the expanding wave of plasma energy did not stop there. It continued at exponential speed until it had caught up with the fighters which floundered momentarily in the air before nosing downward toward the ocean.

Lindsey sunk to the ground as the jets crashed into the bay. The U.S. military had just been rendered useless.

CHAPTER SIXTEEN

Day Two: 0746 Hours

Sam stayed rooted to the spot. He knew he needed to run, to hide, but what he was seeing was beyond anything he could have ever imagined.

It passed low over the ground about 150 feet to his left directly over the I-8, a dark-blue beam of light pulsing from the nose of the ship. Noiselessly, the craft scanned the highway, throwing cars, debris, and dust into the air as it passed. The only sound that reached Sam was the constant crashing of vehicles landing elsewhere.

The goddamn thing was cutting the highway up like a hot knife through butter. The 500-foot-long behemoth was unbelievably ugly but breathtaking to behold. Along its dark, metallic body ran incessant waves of electric blue, as if the ship were covered in plasmic currents.

The helm of the hideous craft looked like the head of a cobra, flared and ready to attack. Atop the head was an array of black glass that must have been windows, but from a distance, they looked like menacing eyes.

From the helm, the ship thinned to a round thorax with a flattened back which sported a huge tower hundreds of feet tall. To Sam, the engineering and physics of the craft simply didn't make sense. Two short, stubby appendages, which had to be wings (because what else could they be?), looked to contain no propulsion system Sam could recognize. They were, however, outfitted with cone-shaped structures that had to be weapons. A blue glow emanated from the backs of these wings.

The rear of the craft was larger and flatter yet and splayed with mechanical engineering like flaps and rudders of an airplane. Dissimilarly to manmade technology however, these flaps moved, undulated, and swelled along the electric current of the body.

Gaping, Sam watched as the ship flew by, leaving in its path total destruction. It turned slightly and suddenly he could make out something along the side of its tail.

Earth numbers, Arabic numerals.

Growing angrier and more incredulous the longer he stared at the numbers, he scoffed aloud. There was *no fucking way*. He tried to convince himself that what he was seeing was a trick of the light, or that his overly tired eyes were misreading some alien language.

Distant screams of terror arose from survivors in its path, people whom Sam could see. Those who had been searching for missing loved ones, scouring and pillaging empty cars, or looting nearby businesses stopped in horror. Many hid.

Sam's gaze darted from person to person, looking for signs of his wife and children. There were none.

The craft floated effortlessly along the length of the highway, beam cutting the road in half. It paid the fleeing people no heed; the ship only seemed interested in destroying the roadway. The more Sam thought back over the last day, the more he realized that he hadn't actually seen anyone killed by the ships. Sure, there had been a myriad of deaths, but those people had been in the wrong place at the wrong time.

Collateral damage. This struck Sam as odd. *If it's an attack, why not kill anyone?* He pondered on this. *Since the craft are so big, why waste time with singling out individuals?* But as Sam looked around, he noticed that no buildings had been destroyed (at least not on purpose) and all major civic centers remained perfectly intact. *They are going after transit areas. Holy shit, this might just be the first wave, rendering reinforcements obsolete for the real invasion.* Sam blanched at the thought. *More have to be coming.*

The craft methodically made its way down the highway, lacerating the cement. He watched as the beam whipped up dust and debris along the highway, obscuring the awful scene, and launched a white, commercial van into the air. Was it a trick of the brain or had he seen what looked like movement in that van seconds before?

The craft was vaporizing everything in its path; anyone with any sense would have cleared the roads a long time ago, especially his wife and kids. He watched motionlessly for a few more minutes as the unit continued to mangle the highway before a thought struck him.

Sam turned on heel and began to run along the side of the now destroyed building, eyeing the roof. He had to get up there. He *had* seen movement near that white van. There *had* been people there, familiar people.

Frantically, he churned through the overgrowth of vegetation that had accumulated alongside the building, clambering over debris as he searched. He found a rooftop maintenance ladder that looked in damn good condition considering the shape of the building, and made his way up. Although D&B was poised to collapse at any moment, Sam ignored the risks. He didn't need to be up there for long, only enough to get some answers. The more he reviewed the scene, the more certain he became — he had *definitely* seen three people scurry away from that white van on the highway before it was blown to hell.

He had a good vantage from the roof and watched the aircraft fly away. He surveyed the highway, seeing no evidence of the three survivors. With a sigh, he frowned. *It's not them. They would have left by now.*

His eyes returned to the massive ship lumbering through the air no more than half a mile away. It seemed to defy gravity and a number of other universal physics. How could it move so slowly, so gracefully with such little noise? Whatever this technology was, it was not of this world and was centuries ahead of anything he had ever witnessed or knew about.

He made his way to a boxy A/C unit, but paused in step as he spotted another smaller, more intimidating craft scream into view to idle near the larger one. It looked as if there were several converging on the same place. The same building. A stadium.

The stadium, once called Qualcomm, was approximately one mile, perhaps a 30-minute walk, from his current location at the demolished Dave & Busters off the I-8. His mission to set off in the direction of the zoo would have to be delayed. He had to know what the hell these things were and, more importantly, figure out what the hell they were doing.

Sam scaled down the ladder and took off in the direction of the stadium. As he cautiously went to find cover, yet another smaller ship zoomed overhead, stopped, and descended into the stadium. That put his running count up to a dozen. *What the fuck is in there?*

Heart hammering, he picked up his pace to a brisk walk and headed for a section of the bridge that had not yet been destroyed. He made his way over the five lanes of Camino Del Rio without a problem, hopped the guard rail, and trundled into the vegetation of the dried San Diego River. The overgrown riverbed was only 250 yards wide, but Sam thought sticking to the jungle-like ravine would be safer than trying to navigate the roads, especially with those *things* flying overhead.

The river, although without water, was marshy in places and full of garbage. It smelled of rot and trash and there were, just in his field of vision, at least 75 tents set up there. This place had become a homeless town. Overpopulation and homelessness had been a tourism killer of San Diego for almost a decade now.

Sam was in no mood to talk to, or listen to, the drug-induced ramblings of the dispossessed no doubt in stupors over what was taking place above them. If they were even conscious of it. So, he stayed hidden the best he could and sneaked his way through trees and bushes to the stadium.

After several hundred yards, he popped out of the thicket to find a pair of train tracks that stretched the length of the river. He knew the tracks would lead directly to the stadium; there was a stop there aptly named Stadium Station. It was the light rail that he remembered taking as a kid to this very stadium for concerts and sporting events.

In the last ten years the U.S. had finally caught up with the rest of the world as far as public transportation was concerned. The archaic light rail had been replaced with the *ultra-light* rail, a magnetic railing system that allowed trains to travel upwards of 300 miles per hour on almost no electricity at all, technology the Japanese and Europeans had been using for decades.

He knew it would be a fantastic risk getting on the tracks, but it was worth his while. He knew the Ultras weren't running right now; hell, nothing was running right now. He just prayed that the craft wouldn't see him. It was approximately three-quarters of a mile to the stadium and he needed to complete it fast. So, he took the risk and set off at a hurried jog.

He made it the length of the tracks in less than 15 minutes, half-walking and half-running. To his amazement, no more craft flew directly overhead and for that he was grateful. But he did see several more fly in from the north; all seemed to be landing in or hovering over the stadium. Were they dropping supplies or picking cargo up? Maybe they were depositing troops or organizing weapons. He didn't know, but the closer he got to the stadium, the faster his heart beat – and the more scared he became.

He made it to the station without incident and walked down the two floors of zigzagging concrete ramps to the street level. Using the trees lining the walkway to the stadium as cover, he surreptitiously hurried to the entrance. The place was remarkably empty. But a strange hum and commotion seemed to be coming from the facility's innards.

It was awkward and disquieting how easy and simple it was to walk right into the huge stadium. No guards, no people. The closer he got, the hum evolved into a rumbling like that of moving machines and bustling feet. He carefully made his way across the concourse to the edge where he could get the best view of the field.

Initially, looking down across the expanse of the now-brown and dying grass, Sam saw what looked like thousands of walking war machines. *Manned body suits*, he thought. By the looks of it, there were several hundred. The machines looked human enough, but the technology was another story. *These had to be extra-terrestrial.*

Sam shifted his gaze to one of the vessels hovering 50 feet above the pitch with the number **506** emblazoned on it in military stencil font. Although intricate and built of materials he could not begin to name, it was the front of the ship that drew his attention.

Eyes wide and unblinking, he read the neatly printed 20-foot-tall white stenciling along the ship's port:

United States of America

PART TWO

"The thing with darkness, I acknowledge mine."
Shakespeare

CHAPTER SEVENTEEN

Major Hax Packard, or Officer 4543: Blue Battalion as his military fatigue stitching offered, sat on the edge of his small, white bunk in a bare domicile, questioning if he had what it took to actually go through with what his commanders had ordered of him. Of the 5,000 or so onboard, was he the only soldier capable of disengaging from military "think training," as the indoctrination was euphemistically called, and have thoughts of his own? Anxiety swelled in his gut as the seconds on his wall-mounted screen nearby counted down. Everything his commander had instructed them to do was against all that he believed to be good and just, but it seemed he was the only one to have such perceptions.

The culmination of countless years of training, inculcation, and military machinations had boiled down to a three-hour countdown featured on the wall screen in his four-by-three-yard dormitory in this city-sized maze of steel and carbon.

He lay on his bed, staring at the ceiling and hatching detailed daydreams of escaping, finding a terrain lander, and abandoning this senseless mission, but he knew that was no real option. If he refused an order, he would undoubtedly be executed for insubordination. He had seen people eliminated for far less. Besides, they were the military of the United States; this was what most of them had been born for, what many had waited their entire careers for.

Only after traveling in the abyss of space to the point of no return had the fleet's commanding officer, Major General Trokker, finally briefed Hax's cohort of officers about the mission at hand. Out of 150 officers on this particular ship, it appeared to Hax that he was quite possibly the only one who had found everything the major general had announced to be absolutely reprehensible. Subsequently, he had taken his time returning to his room on the fourth main deck of the ship after the five-hour-long briefing.

He had never been the kind of soldier to blindly follow orders, which had become perfectly clear several years ago when he had received his first promotion to captain. He had been placed in charge of a company of men who had just finished training with virtual reality combat simulators. None of them, including Hax, had ever been in any form of real combat when they were given their first assignment in the Middle East.

At the time, the U.S. was sending war ships and troops to quell an uprising in the area where the country of Saudi Arabia used to be located before its dissolution in the early-2100s. The area had become a failed state, a hotbed for terrorists. His first day there, Hax and his company had been ordered to enter a small, local village and "terminate with extreme prejudice" anyone there of military age. Of course, Hax had decried – and ultimately refused – the command, citing the high possibility of civilian casualties. He had lost his company, faced a military tribunal, and been sentenced to jail.

But it helped to have friends in high places and he was let off the hook. His company was taken charge by another upstart officer who led them into the village, attacked its inhabitants, lost 70 men, and killed ten times that many innocent civilians. Ever since, Hax had learned to trust his gut, especially in matters of right and wrong, life and death. And right now, his gut was warning him that everything about this mission was wrong.

He still ached all over and he swore every time he went to the bathroom as it felt like he was pissing razor blades. The stiffness in his neck had only resolved itself yesterday. His blurry vision seemed to have disappeared. Being in a hibernative state for so long, as he had been briefed many times, was incredibly hard on the human body. He had woken up only a couple days ago, still in utter awe that he could have traveled so far in what he perceived as a short amount of time. But as he had learned in endless hours of lectures, time travel was tricky business.

Being an officer, Hax was one of the lucky ones onboard who had been granted a dormitory of his own with relative privacy. The room was tiny, but at least it was his. It contained the wall screen, which currently flashed the countdown adjacent to his bed. That was a "luxury" that every officer was required to have, the higher-ups would say, but its primary purpose was to transmit military propaganda, training videos, and updates from the bridge. Anything entertaining was rarely permitted to broadcast on the wall screen.

A small desk with another built-in screen for doing work was situated beside his bed. He couldn't remember the last time he had sat at that desk to do anything meaningful. A lavatory as big as a closet was opposite the bed so he didn't have to shit in front of hundreds of fellow soldiers. The only thing that made it all worthwhile, that he considered truly luxurious, was the dinner-plate-sized porthole on the wall above his bunk.

The porthole showed a mind-numbing blackness most of the time, but the last couple of days, breathtakingly gorgeous swirls of reds and oranges had filled the window. He had been close to Jupiter before, but this time he had really stopped to take in its beauty.

Momentarily, the glowing holographic form of the ship's decidedly female computer module appeared a foot from his face and announced that all personnel must begin preparations for infill and to stand by for a message from Trokker.

Hax took a deep breath and readied himself for the three-foot-tall face that was to appear on the wall screen. The major general's name alone was enough to evoke a visceral response of hatred and distrust. He knew the face – and the man – well. To be honest, he never wanted to see or hear from the commanding officer again.

Trokker appeared on the wall as a face with piercing, black eyes that had seen far too much death and destruction shadowed by heavy brows. The massive scar which ran from his ear to lip gave him a perpetually angry grimace. He wore the black, gray, and red beret of the Fourth Space Wing. His voice was deep, raspy, and grave.

"Men, this mission, although tenuous and long for every one of us, is of paramount importance. What you are about to do in the next hours, days, and weeks will make not only your country proud, but ensure the survival of our great nation. For a vast majority of you, this will be your first time in real combat. Remember that what we are doing here is for the betterment of the United States and its people. Remember in your hearts that that is the reason we are here. Remember that you are soldiers and that no matter the mission, no matter your orders, you are doing the bidding of the president of the U.S. We are saving millions of lives with this mission. You may be faced with difficult situations and decisions, but follow commands, make us proud, and don't forget that the future of our country hangs in the balance. Godspeed."

The screen faded to black, leaving Hax to look at his

reflection in the screen. *That's it?* he thought. *We traveled 190 years for that?* Hax got even angrier at how glib and ephemeral the major general's words had been. He had been expecting some kind of explanation, something to actually reveal to the men what was going to happen. But no. It was just the same old bullshit he had grown so tired of hearing in his years in the service.

A red light appeared above his door accompanied by a soft buzzer. The AI face, a computer-generated version of what people were supposed to perceive as an attractive non-hostile woman, appeared on the screen to his right. The manifestation of the onboard AI informed him that it was time and that he was to make his way to the landing hangar. Hax's mind was racing, but he knew the time for second thoughts was gone. He would have to come up with some method to divert this crazy mission once they had landed on Earth.

He pressed the small, glowing green button to the left of the door. It slid open with a hiss and he stepped into the vast hallway where scores of men were leaving their sleep halls and walking in uniform toward the landing craft bays three-quarters of a mile to the stern. Hax reticently turned and vanished into the immense herd of gray fatigues and hairless heads. Being an officer, his landing bay was closer to the living quarters than the grunts, but he still had to march hundreds of yards in this river of soldiers to get there.

He tried to keep the panic in the pit of his stomach from showing on his face. Crowded in the mass of soldiers, he scanned the sea of empty faces, all impetuous and vacant. With every step, his convictions of duty magnified. But not duty to the mission; rather, duty to justice.

An urgent update rang from the com-band control module on his right forearm. All soldiers had an eight-inch multiplex screen affixed to their right forearms which constantly updated with mission information, bodily vitals data, and other info the brass deemed pertinent. Normally mission updates, or changes in rules of engagement (ROE), were only sent to officer com-bands, but this one seemed to have been sent to every soldier. Hax noticed everyone around him invariably glance down at their screens in unison. His com-band radiated a flashing message and immediately every soldier's face in the immense hall was painted in the crimson red glow of their respective screens.

URGENT: UPDATE ON ROE
ALL ENEMY MILITARY PERSONNEL AND CRAFT ARE TO BE FIRED UPON.
AVOID CITIZENS IF POSSIBLE.
CITIZENS MAY BE DESTROYED IF PRESENTING AS HOSTILE.
ALL WEAPONS TO BE SET TO LETHAL.
DESTROY ALL INFRASTRUCTURE PRESUMED VITAL.

Hax didn't understand. Changing the rules of engagement? Enemy personnel? Weapons to lethal? These words made it sound as though they were on a mission to eradicate, destroy, and kill. Just last night during an intelligence update, the commanders had proudly boasted that this would be the first peaceful invasion in history. "Near zero casualties" was the phrase that had been used over and over. This latest armband directive came as a complete contradiction to that.

Hax scanned the area for someone of rank to see if they had received the same message; after finding no one, he settled for a nearby private. "Hey bud," Hax murmured to the young man to his right.

"Yes sir," the kid replied, saluting.

"Did you get this same ROE update?" He showed the private his armband. "You think this is a mistake?"

The soldier peered at Hax, utterly confused. "Just following orders, sir."

It was the response he expected, but it made his opposition all the more stalwart.

"Just following orders," Hax mimicked flatly. The response had become the battalion maxim during their last months of training and had even been recently adopted by the top brass. With consuming disappointment, Hax realized he was the only one asking questions.

The long walk to the landing craft hangar was mostly silent broken by an occasional cough or whisper of orders on the ROE update. Hax was now certain he really was the only one in the battalion, possibly in the whole invasion force, who believed this whole thing was wrong. But still, he marched along with the hundreds of others.

He reached the officers' hangar threshold, opened the coded door, and entered. The amber light of the landing bay spilled onto him. Each hangar in the massive transport ship, once attack orders were given, detached itself, thereby allowing the hangars themselves to become the landing transports for various troops and invasion machines.

With less purpose than he should have exhibited, Hax meandered to his personnel landing attack vehicle, or P-LAV. Fitted for each individual, these machines were 15-foot pilot-operated walking robots outfitted with ungodly amounts of firepower.

Hax climbed the small ladder in the back of his P-LAV and sat in the cramped driver module. He slid the arm and leg sensors on, which tracked his movements and transcribed it to the machine. As the machine continued to boot up, he slipped on his carbon-fiber helmet. His eyes were instantly overwhelmed with endless amounts of data which appeared before his nose and streamed along the polycarbonate screen of his helmet.

Hax always felt claustrophobic in his P-LAV. Being an officer certainly had its benefits, but he hated these things. They were cramped and encroached on every inch of his body. Of course, this was by design as they were engineered to sense every move of his muscles and propel the massive mechanical suit in conjunction, but he just felt constricted.

He looked out at the other rows of P-LAVs attached to large metal racks hanging from the hangar ceiling, wondering if every soldier inside hated them as much as he did. As the P-LAV was locked into place for the landing, he vowed to himself that he would do anything in his power to stop this atrocity, or at least help anyone if he could.

The reality – and finality – of the situation struck him hard as his landing transport hangar was released from the clutches of the mother ship. He glanced again at his armband still glowing with the new rules of engagement. He opened his mouth to decry his repudiation of what was happening or about to happen, but no words came out. Everyone around him was in the role of soldier, another automaton just "following orders."

He had been with a lot of these men for five years, through relocations, conversations in galleys, training in simulators, and tactical discussions. But in the belly of this dark, cold vessel, he realized he truly knew none of the men around him, that he was surrounded by strangers. He was surrounded by enemies on the precipice of an invasion unlike any other in history.

CHAPTER EIGHTEEN

A Week Before Embarkation

Hax stared up at the sky thick with smog and pollution that blurred the hot desert sun. The vast base, five miles south of Tucson, Arizona, was located where the sizable Davis-Monthan Air Force Base had once been before its restructuring into the west's largest Space Force base. The horizon was littered with ships of every class and size, silently darting every which way, each attending to its own mission or assignment. He marveled at the size and scope of the United States' military might as a battle cruiser, nearly three-quarters of a mile long, hummed its way to a docking bay just 500 feet overhead. He had a terrible sinking feeling in his stomach that this would be the last time he would have boots on dirt and *not* be at war.

He kicked a thick layer of dust off his perfectly polished black, dress boots, deep in thought. After brief reflection, Hax began to regret the decisions he had made over the last two years that had brought him to this point. As a Medium Personal Attack Vehicle, or MPAV, passed noiselessly overhead, Hax was buffeted and he shielded his eyes from flying particles.

Activity of long-range spacecraft at the compound had quadrupled in the last two weeks, signifying the imminence of a massive operation. From the buzz around

Blue Battalion, one of six battalions in the Fourth Space Wing, it sounded as though they were going to be spearheading whatever enterprise the higher-ups had drummed up. Although he was an officer, the higher-ups were keeping everyone – including all officers – in the dark about big things. About *dark* things.

But they told them enough. They were going to "nonviolently" invade and besiege a country that they had yet to name. Nonviolent and peaceful was the nomenclature that the brass had used, but the irony of using *nonviolent* in the same sentence as *invade* was not lost on him; it actually made Hax laugh aloud. A "peaceful invasion" was as much an oxymoron as "military intelligence," he joked. He understood the reasoning well enough; this unnamed country had resources and the U.S. wanted them, but they were leaving so much undisclosed. He didn't need a formal briefing to know that whatever Trokker was really planning had to be reprehensible.

Hax thought back to his dad, which he had been doing a lot recently, and couldn't help but feel raw regret. They had once been close. No more than a year and a half ago, they had been the epitome of the filial relationship – until Hax had decided to make a name for himself and stop standing in his father's shadow. He still looked up to his old man, the powerful and distinguished Lieutenant General Packard. Hell, his father was the reason Hax had joined the military in the first place. But the path Hax had chosen was quite possibly the worst choice.

Trokker, the commanding officer of the Fourth Space Wing, had a way with words. He made everything sound as if whatever machinations they were drumming up would be a shrewd fix to the problems the nation faced. The major general was renowned for succumbing to all levels of depravity to reach his end goals. One such story Hax had heard had been about the major general's commanding of a special forces operation in Namibia years ago.

The mission was simple: kill or detain the militant faction run by the psychopathic warlord who had commandeered a huge mine and the subsequent neighboring town. Trokker and his loyal soldiers went in, guns blazing, and started killing indiscriminately. By the end of the gunfight, the village had been razed and most of the faction members and villagers were dead. It was a massacre.

Trokker had returned, claiming they were ambushed. He was awarded medals and the U.S. was awarded the mine. It was clear the major general would do anything to further his aspirations and kill anyone for the sake of claiming resources for his country.

Hax stood at the threshold of right and wrong, life and death, duty and morality. He knew, from the number of ships landing and the overall buzz on the base, that this mission was less than a week away, maybe a few days. He had a duty to the chain of command and to the oath he took, but he also had a duty to the people he swore to defend. What he chose to do in the next couple days would only benefit one of those two. If he didn't do something drastic soon, one way or another an unimaginable amount of human life would be lost.

There were two men alive he knew he could count on to talk this stuff out and get a real response from. A response that wasn't full of military bullshit or laden with the latent threat of ratting him out for insubordination. The first of these confidants was a captain in his battalion named Sumpter Dixon with whom he had been best friends since high school; the other was his father. Unfortunately, he hadn't spoken with his father in over a year and, if he brought up the dilemma to Dix, he legitimately did not know how his friend would react.

Hax kicked the remaining specks of gray dust off his boot and headed in the direction of the officers' headquarters half a mile from where he stood. He tried to ignore the other ships passing overhead or landing at their respective docks. He needed to focus; he was seriously considering reaching out to the only man who had enough power to do something – his father.

He had been a military brat his whole life which meant he had never seen much of his old man. His mother was an angel and had supplied for all the needs of her three children, but Hax had something in him his mother's love and care couldn't soothe or alleviate. Passion. All he had ever done as a young man was stare up at the sky and wonder when it would be his turn to take off into the cosmos and fight the good fight.

He had abhorred school probably more than he had hated anything else. Most of his classes had been mandatory, state-approved humanities and, as his father would complain, sociology lessons loaded with propaganda and government-approved literature. His history classes were the only courses he felt he wasn't being fed misinformation. Even still, anything that involved state-approved school lessons, he had been dubious of. Interestingly, his father, who was a history buff, had shared with Hax many historical situations which seemed strikingly different than the ones administered by the teachers.

A lesson his favorite history teacher had given in his senior year history class had fueled his imagination and inspired Hax like never before. The lecture was from a class taught by Mr. McJames, a man Hax remembered vividly not only for his lessons, but for his one-of-a-kind looks. He was a short, stumpy and balding man with a belly that didn't match the rest of his fragile frame. He had a white, short-cropped wispy beard that tried to make its way to his sideburns without much luck; his thin, pink lips looked alien on his white and dry skin. He had bug eyes that always held a twinkle and he was always quick with a playful obloquy for anyone brave enough to question anything he said. His classes loved him for his enthusiasm and his innate ability to answer every question anyone asked about any subject. His frank and brutal honesty were much appreciated by all.

One of Mr. McJames' more notable lessons, which garnered much approval from Hax's father and had subsequently encouraged Hax to join the military as an officer, had involved the three-year war of 2136 which, at the time, had occurred about a century prior.

The Korean Peninsula had been completely taken over by the Russian satellite state, the Democratic People's Republic of Korea. The first of the Negative Gravity Quantifier technology had been developed and used in the U.S., allowing massive attack craft to hover effortlessly and at never-before-seen speeds and altitudes. Of course, the technology was stolen and placed into the hands of evil people with sinister plots of destruction and power. The U.S. sent a massive attack group, led by Commander Bryen, to fight over the peninsula. The stories of his charisma, bravery, and leadership skills were legendary.

During one particularly brutal battle, Bryen was shot down, along with several other ships over the country, leaving himself and 85 soldiers stranded behind enemy lines. Bryen helped his whole company evade capture as they fought their way back to friendly borders. He then went *back* across enemy lines to rescue several more platoons before he was captured and publicly executed.

Hax loved the story. The courage, the sacrifice, the honor. He wanted to be just like Commander Bryen. He hoped if he had the chance, he would be brave and fight for what's right just like he had.

While in school, Hax had tried to hide the fact that he was a well-known officer's son; he never brought it up to anyone in conversation, but everyone knew. It helped get him the best education available and, some would say, was the real reason he always graduated top of his class. For as much as Hax tried, people gave him looks and whispered behind his back words he could always hear. But not his best friend Sumpter Dixon.

Dix hadn't cared less who the hell his parents were. The two had been friends simply because they liked hanging out together. The two did everything together, which included getting into and, more importantly, getting out of trouble. A bond like that was a rarity.

CHAPTER NINETEEN

"*There* he is!" Hax heard a voice proclaim from his left, the words reverberating through the expansive main hall he had just entered. The blast of cool air that hit his face and lungs always took him by surprise when he entered buildings on the base. It was such a stark difference from the dry, sweltering desert heat outside. Hax turned, knowing full well it was Dix and his flare of red hair.

With a perpetual grin on his face, Hax's friend waved to him enthusiastically. The man was not handsome per say, but he remained extremely popular with the ladies. Hax understood why though; Dix had a magnetic personality. He was the kind of guy everyone loved to be around. He walked with a commanding gait and was much more of a hardass then the fuzzy crop of red hair and goofy grin conveyed.

"Hey Dix," Hax greeted.

"So, what's the word? We going out tonight?"

Hax rolled his eyes and laughed, knowing that "going out" usually meant an all-nighter. "How did I know those would be the first words outta your mouth?"

"Well shit, Haxy. We only have a couple single-night-leave allowances left. We never know when this battle group with enough firepower to fuck the world into the Stone Age will be launched!" That was a term Dix had been using more lately and it was beginning to make Hax uncomfortable.

Hax considered his friend. He had so many questions, all sitting on the tip of his tongue, but he found himself unable. After a moment, he sighed. "Ah shit, let's do it... You're paying this time though!" Although going out with his buddy on one of the last nights he could be alive did sound great, he was beginning to go with the flow as if he was done fighting a current he couldn't outpace. He hated the feeling of not being honest with himself or the people around him, but he decided to keep his mouth shut.

"Yes! You da man! I mean, good plan, Major," Dix cheered in a blithe, caricatured tone upon spotting another officer walk by. He straightened himself comically.

The two of them had only been on this particular base for a short period of time, but they had already garnered a poor reputation. Other officers did not like that Hax treated Dix like an equal even though he was his commanding officer. He had already received warnings regarding adherence to the chain of command by several higher-ups. The two liked to break the rules and, just like in high school, they liked to do it together.

"Prick," Dix murmured so the short and stocky Captain Brian Killein couldn't hear it as he strolled by with his fat-man waddle. Captain Killein eyed them over the top of his thickly-framed glasses. He was always sweating profusely and was incredibly insecure about it which, in turn, made him an asshole to everyone he was around. The battalion hated the guy. Plus, he was a terrible leader who only got rank for classroom work.

They let him get safely out of earshot in an awkward silence which Dix finally broke.

"What ya thinking, Major? Looks like something is really heating up, eh?"

"First off, stop with that major crap. We have known each other for way too long for you to placate me with that rank BS. Second, yeah, by the looks of things, I bet we are shipping off in less than a week."

"Pretty crazy shit, huh?"

"Pretty crazy." Hax still wasn't sure how much of the mission Dix had been made privy to. Hax had had a few cursory briefings with his higher-ups that had been "strictly confidential." The only thing they had purposefully and repeatedly omitted was where it was actually taking place, something that grated on Hax.

Unfortunately, Sumpter Dixon was a man who followed orders no matter what. He believed in Major General Trokker with all his heart and Hax had a feeling he would not take lightly any conversation about how misguided the man may be. Although Hax had mentioned the major general's motives several times over the last month, Dix had always been them off, going so far as to become angry.

As recent as a week ago, the two of them had been sitting in the mess hall well after lights out, as many privileged officers were allowed to do, sipping on a bourbon Dix kept hidden in his footlocker. They had started reminiscing about the good times and the commanding officers they hated, when Hax had accidentally let it slip his real feelings for Trokker. It wasn't much, but it had been enough to get Dix riled up to the point of leaving the conversation halfway through.

Hax knew Dix respected and admired the major general, but he had no idea the true reverence and faith his friend had in him. He was amazed how easily Dix angered by a simple, off-putting comment regarding the major general's loyalties. Their conversations for the rest of that week had been glib and nonexistent.

"Well, I'm off to rummage around battalion HQ, see if I can't rustle up some intel," Dix said with a wink, glancing down at his multiplex armband.

"Hey Dix?"

"Yeah, boss?"

Hax met his friend's gaze and held it for a long moment before saying, "You believe in all this, right?"

"Ah hell, there he goes. What do you mean *this* this time?"

They had had many talks about politics and philosophy over the years and countless chats over the pride they had in the military, in the country. Hax knew his friend was dedicated to everything they were doing, but he could sense the tension of last week's conversation hanging between them.

"Shit, nothing. I'll see you tonight," Hax replied, deciding against asking the questions and sharing his doubts. This wasn't the time or the place.

Dix gave Hax a dubious look, spun on his heels as he so often did, and strode to the elevators, looking over his shoulder only once.

CHAPTER TWENTY

Sumpter Dixon stared out the window of the fantastically ornate office on the third-floor officer's deck. He had been called on his com-band by Trokker's assistant only moments ago while standing in the main entrance of the building talking with Hax. He had been let into the office by a baby-faced soldier whose head was too big for his beret and body too long for his fatigues. His slender frame stood at bolt upright attention as he guarded the door. The major general had yet to arrive at this ad hoc meeting. The lanky soldier had told him to go inside but to not sit down or touch anything.

The view from the third floor was amazing. In the distance was the impressive skyline of the city which seemed to go on forever. It was hard to see through the dense, gray-brown hue of smog but he could still make out the horizon and countless aircraft. He had read recently that this was the cleanest the planet had been since the turn of the twenty-second century, but from what he could see, he didn't believe a word of it.

Nose almost touching the glass, Dixon daydreamed of being an important general like Trokker someday, peering over an endless sea of military personnel and equipment all under his direct command. He believed he would be a good one too; he most certainly liked the thought of near-limitless power. He would be fair yet disciplined and rule with an unforgiving sense of loyalty.

The thought put a smile on his face. He loved the military and loved his country, but Dixon *really* loved himself.

His daydream was interrupted by a voice in the hallway. He glanced around the office quickly before the major general entered. Why the hell had the major general called *him* there? Dixon was, in the overall scheme of things, pretty low on the totem pole. He had only met the major general a couple of times and knew he had never left such an impression that the major general would seek his counsel or company.

"Ten-hut!" the baby-faced soldier guarding the door called. Dixon straightened his posture and saluted.

"Thank you, Corporal. You're dismissed, but do *not* let anyone close to this room. Do you understand me?"

"Sir yes sir. Where would you like me to station, sir?"

"I don't give a shit, just do not let anyone down that goddamn hallway."

"Yes sir."

The hard rubber patter of glossy boots on concrete quieted as the guard hurried off.

The major general walked into the room, his perpetual scowl and glaring eyes under bushy eyebrows hitting Dixon like a bullet. Just standing in the same room as this man made Dix feel important. Dix did, however, sense that this meeting was verboten.

"At ease," major general Trokker rasped. "Captain Dixon, thank you for coming up."

"Uh, yes sir. No problem, sir."

"We need to have a talk. What we say in here is of the utmost confidentiality. I mean, court-martial-and-have you-executed kind of confidentiality. If I learn that what we discussed here today gets out, you're done. Do I make myself clear?"

"Sir?" Dixon replied, his face twisted with wonderment.

"Do you understand, Captain?"

"Yes sir. Absolutely confidential, copy that, sir."

The major general glared for a moment, driving home the gravity of the situation, before striding across the room and pressing a button on the wall. A small, glass door opened to reveal two crystal bottles. The major general reached for the one with only half an inch left and poured it into an immaculate glass with the American flag engraved on it. Dixon eyed the bottle, knowing it was most likely worth a month's salary for him and from some distillery that doesn't even exist anymore. He was hoping the major general would offer him a snifter. He did not; the bottle quickly found its home back in the darkness of the cabinet.

"From what I hear, you are one of the most committed officers we have," Trokker said. He spoke as if he were reciting a Shakespearean play with dramatic pauses and emphasis on words and silences. "I hear you live and breathe for the Force."

"Yes sir, there is nothing else on Earth I could imagine myself doing."

"And you would do anything your officers commanded you to do, even if it had deadly consequences?"

"Um... Yes sir."

"Good. We need to have a talk about your friend, Major Packard... and something you will need to... to do about him..." The major general drained half his glass and then glanced at Dixon with a conniving and sinister glare.

CHAPTER TWENTY-ONE

"From what our intel was able to garner, Captain, you have known Major Packard and the Packard family for a number of years, yes?" Trokker asked, seating himself on the edge of his desk. He studied Dix, a scowl chiseled into his hardened features. He obviously knew the answer to the question, much like a lawyer who knew the answers to the questions he was asking while cross-examining a witness. Dix could hear the deliberation in the officer's words and see the hawk-like observance Trokker now trained on him.

"Yes sir," Dix replied slowly. "I've known Hax Packard most of my life. We went to school together all the way through officer candidate school."

"Mmm, right," Trokker sighed. "And his father, the lieutenant general, what do you know about him?" His eyes never left Dix's face.

"Well, sir, they don't talk much anymore, but I know he was the commander of the expeditionary space division at Bolton Air Force Base Florida, highly decorated and..."

"No no no, I know all that. I mean, what do you know about the man personally? What kind of man is he?"

'Sorry, sir. I'm not sure I follow…" Dix hid his discomfort. It was becoming clearer as to why he, out of all the others on the base, had been chosen to have this clandestine meeting with the major general. "Lieutenant General Packard has always been very cordial and –"

"The man is a coward," Trokker interjected. "He wanted that position; *he* went out of his way for it, fought for the role as

commander of a non-militant wing for *exploration*." The
major general's face twisted in disgust. "He has turned this
branch into the laughing stock of the world and made us
look like some kind of shitty science-fiction movie plot.
We are goddamn warriors, not pioneers, not explorers."
Trokker eyed Dix vehemently, a pronounced vein
pulsating along his temple. "He is *weak*, and he is making
this country *weak*."

Dixon nodded meekly in feigned agreement.

The major general took a deep breath to compose
himself. "It's men like that who will fuck everything up for
us *real* warriors. Men like that can't see the bigger picture
because they are too caught up in political bullshit and do-
everything-the-ethical-way exploration…" The major
general turned from the table and walked to the window,
hands clasped behind his back. His nose was inches from
the glass as he continued in a calm, collected growl. "The
apple does not fall far from the tree, Captain Dixon."
After a moment, he turned to him.

Dix remained speechless as he stood at half-
attention, not sure how to react to what he was hearing.
He swallowed the thick knot in his drying throat, praying
the officer couldn't sense his consternation. It seemed
Trokker didn't want to hear anything about his friend's
father after all, but was just setting the stage for his own
diatribe.

"That brings me to your friend the major."

Dix's heart shook painfully in his chest. He felt as
though he was in an interrogation. Already sweat had
begun to form on his brow and upper lip as he tried not to
show any emotion to this steel-faced man.

"Is he the same kind of pacifist his father is? Is he
cut from the same weak cloth? Or is he like us, a warrior

prepared to give it all for the sake of his country? Like I do... Like you do."

Dix gazed at the officer longer than he meant to, his mind feverishly searching for an appropriate yet non-inflammatory response. Hax was his best friend, someone he looked up to. He was an admirable student and an effective leader. Dix himself had come to Hax with problems both professional and personal. Hax had been there when his father had died and had been the one to get him back on track at OCS. Hax had been there for bar fights, late-night study sessions, and leisurely outings. He loved the man.

But that didn't stop him from telling the major general everything he wanted to hear.

Strategically removing parts that would make him look overly empathetic, Dix briefed the major general on his best friend. He painted Hax as the major general had put it, "Not far from the Packard tree."

A smile that showed no warmth or humor spread across Trokker's hard, gray face. "Good, that's what I figured." His voice was low and raspy. "Now it's time for where you fit into this picture." Trokker again strode to the window, his breath visible on the glass. It must have been his way of delivering hard-to-hear orders. "Captain, you know this mission is highly classified, and in many circles, would be considered treasonous. It is the single most important thing we will do for this country; we will go down in the annals of history as the turning point for American long-term success." The major general continued without leaving as much as a breath for Dixon to respond. "We are going to have to make near-impossible decisions and do things that are selfless and tough."

Trokker finally turned from the glass and approached Dixon, his boots making such a menacing *click-clack* on the polished floor, that it seemed even the tiles beneath his feet cried out in petrified intimidation. "We know that Hax Packard is against this mission and that he has talked to you about such concerns."

Dix noticed with alarm Trokker's title-less use of Hax's name and a horrifying thought crossed his mind – they had probably been bugged and spied on.

"We fear," the major general asserted, "that when we commence this defining operation, Hax will do all he can to thwart it. If Hax shows any, and I mean *any*, signs of weakness, hesitation, or second-guessing when on the field of battle, your orders are to remove him from duty."

"What do you mean by –"

"You are to *remove* him from command and in doing so, you will receive an instant commendation and field promotion." Trokker watched Dix, allowing the gravity of the command to sink in. "Failure to do so will be perceived as insubordination and the two of you will be considered deserters and punished as such. Do I make myself clear?"

Unable to say much else, Dix just cleared his throat and said, "Sir."

And with that, Trokker dismissed him. Dix saluted and left the major general's office. With a final glance back, Dix's eye caught several framed pictures situated on the wall nearest the door. Even from a distance, he recognized the secretary of veteran affairs, the secretary of defense, and the president's portrait – his commander-and-chief, the man who presided over him and the country for which he had taken an oath to protect. The cognitive dissonance within Dix swelled as he turned and left.

The guard stationed at the far end of the hallway hurried to meet him, but Dix didn't notice. Despite the war raging in his heart and mind, another powerful sensation had risen. Ambition. Already he could picture himself wearing the gold star of a major, shaking hands with the president of the United States. Medals and ribbons marking his valiance and loyalty would be pinned to his chest. Dix grinned.

If it meant a pay raise, widespread recognition, and more, he could possibly – maybe – get over the feelings of betrayal and immorality that simmered in his gut. The major general had more information than him; Trokker knew what was best for the country.

The pipsqueak of a guard passed Dix, saluting as he passed. Dix didn't even acknowledge him, a broad smile painted across his lips.

CHAPTER TWENTY-TWO

Hax sat at the bar working on his second beer while he waited for Dixon who was running late, as usual. He glanced at his reflection in the beer mug, noting the scar high on his pronounced cheekbones which he had received, along with several chipped teeth, from a training accident years ago. He thought it gave his handsome face a tougher look, but the dental pain had never gone away. This line of work consumed his life, body, and mind.

He glanced down at his armband. *Forty-five fucking minutes late.*

The holographic screen that covered the entirety of the back wall, as well as the bar top, showcased the usual military propaganda. Located just outside the base's fences, everyone knew it was owned by the government as a place to feed their news and to listen for gossip of insurrection or mutiny. Times in the country were, as many would say, at a "tipping point, with revolution just around the corner." This made the government nervous and caused them to tighten their influence on soldiers, politicians, and citizens alike.

When all that was left in his second glass was a brown film of liquid along the bottom, his courage caught up with his buzz and he began making eyes at a pretty brunette seated two seats to his left. He assumed she was the typical bar fly, frequenting the base watering holes in search of guys in uniform. He didn't care; he liked the attention and the thought that this might be the last contact he would ever have with a woman. Plus, she was just his type with dark, brown hair done up in curls, olive skin, and facial features that revealed a vibrant Hispanic heritage.

He glanced at his wrist again; Dix was now 55 minutes late. With a coy smile, the woman asked if he was waiting for someone special. He replied charmingly in the negative and slid over to sit shoulder-to-shoulder with her to prove it. "Can I buy you a drink?" he asked, a boyish grin curling the sides of his mouth.

Her response was a laugh that was so unadulterated and real that it actually made him jump. Taken aback, he shyly met her gaze. "I'm sorry, I'm sorry!" she said with a Southern draw as she tried to hold back more laughter. "You're just really cute and that line is so cheesy!" Her green eyes struck him immediately as both passionate and jovial. His face reddened as he desperately searched for a clever line to recover with, but ultimately failed. His only answer was to gaze back at her and join her in the laugh.

"Sorry, I'm, uh, not out a lot – and it's not a line! You just look thirsty, that's all."

"Really? A handsome officer like you? I can hardly believe that! But yes, I'll take you up on that drink." She pressed the button on the bottom of the glass in front of her and the bartender brought her another Cosmo.

"There ya go, Meyah," the bartender said, seemingly intimidated by her attractiveness and by the now-uniformed man sitting next to her. He was right about the bar fly-thing. But Hax couldn't care less. He could tell she was a couple drinks ahead of him, but her candor was appreciated and her looks were as intoxicating as the beer. A short sensual moment lingered as she took a sip of her drink.

"So, uh, they know your name here, huh?" Hax said with a smile. Without waiting for her answer, he continued, "And hey, how did you know I'm an officer?"

"Oh please, this entire city is military boys. Y'all are so easy to pick out, especially officers. You practically walk around with a sign that says it." She winked. "Plus, I'm a military brat myself. I could prolly tell you what every commendation medal on your lapel is for." She reached inside the plain, brown leather jacket he wore to help him blend in more when off-base, and grabbed the lapel of his pressed gray shirt. "Not a whole lot, huh?" she murmured with a cute laugh.

"I just like to think the most impressive work I do is more of the personal and intimate kind," he replied, raising his eyebrows flirtatiously.

The coquetry and laughter continued after proper introductions were finally made and the two found themselves quickly engaged in conversation. After another half hour, Hax was stuck in her gravity.

Dixon finally showed up halfway through Hax's third beer and five minutes after his date's hand had landed itself sensually on his thigh.

"Whoa whoa whoa! And what do we have here?" his friend teased loudly.

"Right on time, bud," Hax remarked dryly.

"So sorry, Major!" Dix said sardonically as he theatrically saluted him.

Meyah battered her eyelashed. "He says you're always late."

"Dix, meet Meyah. Meyah, this is the guy I was talking about, Captain Dixon. I call him Dix. Partly because his name, partly because he is, in fact, just a dick."

Meyah laughed heartily and Hax couldn't help but be absorbed by her mirth.

"Talking about me, huh? Well, hi, pretty lady. Sounds like you two are already best of friends." Dixon made obnoxious kissing sounds as he stumbled forward.

"See you already tied a couple on, eh brother?" Hax observed.

"Had to drink my fucked-up sorrows away, I guess!" Dixon babbled. Hax gave him a curious look wondering what the hell he meant by it. "Just a last toast before we fuck this world into the Stone Age!"

There it was again, that weird line.

"What are you talking about, Dix?" Hax gave Meyah an apologetic look, asking her to excuse him for a moment as he dealt with his inebriated friend. Meyah turned to leave and her chair was promptly commandeered by Dix. "Just give me a minute," Hax said, grabbing Meyah's hand. "I'll be back in a sec." She gave him a smile and wandered off. Hax waited until she was out of earshot before turning to his friend. "Dude, I saw you, like, three hours ago. You were fine. What's going on?"

"Yeah man, you wouldn't believe my day," Dix said as he leaned on the counter and shouted for a beer from the bartender.

"Come on, let's not talk about work or any of that shit right now," replied Hax. Dix gave him an odd, almost sad look and then turned to his waiting beverage.

Hax found Meyah's gaze from across the room and motioned her back over. She sat on his other side, reclaiming the clandestine space along his inner thigh with her hand, and grinned.

"So, now that you're spoken for, where are your friends? We gotta celebrate!" Dixon said cheerily, and again so loud that everyone in the bar could hear.

"Oh yeah? And what are you boys celebrating?" Meyah said, the coquettish look directed purely at Hax.

"Well, looks like we are shipping off in a day or so to go save the world!" Dix drunkenly spewed.

"Ooo, my heroes!" Meyah crooned.

"Well, he isn't supposed to offer any indication of what we are doing or when, but yeah," Hax interjected with a look at Dix, "it looks like we are going to be shipping out in the next day or two."

The three of them stayed at the bar for another three rounds, laughing and telling stories. Meyah quickly warmed up to his drunk friend and the three of them eventually found themselves lost in an evening of smiles and good-natured flirtations. Meyah's hand remained on Hax's thigh or his hand for most of the encounter. After her first shot of tequila, she pulled out her phone to call a friend for the third-wheel Dix. The friend, a shorter and less attractive woman with massive breasts, came in after midnight.

Last call was announced by the bartender and they had a shot of tequila and a beer each to finish. Dix, of course, ordered another round against all their pleading and told them to raise their glasses for a toast.

"To you Hax, I love you like a brother and no matter what happens when we go down range, I want you to know that I will have your back and will always take care of you." Dix's gaze settled on Hax's. "And to new friends," he gave an award-winning grin to Meyah, "and to you, Nicole." He winked at the buxom woman seated beside him.

"Uh, it's *Nichelle*," she interrupted.

"Shit. And to you, Nichelle," Dix promptly corrected.

"And here's to you, bud!" Hax replied. And to Nichelle, he added, "And um... Good luck with this one."

They clinked their glasses and shared a last laugh. But Dixons' mirth was short and forced, Hax noticed. When he caught Dix's eye, Dix gave him an empty half-smile and a tilt of his glass. Hax thought about that strange moment on the entire cab ride home, a ride he shared with the beautiful Meyah.

Hax woke long before his date the next morning, a product of a decade of military life. Head pounding, he cursed the tequila he had consumed the night prior. Lying motionlessly in bed so as not to anger his migraine, he glanced at Meyah, focusing on the smoothness of her hips and buttocks. With a soft, caressing finger, he followed the contour of her naked body exposed in the dim light of dawn.

The room was small and bare, as all cheap hotel rooms were, but there was no way that he would risk bringing her onto the base. They were way too drunk and she was way too pretty. She'd undoubtedly bring too much attention to a commanding officer. Plus, the one-night-leave allowance let them stay off base for occasions just like this.

He was almost certain this would be the last woman he would ever be with and he wanted to take in every detail of the moment. Every curve of her body, every delicate waft of her perfume, every sigh she made – he stored them in the deepest part of his brain. He wouldn't exactly say why, but the last 18 hours on had been some of the best of his life. The air had never been cleaner, the sun had never been more glorious, and his love-making had never been so selfless. He actually wondered if he made the right choice joining up at all.

Meyah rolled over and batted her eyes with a smile. He grinned back, but kept it short, knowing that it was all meaningless; there was no future here. "I had fun last night," she said softly.

"Yeah, me too... I wish we had more time together... or we had met each other sooner..."

"Me to. I really like you…"

He had no reply, just a weak forced smile. "I gotta get going. I have to be at the base soon."

"What about all those plans of mimosas and brunch?"

"Oh yeah, forgot about that. God, I wish I could, but no drinking for me today."

He kissed the top of her head, got up, and dressed. Once ready to leave, he wrote his number on a piece of hotel stationary, telling her to look him up someday for a second date if he ever got the chance to come back. He knew though, somewhere deep in his gut, that he wouldn't be coming back. He kissed her deeply one last time, taking in the beauty of her face and body, then he walked out the door and out of her life.

Hax had never really been the kind to get involved with women he met at a bar and definitely not the kind to sleep with someone he had just met. But given the circumstances, he thought, *To hell with morals!* He wanted to feel human one last time.

CHAPTER TWENTY-THREE

From the outside, West Command for the Space Force appeared as a massive, upside-down steel dinner plate. The building, erected during the height of the last nuclear standoff, was designed as such that a blast wave would ripple over the structure, leaving it intact – at least, that was the logic used to get Congress to appropriate the $25 trillion for the construction. Seventy-five years ago, when it was determined the archaic and crumbling Pentagon was far too small for the growing U.S. military, all six branches had several respective headquarters built throughout the country, each just as massive and expensive as the next. This was also an attempt to decentralize the DoD so that, in the event of a nuclear attack, a single blast couldn't take out the military's brain center.

West Command, aptly named the Bunker, was the western hub for everything outer space-related in the United States. NASA was dismantled and folded into the Space Force decades after President Trump created the branch. It started as part of the Air Force, but as the need for a strong presence in space became essential and other countries began capitalizing on the power vacuum amongst the cosmos, it quickly became the largest and best-funded branch of the military.

West Command was primarily underground and extended more than 30 stories into the dense bedrock of the American Southwest desert. Coincidentally, the conspicuous building was also the birthplace of the Space Force Intelligence Sector, the division behind space and time travel, the latter of which was less than a decade old and all but perfected.

Hax entered the Bunker through the officers'
entrance on the north side of the expansive building. He
usually tried to avoid going there at all costs as the process
of making it through security took an hour alone. When
partaking in deep space navigation or time travel, however,
the journey was necessary. All officers underwent
mandatory medical and psychological examinations before
venturing into the heavens.

He and Dix had planned to meet up in the forward
foyer of the officers' entrance at 0930. Of course, Hax
knew he would be waiting in his uncomfortable officer
fatigues for at least 30 minutes before his friend would
saunter in. To his surprise, however, he found Dix actually
waiting for him. It may have been the first time Dix had
shown up to any kind of meeting punctually, and it was
definitely the first time his friend had *ever* showed up
before him.

"Ready to get your pickle tickled?" were the first
words out of Dix's mouth.

"Ha, yeah buddy."

"Sucks it's all machines now, takes all the romance
out of it," Dix chuckled.

There was something off about Dix that Hax
couldn't quite put his finger on. Was it his body language
and the way he didn't hold Hax's gaze too long? Hax
pushed the idea aside, chalking it up to nerves. They were
preparing to deploy. They were both nervous and
apprehensive.

The two made their way down the low-lit hallway
toward the med unit for their preflight checkup. The click-
clack of their polished boots echoed down the long and
bare corridor. This would be the first time either of them
was actually to go through the whole gambit of a preflight

checkup for long-distance space-time travel; Hax didn't know what to expect. Few who had made the ultra-long journeys ever retired to tell their tales. With some uneasiness, Hax thought about what it would be like to be cryogenically frozen. Dix roused him from his worries.

"So Haxy, what do you really think about Trokker?"

Taken aback by the question, Hax stopped mid-step to face his old friend. "Why? What have you been thinking about?" He hoped this would be the moment they could finally speak their peace to each other about the upcoming mission.

Dix shrugged. "Well, I think he is one hell of a leader and I believe in this mission wholeheartedly." His sentence trailed off, leaving Hax in some suspense.

"But?" Hax prompted.

"Nothing... No but, I was just wondering what your opinions were about everything."

"Well." *Fuck it, just lay it out.* Hax gathered himself and calmly said, "Well, I have my doubts, to be perfectly honest. None of this seems right, none of it seems ethical. Shit, I don't know if the true nature of this operation has even been cleared with any of the D.C. top brass. I just don't see the president of the United States of America signing on to something so..."

"Drastic times call for drastic measures... Major," Dix interjected. "You gonna be able to carry out your orders, bud? You gonna be able to do this?" The timbre in his voice was alarmingly aggressive.

Hax paused longer than he intended to. He didn't like where this conversation was going. He didn't like the tone of Dix's voice and he didn't like how he felt cornered in an empty corridor. Something was off. "Yes," Hax finally said in a voice that fooled no one. And with that, he stalked off, leaving Dix to his own devices.

Following signage that read OFFICERS, Hax lost himself

in his thoughts. He needed to talk with his father but their relationship had crumbled away to a mere blood connection over the last 18 months. He felt ashamed and too foolish to even try to reach out to his father, even though right now, he needed him more than ever. It was beginning to feel like a life-or-death decision.

CHAPTER TWENTY-FOUR

Lieutenant General Danyel Packard sat at his desk, sorting through a large archive of personnel transfer requests that had been staring at him for over a week. A picture of his wife remained close enough to touch the edge of his leather blotter; it was what he settled his gaze on several times an hour in thought. A picture that had at one point been its equal, a picture of him and his son at his boy's officer graduation ceremony, had taken a seat further back on his desk and gained a layer of neglectful dust on its gold frame.

Danyel glanced at it rarely, purposefully avoiding the feelings of loss and sorrow that the image dredged up. He knew the breakdown in their relationship was almost entirely his doing and, as his wife liked to point out, it was his temper that was to blame. He knew it was his fault his son had begun to hate him, and that killed him inside. In the last month, he had kept his son's number dialed and ready to call to finally rectify the relationship, but had never been able to go through with it. Pride was still one of his biggest foibles.

The Packard family, which included a long line of high-ranking military men and, before that, family money passed down through the generations, was well-off financially. Because of the nature of the job, the family moved often, settling in ornate houses located in well-established neighborhoods. Hax had always gone to the best private schools and, though hating it, had excelled at all of his educational endeavors with the help of highly-paid tutors. Danyel had wanted him to continue the Packard family tradition of military leadership, but he had also wanted his son to be as educated as possible in case he found something else that challenged and fulfilled him. Early in Hax's childhood, however, it became obvious that Hax would someday wear the uniform.

Danyel and Hax had been close for the better part of Hax's youth, sharing not only each other's dimpled chins and fierce eyes but their interests. Danyel had often taken Hax to tour magnificent flying craft and battlements. More than once, the major general had heard his son proclaim that he was his hero, that he loved the military, and that the United States of America was his true love.

Of course, Danyel had explained to his son that most of the craft on this particular base were non-aggressive and for exploratory purposes only. The U.S. military now was more than brawn and guns.

As an example, Danyel had disclosed that while he had in his power an impressive amount of firepower, the purpose of his newly-created fleet was peaceful space exploration. Weapons were to be used in the case of self-defense only. In fact, the fleet had been sequestered and funded by unanimous congressional votes with a near endless budget with peaceful exploration in mind. The point the major general had wanted to drive home to his ambitious son was that high-power weapons and ultimate military might alone did not define the U.S. military.

Danyel had been so proud of Hax knowing that his son would be a better man and an even better leader than him one day.

Unfortunately, his relationship with his son had taken a precipitous turn when Hax signed the paperwork to be transferred out of his father's division and into Trokker's. Danyel had been devastated and felt a level of betrayal he didn't know possible. Hax's choice, Danyel knew, would lead him down a road of willful ignorance, regret, obfuscation, and death. But there was no going back.

Danyel knew of Trokker's ambitions. The intense and visionary general was recruiting by way of volunteers and developing a group of highly-aggressive soldiers. When the order came from the top that all Space Force ships were to be used exclusively for deep-space exploration and natural resource acquisition, word was Tokker was furious. He sent a memo to fellow leadership imploring them to ignore the president's decree. The memo stated, in short, that they were warriors, not emissaries. They were hunters, not gatherers. And exploratory missions like this were a waste of a deadly fighting force. Although it had not been said forthrightly, Danyel had understood that Trokker would end up utilizing tactics that were frowned upon and borderline illegal. When Danyel was being honest with himself, he would admit that Trokker scared the shit out of him.

Danyel had pleaded with Hax not to align himself with Trokker, but his son had adamantly refused, stating that he wanted to make a name for himself outside his father's shadow. As if to emphasize his grim determination, Hax had even gone so far as to declare his hatred for being a Packard, saying that he was always deemed a pussy because of his name. He called his dad the same for being an "explorer" and not a real warrior. He told his father to that a real warrior had finally been born in the family to repair the family name that Danyel had aptly destroyed.

Danyel had beseeched Hax to reconsider, encouraging him to look beyond his own cowardice and focus on the big picture, saying he never raised such a dim-witted, narcissistic son. Their next conversation had been shorter and even more bellicose. Afterward, they had stopped talking all together.

CHAPTER TWENTY-FIVE

In the med unit, Hax was greeted by a large woman with short-cropped hair and black eyes. She was nice enough, but her gaze revealed her hatred for her job and, more importantly, her abhorrence for the patients who passed through there. Hax was gracious and tried to win her over with joviality and proper manners, but her expression did not change and her coldness only grew. After being checked in, Hax went to sit in the waiting area.

Eventually, he was called back to a small room illuminated by white lights that littered the ceiling. The screen on the wall, which now showed an AI-generated face of a 20-something-year-old nurse, immediately welcomed him by name and rank and politely asked him to take off his shirt and to press the self-vital check on his armband. With grim humor, Hax marveled that a computer program made to diagnose and prescribe was the warmest and most pleasant interaction he had yet to have. The latently coquettish AI reviewed his medical information and asked a bevy of relevant questions before finally informing him that the physician would be in shortly.

A few minutes later, a doctor strode into the room, knocking on the doorframe more as a formality than anything else. The short, stocky woman stared at a paper-sized piece of glass decorated with numbers and graphs as well as the rhythmic projections of his heartbeat. She said no words as she touched his armband and sent more information to her electronic medical record.

When she did finally ask a series of queries, her voice remained cold and detached. The conversation was succinct and humorless, like all conversations he seemed to have with doctors. Once complete, the increasingly peevish doctor left.

The AI-generated nurse appeared again and kindly asked that Hax go down the hall to room A-45 to wait for his psychological exam. He thanked the pretty girl who vanished from the screen. Mildly embarrassed that he had just thanked a computer, he left.

He always got nervous for his psychological exams. Every person going into space had medical checks, officers and enlisted alike. For those who were not officers, checkups were so routine that they would last no more than ten minutes; in fact, a quick brain scan would suffice. Officers, on the other hand, had to undergo a gauntlet of tests – and for good reason. They, unlike their unranked counterparts, were valuable. They were the ones who needed to wake up alert and ready after a cryogenic sleep for the multi-century trip.

Hax sat patiently in room A-45 thinking about the endless lectures in OCS he and Dix had attended and about late-night office visits with the greatest military mind of the twenty-third century. Every officer candidate had to go through extensive astro and theoretical physics courses to learn exactly how the technology of time and deep-space travel worked. The DoD figured it was better to have well-informed leaders grounded in facts than bedtime fairytales.

He thought back on the ebullient and brilliant Dr. Monark whose research and guidance were the reason this kind of travel even existed. Hax had been exceptionally lucky to be a part of his lectures.

"You don't need to be a goddamned genius to know that

time travel is bloody impossible, Mr. Dixon," Dr. Monark had replied abrasively to Dix in his third lecture with the man. Dix had shrunk in his chair embarrassed and looked over at Hax who wore a deer-in-the-headlights kind of expression. They had taken several courses with the doctor to pass the required didactic time for OCS, and it was becoming increasingly clear that some of them were grasping the material more than others.

Already, they had finished two weeks of the Applied Theoretical Magnetism which Dix had barely passed with Hax's tutelage. Unfortunately, those lessons which Hax knew Dix didn't fully understand had been brought into the complicated theoretical landscape of Trans-multiverse Nomadizing. Understandably, Dix had struggled with the concept that they were not technically traveling through time, but changing the location of themselves in the multi-universal continuum. Even after Dr. Monark had dumbed it down, Dix had still been unable to comprehend it.

The theory of infinite universes or what became known as the multiverse had been around for several hundred years prior to being proved by a physicist using incredibly powerful magnets in the late-2100s. The first time the Superconducting Magnetic Transponder, or SUMAT, was tested, it reached 50 percent total power output and generated nearly 500 Tesla.

The ultra-secret magnet built in the last half of the twenty-second century in an even more top-secret military installation in the desert of New Mexico could create magnetic fields one million times stronger than that of Earth's. The output was so phenomenal that the experiment was shut down a millionth of a second after it reached the massive power level in fear that there would be worldwide catastrophic failures of all electric equipment. The technology was being primarily researched for its impact on space travel and how, if it could, minimize fuel consumption. But what they discovered instead was a new way of traveling all together.

The physicist and his cohorts soon realized that such incredible power pulled on magnetic fields from other universes. If they generated enough power, they could bring the universe most similar to their own close. This was because it was pulling on (almost) the exact same SUMAT and generating the same amount of magnetic power, but located in another universe all together.

Hax remembered the way his professor had explained it.

"Imagine our universe is a stateroom in an infinitely massive cruise ship. Each stateroom room, for all intents and purposes, is exactly the same, except for one tiny detail. Let's say the toilet paper was put on over the top instead of hanging from the bottom in the room next door. There are infinite staterooms on this ship, all with minute variances that grow increasingly different as you walk down the hallway. The differences become bigger and more meaningful the further from our stateroom you get.

"The superconducting magnets are used as place finders for the universe next door. If you create one strong enough, the two will match up on the same places in your room and the one next door, meaning approximately the exact same place in each universe. All you have to do is figure out how to get through the stateroom wall and *voila*! You're in the next universe that is identical to ours. If you create magnetic fields strong enough, and then create a massively powerful explosion in that magnetic field, you can tear through space and get there. But here is the amazing thing – the longer you maintain yourself in the magnetic fields after the explosion, the further down the hallway you can go. Unfortunately, it takes unbelievable power and time to go any significant distance.

"'But what about the different decks?' you cry. Each of these staterooms is the exact same except they exist on a different part of the time continuum. Each hallway on the x-axis is a different location in the space continuum, but each deck on the y-axis is in time. So, using the same massively powerful magnets and corresponding explosions, we can rip a hole to decks beneath us and travel to different universes identical to ours, but at different locations in the timeline. Here on Earth, we can make powerful magnetic fields, but nothing strong enough to realize the energy needed. So, we figured, let's use fields already in existence.

"Jupiter's magnetosphere is the largest in the solar system, a magnitude of 18,000 times that of Earth's. All we have to do is get our ships into the outermost part of its clouds, turn on our SUMATs, initiate the explosion, and we are in business! How we got to this point however is a different story altogether.

"When we first started to investigate the validity of these concepts decades ago, we assumed we were experimenting with some kind of transportation system. After a massive amount of power and magnetism was applied to singular atoms, they would seemingly disappear and then reappear fractions of a second later. As the experiments grew more complex, physicists soon realized that they had to address a very difficult question – and it wasn't to what location was the matter being sent. The question became: to what time was the matter being sent? That's about the time the U.S. military took over our research and I officially got on the payroll of the Department of Defense.

"A decade after that initial test was launched under some 20 stories of dirt and bedrock, the DoD was finally ready to try out its most expensive and largest scientific discovery since electricity. So, what did they do? The U.S. DoD sent a research vessel to the exosphere of Jupiter, carrying a powerful neodymium iron-boron superconducting magnet. Now, at the time, it took the crew nearly three months to reach the gas giant, an unimaginable time frame. With recent developments in technology, we can make the trip in a little over a week.

"Turns out that it takes time to travel along the time continuum – who knew? If you want to go back 50 years to another universe to see your parents as kids, it takes 50 years to get there. But what will really blow your noodle, scientifically speaking, is that when you return home from your cumulative 100-year journey there and back, not a second will have passed in this universe. And lucky for you bright-eyed cadets, thanks to cryogenic sleep, your metabolism will be slowed so much, that the 100-year trip would age you, eh, about six months. Wormholes are weird like that; time and space don't really exist in them, but that is a lecture for another day."

CHAPTER TWENTY-SIX

Hax left the medical unit, rubbing his right shoulder. They always told him that they were just injecting him with the standard cocktail of prophylactic vaccinations and other "health stimulants" when he went in for his yearly physical. This year, since they were about to embark on a mission that would take him centuries away, they added several more assessments and what felt like a never-ending succession of shots. These, they had explained to him, were to keep him from going into a coma, a possible side effect from the long period of time he would be kept in cryogenic sleep. That didn't help with the sense of dread already growing in the pit of his stomach. Whatever the hell they were pumping into him with those needles hurt like a son-of-a-bitch.

Dix finished a few minutes after him and they met in the foyer of the med building. He sat beside Hax in one of 50 dark-gray chairs and rubbed his arm. The expression of smugness which frequented his face was slightly muddled by nervousness. "The fuck they load us up with this time, goddamn plasma acid?" Dix growled, excessively rubbing his right shoulder for dramatic effect.

"Heh, no kidding. I felt like a stuck pig that whole time, hoses and wires and needles in every inch of my body."

"Yeah, every orifice too," Dix added.

"Well, I guess that means what? We ship off tomorrow?"

"Normally yeah, I think they do the med checks the day before so they can be assured there are no physical changes in the 24 hours. Apparently, they underestimate my ability to put my liver into toxic shock."

Hax laughed but noticed Dix didn't – or couldn't – meet his gaze.

"Speaking of liver failure," his friend continued. "How'd it go with that chick you brought home the other night? She was a cutie."

Hax's response was a slow theatric wink, involving his upper lip and a click of his tongue, a tried-and-true statement of "I don't kiss and tell, but I do fuck and wink."

"My man! Well, her friend was a dud. We ended up at my place and before we did any more than some tit squeezes, she was passed out."

"Playing catch up with people six drinks ahead of you always seems to knock people out hard," Hax finished, standing with a groan.

They had just made their way out of the echoes of the perfectly air-conditioned building when both of their multiplex wrist screens flashed and vibrated in unison. They exchanged confused looks before turning their arms up to eye level.

URGENT: ALL COMMANDING OFFICERS
ALL COMMANDING OFFICERS O-3 AND ABOVE TO REPORT
IMMEDIATELY TO HQ
MISSION UPDATE TO BEGIN AT 1300 HOURS
COMMAND STAFF PRESENCE MANDATORY

Hax's eyes shot straight up to meet Dix's and his heart jumped 20 beats as he felt a powerful surge of adrenaline pump through him. This had just become real. He had been sure that when he had joined this unit, the news that they would be shipping off for some risky and possibly covert mission would fill him with excitement and pride. What he felt now was anything but.

"Jesus," Dix said. "Looks like it is about to begin, huh? Finally get to find out exactly what the fuck we are 'bout to go do…"

A thought occurred to Hax and he met his friend's gaze in confusion. "Why did you get that?"

"Get what?" Dixon replied, face painted with a perfect tell of his uneasiness.

"Why did you get that update? That was for majors and higher-ranked officers only. There is no reason for you to be attending a mission update. I'm a major and I'm barely ranked high enough to be invited to these kinds of things…" There was a moment of silence between them. "So… what aren't you telling me?" Hax folded his arms across his chest, taking full possession of his higher rank.

"What do you mean? It's nothing, Haxy."

"Dix, I have known you for most of my life. I know when you are not telling me something or lying. What's going on? You've been acting weird the last couple days and now… Is there something you're not telling me?"

"Nothing, dude." Dix fidgeted. "Sir." It was obvious his friend was shaken by Hax's sudden command. "It's nothing with you. It's just my nerves or something. That's all. Didn't mean to take it out on you."

"Why did you get the HQ update?"

Dix sighed. "How should I know? A mistake? Maybe they're calling in everyone down to the captains?"

Hax observed him for a moment longer and then strode off toward HQ a quarter of a mile away. He had no intention of grilling his subordinate, his friend, right then and there; he was sure the answer would come out shortly. Dix fell in a few paces behind him.

They entered HQ together and made their way to the large, darkened room of sub-basement three of the building. Hax had said nothing and his friend had, likewise, remained quiet. Appropriately dressed in his officer fatigues and carrying his black and gray service cap bearing a golden eagle and blue and gold shield, Hax greeted the ranking officers, strategically avoiding contact with Trokker. Eventually, he found a seat in the middle of a row of chairs which surrounded a small stage.

Hax had expected Dix to stay close since this was more his show than Dixon's, but upon finding his friend greeting Trokker with a warm handshake, grew concerned. What the hell was a captain doing shaking hands with and talking to the highest-ranked man on the base? Hax pretended to be interested in the lighting overhead, but continued to glance at his friend and the major general in interest. After a moment of discussion, Trokker guided Dix to a seat near the front of the room and then took the stage.

The major general cleared his throat as a holographic map of the United States of America materialized in the middle of the room. The map showed all U.S. states, including Puerto Rico, North and South California, and the state of Baja which had been annexed in the mid-2100s as the 54th state.

As the room fell silent, Trokker began.

"Gentlemen, thank you for hurrying here in such short notice. This briefing is for command staff only; the information we will be discussing is not to leave this room under any circumstances." Hax glanced at Dix but found his friend entranced by the major general. "I, along with members of the intelligence team, have finalized our plan. Now, all of you volunteered to be in my division because you are bold, courageous, and visionary. Well, that is *exactly* what I expect from you now. As most of you know, our top directive from the White House for the last 24 months has been primarily focused on securing the future of energy resources for the country and affirming our military power. Plainly stated, the world is out of nuclear ore of pretty much every stripe, thus we have been tasked to look elsewhere.

"There are other divisions in this great force that are more of the exploratory ilk and think it wise to spend a hundred years flying from planet to planet and moon to moon with little to no intel that there are even significant stores to be mined. The brave minds of this division have a bold answer to this question. Using technology that is of the utmost confidentiality, we have selected a place to launch an offensive that will secure us a hundred years' worth of fuel." Trokker thought and then clarified, "Well, to be more exact, we have identified a time."

"This will be the first non-violent military offensive of this size in history," Trokker said proudly. "This is a simple and straightforward op. We will come out of cryo after traveling approximately 190 years. The target is San Diego and the massive cache of Uranium that had been stored there." He paused a moment, marched to the other side of the stage, and continued. "Destroyers will go in two hours prior to foot invasion, rendering military counter-ops ineffectual and dismantling major thoroughfares. We will then send in our P-LAV battalions and transports to secure the payload. Simple in-and-out mission. We shouldn't be there any longer than three days. If all goes as planned, not a single innocent loss of life will occur."

Trokker stopped and scanned the room as if wondering if he should continue. He didn't. The major general's briefing was purposefully vague and rushed.

Plausible deniability or purposeful and malicious obfuscation? Hax assumed the latter.

Trokker turned the floor over to his highest-ranking intel officer Colonel Frank Piltez. The colonel, in his perfectly starched and pressed black uniform, appeared like a character out of a children's movie. His beady eyes were sharp but hung in dark, sunken sockets while his hairline was far past the point of saving. A long, crooked nose added to the caricature.

Colonel Piltez continued where the major general left off, explaining in further detail the intricacies of the mission and the expectations. He went battalion by battalion explaining where they were to land and their core objectives. Finally, Hax's battalion designator popped up on the hologram in the middle of the room and the colonel turned to Hax.

A map of twenty-first-century San Diego appeared cloaked in grays, greens, and browns. Two bright, red dots shown alongside numerous other smaller ones. One red dot was marked NAVAL BASE SAN DIEGO in skinny, black lettering while the other read NAVAL BASE POINT LOMA.

"These, Major Packard," the colonel continued, "are your primary objectives. Remember, as the major general said, we are taking out military installations, major thoroughfares, and integral infrastructure only. There is to be as close to zero civilian casualties as you can possibly manage. But again, as mentioned before, every piece of military apparatus and structure is to be neutralized."

Hax spent the next several minutes in stunned silence, working to block out the colonel's droning as he briefed the other battalion officers. Hax only snapped from his daze when Piltez raised his voice and continued.

"Further details and maps, pictures, and other relevant intel have already been sent to your com-bands. I know this is still little information for you, but we have two centuries to fill you in on all the rest. We are telling you this now–"

"We are telling you this now," the major general interrupted as he strode back into the middle of the stage, distorting the map, "because this is your last chance to leave. Any of you who decide to make that unfortunate decision however, will instantly be met with a dishonorable discharge from the military. Furthermore, if anything we have talked about here today is leaked, you will be disposed of. Clear?"

There was no response in the room, just a heavy and palpable silence.

"If there are no questions, then you are dismissed," the major general concluded, leaving the stage and subsequently the room.

Hax's brain was going a thousand miles an hour; his heart raced even faster. He was in utter disbelief at what he had just heard.

They were going to invade their own country for resources.

He refused to believe it. Was everyone else going to follow blindly? The room was tense, but by the looks on the faces of the men surrounding him, all had been accepted with no questions or reservations. Hax found himself shaking and worked to keep the disgust from his face.

Most of the brass filed out of the room shortly after Trokker left, silently, complicitly. Hax remained. Alone, he let the dread show as he stared at the chair in front of him. Movement caught his eye and his gaze met Dix's.

At that moment, Hax knew in a very real and dangerous way that he was completely, entirely alone.

CHAPTER TWENTY-SEVEN

Hax lined up with 20 other officers as a large, ominous thunderhead in the distance threatened to soak the parched dirt. It was that perfect time of the morning when the desert held a charming beauty and the birds happily sang about it, greeting the rain enthusiastically. They were a mile north of the now-empty base as massive spacecraft, which not long ago were preparing for war in droves, made their way to their original ports of berth.

Someone had leaked.

There was a spy or a rat. Somehow the men with all the stars on their shoulders in their offices in D.C. had discovered the intent of the operation and had sent the might of the entire Space Force's Eastern Command to prevent the unbelievable from happening.

Hax looked down, indifferent to the dirt piling on his once immaculate boot, thinking how this was the last time he would ever be wearing them. He had actually been relieved when the ships had come and arrested them all. The idea of Trokker and his traitorous men being executed brought a slight smile to his face. Hax hadn't been the one to let slip news of the operation, but he was grateful nonetheless.

Pop. Pop. Pop.

One by one, the officers fell dead into the red dirt of the desert.

Hax woke from the dream covered in sweat and heart racing. He lay in his small bed for several minutes, eyes swollen with exhaustion, brain afire. He had barely slept all night; the last 12 hours were a complete blur. Not for the first – or last – time, he contemplated the insanity he had heard the day before and laughed aloud in an out-of-body chortle at the absolute madness that was to transpire.

For a brief moment after leaving HQ the day prior, he had actually thought about going directly to the major general and telling him that he wanted nothing to do with the operation. But he knew Trokker was gravely serious and would perceive his resignation as a threat. Maybe if the major general was clever enough, Hax would die in a *training accident.*

Hax had thought of bringing up the matter with Dix, but he wasn't so sure that he trusted his friend anymore. So, instead of doing something, he sat in the dark and stared at the ceiling.

Momentarily, the wall clock interrupted his grim musing. "Good morning, Major Packard. Your schedule today is…"

The usual charming tenor of the female voice was interrupted by Trokker's gruff one. "I am proud of each and every one of you. Prepare for invasion."

Hax hated when they added stuff like that to his personal space. It was meant to give them a sense of pride and meaning, but to Hax, it was just a reminder that he was military property; they could do whatever they saw fit to and with him.

He swung his legs over the side of his bead and put his bare feet against the metal floor of his bunk room. The cold that shot into his foot awakened him instantly, instilling in him a sense of finality as he would be partaking in one of the most treasonous operations the United States DoD had ever executed.

He dressed methodically like he did every morning, but this time, he took his time. He was filled with a deep sorrow and a very real love for this country that he did know he had in himself. He thought back on the girl he had spent that one night with and wondered what she would end up doing the rest of her life. He thought back to when he had visited his dad's base at the age of eight. He had perceived his dad as a goddamn hero. He had been so full of wonder, so full of the thought that the best thing a person could do with his life was to join the Space Force to protect the United States.

He thought of holidays as a young child with his family, unaware of the world beyond their warm living room. But there he was, feet on the icy floor, staring at a man he didn't recognize in the mirror.

An announcement from the wall screen broadcast that he should be preparing for the "most important day of his life." Hax punched the mirror and turned to leave his dorm. Surprisingly, Dix was waiting for him as he walked out of his quarters, an impetuous and dangerous look carved on his face.

"Jesus, Captain. You scared the shit outta me. I think this is the first time in our careers you've been awake before me," Hax joked, but his levity didn't work. The mistrust between them was palatable.

"Ha, come on, Major. I'll escort you," was all Dix said. Hax noticed the formality with which Dix addressed him and it made him nervous.

The walk to their massive transport vessel was long and, for the most part, silent. Nominal questions regarding troop preparedness and when the formal and in-depth briefing would occur popped up, but Dix's silence was new to Hax. It was awkward and foreboding.

Although there were droves of troops, this was one of the smaller divisions in the military. Again, Hax was taken by the size and the scope of what his country could amass. He stopped mid-gait and knelt, much to the chagrin of another officer who had been striding along not far behind him. With a curse, the man barely navigated around Hax who had placed his hands in the warm, red dirt.

"Ah Christ, you're not gonna get all sentimental on me, are you?" crowed Dix.

"No, just amazing, isn't it? We will be gone for centuries, but when we return this will all be right here, like nothing had happened. If we return... Guess I just want to take it in while I'm still here." Hax didn't want to reveal any weakness on his face so he remained looking at the ground.

"We will be back in a week," Dix said without conviction. "Always so damn philosophical. Guess that's why I love ya."

Hax looked at Dix abruptly to find his friend grinning. *There* was the man, the soldier, the friend he had known. He smiled back and reached an arm up. Dix yanked him up and they continued into the shadow of a huge ship.

They made it to the ten-story elevator tower which housed the various gangplanks to board the ship. The officers' elevator was smaller than the enlisted and located on the backside. Hax and Dix boarded the elevator with four other officers for the quick and silent ride to the top four officer decks. The door opened at number eight where Dix and Hax got off, leaving the others still in the elevator car. The officer's gangplank to the ship was relatively narrow but very long and gave Hax a sense of vertigo as he crossed it 80 feet in the air. It was located near the aft of the ship and went directly into the belly of it. The air hummed with a deep, bone-rattling electric purr that could be felt over a half mile away.

Hax always marveled at the way the electric

currents, even at the lowest power at docking elevation, seemed to make the skin of the ship seem alive. But the constant undulating of the ship's outer hull also made him shudder. It reminded him of the time nearly 20 years ago when he had been walking along the perimeter of the latest base where his family had been stationed.

At the time, the bases had automated proximity sentries every 200 feet equipped with impressive firepower. Anyone on the inside was incredibly safe; anyone on the outside was likely to be blown to pieces. It was for this reason his parents didn't mind when he wandered the grounds by himself for hours on end.

One particularly hot day, he had been met by a horrific smell and a shocking scene – a coyote had been shot by the sentry guns. Upon approaching it, Hax had discovered that it was covered in maggots, writhing and undulating. Their presence under the coyote's ragged fur had created the haunting illusion that its skin was alive. The sight had shaken him and he had never again gone out alone to explore.

Hax took a long look at the hull, then cast his gaze back over his shoulder at the ground 80 feet below. He drew in one last deep breath of air, cleared his mind, and carried onward, chin high and shoulders back.

The 50-yard gangplank admitted them to a hallway illuminated with an unnatural pink glow. A sensuous female voice requested that the men go to their respective decks. To the left and up several levels were the officers' bunks, mess halls, and the like; the hallway to the right gave access to junior officers' quarters.

Hax and Dix stopped at the juncture and faced each other. Normally right about now, they would be making jokes and roughhousing with one another. But there was no levity here. Instead, they simply gazed at one another in professional uneasiness, both dressed in their officers' dress uniforms.

Hax's heart pounded and his gut knotted with a mixture of excitement, angst, and a fear of the unknown. With a slight nod, Hax reached out and shook Dix's hand. Immediately thereafter, Dix saluted him and the two turned on their heels and went their separate ways.

CHAPTER TWENTY-EIGHT

Hax made his way to his bunk room, as ordered by the lovely echoing voice. He walked with his proud officer's gait, but felt more and more recalcitrant inside with each step. The ship seemed so sterile, so dead. There was the pitter patter of feet every which way, but he felt alone and confused.

Hax's bunk room door opened with a hiss and he stepped inside. Instantly the wall screen came to life and he was faced with the attractive AI-constructed woman. She greeted him by name and rank and gave him instruction to prepare for what was called "the long nap." The science of cryogenic deep sleep was almost perfected over the last decade, but the pretty girl still explained the myriad of complications that could occur during the sleep as well as the body-altering problems one could have once awake. The thought of pissing and shitting out a tube through his belly just turned him off.

He was surprised at the perfunctory of the whole operation. The ship was in space and on its way to the largest planet in the solar system in just a couple hours. In his head was a whirlwind of anxiety and mistrust.

There must have been over 5,000 aboard and they got them all in and loaded that quickly? Why was there such a rush to get an operation this enormous both in scale and complexity out to space within a couple hours?

Hax felt betrayed. Or maybe he was the one doing the betraying? His dad was right. He was young and starry-eyed following a crazy general into this, and now there was no going back.

He wandered out of his bunk several times much to the

protestation of the AI. He just wanted information or someone to talk to.

Upon returning to his room, the AI asserted that he was to remain in his bunk until it was time to head to the "nap chambers," and that if it was food or drink he was looking for, it would be sent up by a soldier.

They're keeping us cordoned off, he thought. *They don't want us mingling or even talking until we are well-past the point of no return.*

The deeper into the cosmos the fleet of ships went, the more he knew that this mission was, like his gut had been telling him, entirely fucked.

The ships traveled at full capacity with multiple laser thrusters set at approximately one-tenth the speed of light, or about 67 million miles an hour. The trip, when Jupiter was at its closest to Earth, would take approximately six and a half hours. Everyone, for all six hours, was to remain in their bunks. At the six-hour mark, the pretty voice and face appeared once again to announce that all crewmembers were to make their ways to their respective CRYSLER, or cryogenic sleeping room.

Hax left long after most the other officers had departed; he knew he was alone. A hundred yards down the bright chrome hallway, he stopped and stared down at his com-band. He had to do it. It was his *duty*. He hadn't signed on for this.

Over the past six hours, he had thought of only one person, the only person could right this wrong. For so many years he had promised himself that he would never call him to get him out of anything. He had joined this rogue division to do just that, get the hell away from his father. Hax was his own man, and it was about time he did something without hanging off his father's coattails. But this was different…

He raised his arm and punched in the short password to his wrist screen. Momentarily, he found the video call function.

Several million miles away, Lieutenant General Packard's armband illuminated with the word URGENT written in red.

He peered in confusion at the screen. He hadn't received a single message in nearly two years from his son. Fearing the worst, he asked the two colonels currently occupying his office to give him a moment; the two men left.

Packard opened the short message which had a time stamp of 45 minutes ago.

His eyes grew wide as he listened to the short message. His son, who had always been so proud and fearless, looked panicky and anxious. The message, which was staticky and broke up frequently due to the vast distance it had just traveled, finished with a plea that would change the lieutenant general's life forever.

"Dad, we need your help."

PART THREE

"We have met the enemy and he is us."
Walt Kelly

CHAPTER TWENTY-NINE

Day Three: 0845 Hours

Food had become scarce and people had already grown wary of each other, and for good reason. Although the flying things and stomping robots were, of course, enemies, it was painfully obvious that man had become his own greatest enemy.

People have in them, and probably have always had, a dark side, an animalistic side. All it took was a crisis to bring it to the forefront. Once honest, hard-working people were exposed to a grave threat, instinct kicked in and survival became paramount.

People who had once thought themselves passive and loving became violent and hostile as they searched for ways to endure.

Those who had once been surrounded by friends and adoring coworkers now found themselves alone, casting about for encouragement and support.

People quickly found themselves in a panicked state of survival where all thoughts of normal interaction and societal norms were cast out at first signs of unrest. Neighbors, who had had barbecues a week prior, now killed each other for what was in their fridge or gun safe. Extended family members who, not long ago, were thought of as loved ones, were forgotten for nuclear family members.

The veneer of normal dignity and civility cracked into a nightmarish Hobbesian reality of singular brutality and brevity. Only those with a strong constitution and those courageous and forthright would survive. In less than a week, it had become plainly clear who was who.

Maggie dragged a filthy hand along an empty shelf, collecting dust on her fingertips. She wiped her fingers on her jeans in complete amazement at how quickly the world had turned to shit. She glanced at her once perfectly manicured hands, now bruised, dirty, and cut to shreds.

Her two boys also appeared filthy, ragged, and aged past their years. Their hollow gazes were heart-breaking, but Maggie had run out of tears. They had been surviving by hiding and eating whatever they could get their hands on. She hadn't seen Sam and she didn't suppose she would; certainly, he was gone.

She and her boys were the only ones in the relatively large convenience store, but seeing the dearth of products it held on its shelves, it made perfect sense. It had been looted to the bone. The loud but muffled voices broadcasting from the ships flying overhead still warned citizens to stay inside their domiciles and off the streets. The constant barrage of stringent guidance had begun a day ago and become maddeningly monotonous – but no one dared to defy the orders. Of course, the only people on the street were the homeless, those caught without a place to stay, or, in Maggie's case, people with no choice.

Maggie reached to the back of a mostly empty shelf and groped at the small can hiding in the back. When she drew it out, she stared at it for a long moment, simmering. Fucking oysters. Fed up, she chucked it down the aisle with a yowl of frustration, throwing it at the cement block wall at the south end of the building. The thick, milky-gray contents dropped to a congealed blob on the tiled floor. She let out another scream of anger, for the first time in her life hating God for what He had done; her voice reverberated throughout the store.

The only reply she received was a choked question if she was okay from her oldest son.

Initially flooded with anger – she had told them to stay in the back office where no one could see them – her affect immediately changed upon spotting a bearded face pressed against the glass in the front of the store behind them. "Get your asses over here now," she hissed at her children, terrified. She didn't know how long he had been looking in, but without a doubt, he had heard the scream. The man peering in was unkempt, unshaven, and dirty. His impossibly wide eyes looked ferocious and half-crazed.

Heart thrumming, Maggie watched the feral-looking man as he slowly trudged the length of the storefront, heading to the front door, his eyes never leaving the darkened interior. She was furious with herself for advertising her location in that brief moment of heightened emotion.

The man's dirt-crusted fingers drummed on the glass, a sound loud enough that the patter echoed to the back of the store; his other hand held a long, serrated kitchen knife that, from a distance, appeared rusted and dull. Maggie pushed her boys below the aisle divider, keeping her gaze on the man as he licked his lips with mad obscenity. The scream had gotten his attention; she now prayed that he hadn't see them – hadn't seen her boys. But the way his ferocious eyes stayed fixed on the inside said he knew perfectly well they were in there and that he did not have friendly intentions. As he approached the store's door, he allowed his nails to scrape along the glass pane, sending an eerie screech inside.

The three of them had spent almost an hour in the building and knew that the only other exit was located in the back office and was locked with a deadbolt that had been rusted shut. The only way they could get out of this was through the front where this savage-looking intruder was slowly opening the glass door with slow and methodic madness.

Breathing unsteady, Maggie glanced around for a weapon, *anything*.

Once the door was open a few inches, the man brought his face up to the small opening and, in a musical and unusually high-pitched voice, sang, "Helllooooo."

Just then, something made the man pause and look over his shoulder. His face, once maniacally predatorial, folded in fear as two large, metal legs reinforced by three piston-like tubes came into view at the window's edge. The legs supported a metal frame which appeared to have electrical currents running down its body. Two bulky, metal arms protruded from its sides; another wiry one holding a large-barreled weapon was folded over the right shoulder. The machine took two more long strides toward the man then stopped. The torso rotated a quarter turn to face him.

Maggie motioned to her boys to be quiet and still as she looked on. They had been doing everything they possibly could in the last 48 hours to avoid those horrible machines. Although the ships overhead were sparse, the 15-foot-tall mechanical nightmares were now ubiquitous as they patrolled the streets. From what she could tell, they were there to enforce a complete lockdown of the city and the curfew restrictions of the people. And they were enforcing them violently without hesitation. They had begun killing indiscriminately, mowing down anyone who was not following the loud speaker dictates.

"Citizen, you are disobeying lockdown orders," rumbled a baritone, synthesized voice from the armor's speaker.

Before the craft had finished its warning, a diamond-white light accompanied by a sound like the intense buzzing of highline wires, burst into the store. A shelf containing the few remaining cans of fruit exploded above their heads and tin cans melted. Maggie dove to the floor atop her boys as red-hot debris fell over the three. Then everything went silent.

After a moment, the heavy footsteps slogged off out of earshot. Wheezing in terror, Maggie slowly – cautiously – peered above the aisle divider. The glass of the front door was an oozing mess of orange and purple plasma that dripped from the metal frame. The man was gone. A heavy dust hung in the air and pieces of charred bone lay strewn on the sidewalk and linoleum floor.

She had seen it before, those horrifying metal bipods killing people just for being outside, just for disobeying the lockdown orders. But Maggie and the boys had to risk it, they had to find Sam. The one place she knew for sure at which he would eventually end up was his parents' house.

Their feet ached as they meandered through every street, checking any empty store that could possibly have food or water. They were only a mile or so from the quaint little home where her husband had been raised, but the trip was long, tedious, and took the better part of a day. Hiding from looters and all other sorts of depraved people taking advantage of the chaos was hard enough, but now she had to worry about 15-foot killer machines and patrol ships – while towing two children.

Somehow or another they made it to Brookes

Avenue, a street replete with beautiful cottage-style homes and well-manicured lawns. Sneaking down the street as covertly as they could, they finally found Sam's parents' house ahead. They hid behind a hedge across the street – a risk, Maggie knew – and observed the house. It appeared empty and just like she remembered. A pristine brick retaining wall held up a lush garden which gave way to a cute, ambling sidewalk. The house itself radiated warmth with a mustard-yellow adobe exterior; the front door was adorned with a floral wreath. The eucalyptus tree in the front yard was fuller than she remembered.

But something was off.

Maggie frowned as she spotted a broken side window and several liquor bottles in the meticulously-kept yard. She saw the form of a person, tall with thick, black hair, lumber past one of the windows – there wasn't a chance in hell that was her mother-in-law.

Suddenly, a yell came from within the house, hostile and deep. Something was terribly wrong here.

She turned to her kids and ordered them to stay put, holding Zachary's gaze to emphasize her command. When she was sure he was going to stay with his brother, she, having become extraordinarily efficient at staying low and moving fast, crept across the road to the house. She went to the Albert Avenue side of the house, the side with the driveway and small kitchen windows, and stood on her tippytoes to peer in.

The house was in ruin. Liquor and beer bottles littered every counter space; some kid was passed out on the tile floor. It had been taken over by squatters and thugs. After a few more moments of disappointing investigation, she determined there was zero sign of her mother-in-law. But curiosity got the best of her and she sneaked along the side of the house to the back fence. Looking through the cracks in the wooden slats, she saw what she feared most. In the far corner of the backyard lay a heap of a body. Although the face wasn't visible, the woman's hair color was undeniable. Maggie audibly gasped and covered her mouth, running straight back to her kids. Those men had killed her, they had killed her mother-in-law and thrown her out like an animal carcass.

The small amount of hope Maggie had left in her soul was sucked out. She made it back to her kids as quietly and surreptitiously as possible and knelt beside them. They didn't ask; it seemed they already knew the answer. She slumped down and put an arm over their shoulders.

Now what?

Everywhere they went they seemed to encounter gruesome and terrible sights. Some of the killing was at the hands of the robot machines, but survivors of the invasion set forth an even more sickening pattern of ruthlessness. The worst they witnessed had happened the day before in the back room of Vons Grocery where the family had tried to find sustenance.

There had been several others hiding in the back of the dark, empty building, all harmless people in the same dire straits Maggie and the kids found themselves in; none of them had even batted an eye at the three new short-term tenants.

Maggie had gotten up early and awakened the children as she wanted to get to their in-laws' house. Peeking her head out the rear doorway that looked into a small back alleyway, she had seen an elderly couple emerge from a new Mercedes SUV. She assumed the couple was living in the car, trying to hide and stay out of the eyes of both the terrible craft and the roaming bands of looters. The man had gone to the rear, opened the hatch, and pulled out a suitcase while his wife found a bottle of water for herself in the backseat. Mere moments later, several thuggish-looking men had attacked the man and thrown him violently to the ground. The wife had let out a shriek of horror before being hit squarely in the face with a baseball bat, nose and eye socket exploding in red liquid with a horrible crunch. She had collapsed into a crumpled pile.

Maggie had reflexively pulled herself back into the doorway and held her kids against the inside wall. She heard screaming as the gangsters beat the old man mercilessly, kicking his body, legs, and face until they were swollen, bruised, and bloodied. When Maggie had chanced a glance, she found the mobsters still pummeling the old man who was no longer conscious. One especially skinny and grimy-looking thug had hopped on top of the old man and wrapped his fingers around his lifeless neck. He had kept his hands tight as the other two rummaged through the high-end vehicle, taking everything. They then ran, laughing and ecstatic about their latest grab.

Panting, Maggie had watched in disgust and horror, a hand over her mouth, the other pressing her children inside the doorway to keep them from witnessing the terrible sight. She contemplated going to help the two elders lying dead or dying in the street, but she knew there was nothing she could do.

Since that morning, she had been holding on to the hope that she would find Sam at his parents' place. But now, with the knowledge that her mother-in-law had been murdered and Sam was nowhere to be found, she was heartbroken. She assumed Sam had already been here and had seen the state of the place. There were at least five crooks in there; he wasn't stupid enough to try to take them all on. She knew he wouldn't go far, and that they wouldn't either.

Her only constant source of comfort through this waking hell was her sons and their enduring courage. The perseverance they had demonstrated over the last several days was what had kept them alive. There were, as to be expected, several times when the three of them would break down and cry together in fear and hunger, but mostly in fear because they would never see Sam again.

The rest of the day was spent much like the past several – avoiding the invaders and breaking into various stores and buildings in search of food, water and shelter. Most were the same; pilfered and empty.

Their luck began to change when, less than a block from where they sat, Maggie heard a familiar voice yell at the top of his lungs.

CHAPTER THIRTY

Day One: Commence Operation 0900

Hax fought the routine claustrophobia that swelled in his chest. The thought of being strapped in his P-LAV, which was locked into a landing craft docked inside the belly of a transport vessel, was unnerving. He had always scored low on sorties and ground attack simulators in P-LAVs. He hated the cramped quarters and the multitude of buttons and joysticks; but most of all, he hated the heat. And now, as his heart beat into his temples and he needed to take a piss more than ever before, he was locked inside of one of them for the real thing.

Sweat slithered down his forehead and dripped off his nose, elbows, and neck. Internal temperature readings indicated that the P-LAV was "within normal functioning limits," but it was his nerves, not the temperature that made him sweat so profusely.

After leaving the main transport ship, the final descent in the landing craft was remarkably smooth. Then, without warning, everything started shaking violently and the temperature skyrocketed to near unbearable levels. The calm voice that broadcast through his headset informed him that the automatic environment control module was setting to the military-regulated 75 degrees Fahrenheit. The air conditioning in the cabin of his vehicle didn't stand a chance against the robustness of Earth's mighty atmosphere. And to make matters worse, the blowers were set at the perfect level to only cool the face – and the balls.

The unreal amount of noise and turbulence lasted only a

minute, then faded into an ominous silence. Hax, still combating his claustrophobia and excessive sweating, turned his focus inward to control his breathing. His heart rate slowed to an acceptable level, at least according to the soporific AI in his headset that had accompanied him on the whole trip.

He patiently waited in the relatively small P-LAV hangar/landing craft, eying the 200 other P-LAVs in the lander with him. Only 75 yards long and 40 yards wide, the craft was one of several he was to command. A few moments later, four more would land with the remainder of his battalion. He was the highest-ranking officer on the vessel, which meant all the pressure was directly on his shoulders. Normally, pressure would help Hax focus and compel him to be the best, but now it was just that. Pressure. Heavy and burdensome.

The sensation of alloy feet hitting the ground instantly cleared his mind. He became the man he had trained his entire life to be. The stratagem and tactical priorities from the previous day's officers' briefing flooded his brain. All thoughts of quitting, or worse, going AWOL, vanished in the powerful vibrations of the lander as it made preparations for troop disembarkment. He knew he would do the right thing when the time came, but he was a soldier and he would be damned if he were to go back on that sacred creed. The aft of the lander opened and a giant ramp lowered with a hiss. The P-LAVs were unlatched from the sides of the ship at which point they clomped down the ramp to the soft dirt.

His pulse was maintaining a steady rate of 75 beats per minute; his wits were laser-focused, thanks to the adrenaline, and he still needed to pee. He led the way, guiding 200 P-LAVs into the chaos of war.

The grass in the stadium, for the most part, was long, unkempt, and brown; traces of hash marks left dying lines in the turf. It was, by all standards, a football field – 120 yards long, 54 yards wide – except for one thing; on this day, a 40-million-ton spaceship had landed.

The first several steps in his P-LAV were like none of the endless training he had done in these machines. And having the power of three separate state-of-the-art, military-grade weapon systems at his fingertips made him feel uncomfortably authoritative. Back at the base, he had been stuck in the same overheated, tight simulator which could mimic the vibrations and violent movements of combat; there had been few instances of training in an actual P-LAV. The half-dozen times the officers had been able to train in the craft, they had felt nothing but an abrasive crunch of dirt and gravel beneath the feet of the 15-foot killing machines.

Hax took a dozen steps on the wet grass and then looked out. He didn't really know what he had expected to see upon finally exiting the belly of the ship. He had thought going so many years in the past, he would step into a foreign world. But it wasn't; everything appeared eerily familiar. The sky was bluer with centuries less smog hanging in the air, the grass was green, and the air tasted a little sweeter – but he couldn't be sure as he was comparing it to the recycled air of the years-long deep space voyage. He took it in for only a second, then Hax Packard got to business.

He began barking orders into his headset and getting his men in line. His specific mission was to destroy and then secure the major causeway coming into the downtown area from the east. The destroyers had made a cursory flyover prior to landing, ensuring the destruction of all primary roads to deter a military counter offensive. He needed to secure that area.

As commander of Blue Battalion, he was in charge of

approximately 1,000 men and P-LAVs which included the company Dix oversaw. He knew intimately the phrase, "Keep your friends close and your enemies closer," so it was with some disappointment and heartache that he felt he had to keep an eye on his long-time friend.

Companies Alpha and Bravo were ordered to go to the easternmost edge of the highways to oust civilians and maintain order on and around the thoroughfare. Companies Charlie and Delta were tasked with securing the same on the western edge, ensuring major thoroughfares were shut down or destroyed.

Hax decided he would stay with Company Echo, Dix's company, for the entirety of the mission. He had always wanted to work closely with his friend, just now, it was a matter of caution rather than friendship. Echo was tasked with marching to the military bases to contain them and the surrounding areas.

Hax followed shortly as he heard the heavy, electrical groan of the transport ship taking off behind him. His first steps into the streets of San Diego felt alien and ugly. He knew he was an invading force; he knew he was the bad guy. He glanced up to see a wave of flying ships of various sizes and capabilities powering across the region. An hour before they had landed, the attack ships had razed all major bridges, highways, and military complexes. There had been several short-lived counterattacks by the American Air Force, but those had been easily crushed.

He took off in the direction of downtown, completely unaware it would be the last hour of his command of Blue Battalion.

CHAPTER THIRTY-ONE

Day Five: 1630 Hours

Maggie melted into Paul's arms, something she had never done before. They looked like shit and smelled worse, were beaten down and starving, but Paul didn't care. When he held his nephews in his arms, he allowed himself to cry for the first time in years. He felt a little less betrayed by the world and a bit more hopeful when they were locked in those long, tight hugs. But it wasn't long before the joy evaporated.

It took mere moments for Paul to realize he had embraced one less person in the Hunt family than he should have; what he had thought to be the once happy family of four was, in fact, three. More tears were spent on the wordless realization and soon they were promising each other that Sam was alive and that they would find the beloved brother, father, and husband.

Paul had run into Maggie and the kids by pure happenstance. He had seen them – a woman and two children – sprint from the back of a small restaurant to the other side of the street and had thought they resembled his sister-in-law and nephews. Deciding it was better to reveal his location to a stranger than to let his family slip through his hands, he had shouted through his dehydration.

"What the *hell* are you doing?" had been Lindsey's immediate response, while Donovan had just looked at him, obviously taken aback by the dangerous action.

"I think we found them... No, I fucking know it," Paul had beamed.

Paul was struck by how thin and broken Maggie looked, but felt deep pride at how resilient and grown his nephews appeared. Thank God they were alive.

The introductions between Maggie and the children and Donovan and Lindsey were brief and full of distrust, but Paul with his endless charm and charisma quickly brought them to friendly terms. They were going to be allies whether they liked it or not.

"God, I thought I would never see anyone again," Maggie cried through tears.

"Yeah," Paul sighed as he exchanged looks with Donovan and Lindsey. "Yeah, me neither." After a moment, he asked, "So, where is he? Where's my brother?"

Maggie struggled with the sudden onslaught of tears on her cheeks and the children wilted beside her, weak and vulnerable. "There was... there was a terrible attack when we were on the freeway on our way in. Everything just… seemed to explode; it was complete chaos. Our car was completely destroyed. When we all came to, he-he was... Well, we haven't found him yet. We went to your guys' mom's house, hoping he would end up there too, but..." There was a short pause in her story as she stared down at the cement beneath her feet.

"Yeah, but what?" Paul retorted, passionate intensity in his voice.

"I'm sorry, Paul. Your mom is...is dead. It was just homeless peop…"

"No way, fuck that," Paul interrupted. "We're going back. That's where Sam will meet us. That's where we'll all meet up."

"I know. That's what I thought too, but he wasn't there, and they had killed —"

"I heard you the first time," Paul snarled, his pugnacious anger boiling to the surface. He urged himself to calm before the boys. "Well, that's where I'm going and I recommend you all come with, strength in numbers and all. Mags, I don't wanna put the kids in any risk, but you know as well as I do that Sam's alive and he is going to Mom's."

"Paul, the people in the house were armed. They looked... They seemed dangerous."

"Well, I'm no fucking school boy," he argued, holding up his shirt to reveal the gun tucked into his belt. Although Maggie appeared dubious, Paul got sight of Zach who wore an expression he had never before seen, one of intense anger and fire. *Jesus, their innocence is completely gone*, Paul thought.

"I'm not involving my boys in your dangerous bullshit," pronounced Maggie.

"Yeah, fine," Paul agreed. "Let's stick together for now, then when we get close to the house, you and the kids hang back while I... while I get it sorted out."

"I'm in too," Donovan said, taking a step forward. "Let's get this family together."

"Dude, Donny, no offense, but I don't think you're up for this," Paul murmured.

"No, screw that. We said we are sticking together and getting you with your family, right? Well, that's what we're gonna do," affirmed Donovan with more confidence than he had exuded in days.

"Well, you boys aren't leaving me behind," concluded Lindsey matter-of-factly. "I'm in." Paul saw Donovan glance at her admiringly, fondly.

The group shared a moment before the new pack of six headed off the two miles to the hijacked family home.

CHAPTER THIRTY-TWO

Day One: 1730 Hours

They were half a mile from the stadium when Hax
told Delta company to switch to channel 21 for their
coms. He was only about a minute into telling his men
that he would not persecute them if they found the
mission unethical and, if they felt so inclined, opted out;
their secret would be safe with him. He essentially gave
them permission to leave. Desertion without consequence,
at least not from Hax.

Then a familiar voice burst in, interrupting him. At
first, Hax didn't register what he was hearing. It was
random words buried in the cacophony of a wartime
battlefield. But then he heard it, he heard his full name
yelled out by a voice he had known most of his life. His
heart leapt to his throat as the rest of his senses took hold
of his consciousness and he became aware of every aspect
of his surroundings.

Tense, he turned to find Dix and the rest of Echo
company, looking impressively deadly in their battle
walkers, all weapons trained directly on him. Hax could
see the deadly determination on Dix's face through the
carbon reinforced glass of his P-LAV.

"Captain, what the fuck is going on here?" Hax
snarled. "Tell your men to stand the fuck down!" The
visceral rage and fear in his voice made no difference as he

continued to stare down the barrels of nearly 200 plasma ray rifles.

The steadfast look in Dix's gaze told him there was no talking his way out of this one. It was apparent by the intense and rigid look on his friend's face that the man's mind had been made up long ago; this was no sudden change of heart. And with how awkward Dix had been towards him lately, Hax actually wasn't surprised. Hurt and betrayed, but not surprised. After several tense moments with zero change in stance from his once-trusted soldiers, Hax lost his confidence of control and met Dix's gaze, shaking his head. "What happened to you? How could you betray me like this... betray your country like this?"

"No, fuck that, Hax. It was *you* who betrayed *us*," Dix replied lowly, passionately. "I've been listening to you gripe and complain for weeks about how you think we have become the enemy because of this mission. What the fuck happened to *you*? You obviously don't give a shit about this mission, this country, or Trokker!"

"Well, there it is, huh? Trokker got to you. I knew he was bad news, but I didn't know he could flip someone like –"

"Shut the fuck up, Hax. It was *you*; it was your family, your dad, who made the military weak. It was your dad that turned us into explorers instead of warriors. I've known you forever, man, and I love you, but Trokker was right… You guys are weak. The Packards are feeble. You're destroying everything we are."

"Dix, I am your lifelong friend and commanding officer," Hax said, glancing at the others in Echo company. "Cut this shit out before something bad happens."

"You're not in charge anymore, Hax. Look around you. You're at the killing end of everyone's weapon. I was already given control of this battalion by Trokker before we even landed, all I needed was a reason. And telling your men they can commit insubordination, commit treason without punishment? That was

the last straw. He knew you were weak and he was right."
Dix regarded him through the opaque glass.

"That's it, huh? After all we've been through, after
all this time, you're going to commit treason and kill your
commanding officer? Is that how the history books will
remember Captain Dixon through this whole fucking
mess... as a goddamn backstabbing, treasonous *murderer*?"

The words must have hit Dix hard because he
didn't move, nor did he speak. After a painful minute of
silence, Dix finally said, "Just walk the fuck away before I
kill you, Hax. I wish it didn't have to come to this, but it
was inevitable... You weren't strong enough and we all
know it."

Hax took a long breath, allowing some clarity to
overcome him. "Okay..." Hax nodded, scanning the
soldiers in Dix's company. "Men, this is not what you
signed up for. You are all better than this... We are
supposed to be a force for goo –"

"Just shut the fuck up. Power down your P-LAV,
get the fuck out, and go, Hax," Dix interrupted, voice
trembling.

Hax spent another moment searching Dix's gaze,
telling him without words how disappointed he was in his
once-close friend. Eventually, he climbed from his battle
walker, as straight and proud as he could muster. Hax put
his arms in the air in the universal sign of defeat and
turned his back to the company.

He was confused, angry, and heartbroken. He
made it 20 paces before he broke off sharp behind a large,
tan building. The road where he had just been standing
exploded and cement and asphalt erupted around him. He
doubted they were trying to kill him; they would have
already done it had that been the goal. It was a warning.

But one thing was made impossibly clear; his time in the military was over. He would never be able to show his face in their presence again. He was never going back home.

Hax ran until he was sure he was several blocks from his old battalions' proximity. In utter disbelief at what had just transpired, he fell to the ground. A fellow soldier, a man he outranked, his best friend had just betrayed him. If Hax remembered correctly, it was Dante who remarked on a traitor's place in hell. In *Divine Comedy*, the ancient author had placed traitors and those who betrayed in the lowest tier of hell. And Hax couldn't agree more.

CHAPTER THIRTY-THREE

Day Five: 1330 Hours

Sam's week had been a level of hell he wouldn't wish on his worst enemy. He had witnessed more death, morbidity, and suffering within the first hour of the attack than he had seen his entire career. After witnessing the unbelievably technologically-advanced invading forces regroup at the stadium, Sam had become certain his family was dead.

Days after the initial attack, he had made it to his parents' house where he was sure he would find the rest of his family waiting. But the home had been overrun with a gang of street people who, thanks to the cautious peep he had made into the side window, appeared heavily armed. Undoubtedly, his mother was dead. He didn't see her, but she had to be. He had sworn to avenge her once he found his wife and children.

Sam sat alone in an empty set of tennis courts, head down, body slumped against a cold, rusted chain-link fence. He was within a half mile of the zoo and the family home, locations he had been certain Maggie would meet him at given the fucked-up situation they were in. But there had been no sign of them in all the regular places they had visited over the years. It had only been five days and Sam had walked well over 20 miles, searching desperately for his family; he was well past the point of exhaustion, having slept only a couple meager hours when he could no longer move. His throat and tongue ached for moisture. He had only been able to manage a couple of putrid sips of highway runoff early that morning and hadn't eaten in several days. He was a man crazed by his only mission; only death would stop him.

He wetted his chapped and cracked lips, wincing at the pain, and then stood. He wandered in subtle delusion down Texas Boulevard. He had spent almost a week's worth of energy frantically searching for his wife and children, neglecting sustenance and water, and it was beginning to show. He staggered into the street in a daze. From a nearby apartment complex, someone yelled for him to watch out before he got neutralized by the patrolling robots scouring the area. He heard the warnings, but disregarded them all the same, too deep in his half-crazed stupor to care.

It wasn't until the peaceful morning stillness was shattered by the undeniable buzz of machine gun fire followed by screams of panic that he woke from his trance. That was close by.

Sam's first instinct was to immediately surrender, to cower or plead, rendering his body all but motionless. But as the screams became louder and more hysterical, his focus sharpened. Adrenaline flooded his body and the general malaise that had been fogging his brain vanished.

The blood curdling screeches lasted less than five seconds, but it was long enough for Sam to pinpoint their approximate location – one street over and down a block. He ran to the other side of the four-lane road and found temporary refuge behind a dilapidated dumpster outside a small store. The sharp and familiar smell of putrefaction broke through the cracks in the rusting metal of the bin and he drew away in disgust.

The narrow alley which led to the next street was only ten feet away, but the mixture of carrion and garbage from the dumpster made his knees weak and again, he felt as heavy as lead. Mustering what strength he could, he forced himself to the alleyway and peered out onto the empty street – well, *relatively* empty.

Several bodies lay strewn everywhere. Gore decorated the sidewalk and street while fresh blood pooled as thick as honey around the bodies to slowly ooze off into the neighboring storm drain. The cacophony of terror was now nothing but silence. He thought he could hear the slow patter of the blood dripping into the gutter.

Movement caught his eye as he spotted the shadow of a tall robot armor rounding the corner of the next street. As the machine lumbered off from its massacre, Sam released the tight ball of air he had kept in his lungs.

When he was confident he was alone with the bodies, he crept forward. His first step echoed off the walls of the city as his foot fell perfectly on a pile of broken glass alongside the store front. His next several steps were more careful.

With some surprise, he identified a patrol cruiser that had been just out of sight from his position. The vehicle, however, was not like the fast, little cruisers he had seen in his small Arizona town. The cruiser was a large, military-grade hummer with the letters PO painted on the side in white stenciling.

About a decade ago, Mayor Slivio Batrales had signed into law a bill separating "Peace Officers" from "Statute Enforcement Officers." The law, a response to cries from the public to abolish the police altogether, had originally been made to distinguish the POs – the ones people called when they were in trouble – from the SEO's, those who wrote tickets, pulled people over, and wrote noise citations. The bill had passed with almost unanimous consent from the current three parties.

Of course, as many had warned, the boundaries between who could do what and who had jurisdiction where were blurred, and the two police departments had become enemies. Many would argue it had made the city more most dangerous than it had ever been.

Sam inched up to the bullet-riddled Humvee, property of the San Diego Peace Department. The familiar smell of blood and the crushing dread of death hit him in his gut. What was worse, he had been just a block away from the killing; he felt so powerless. Amazed and horrified by the general destruction of the vehicle, he placed a hand on its ravaged body and walked to its rear. That's when he heard a moan.

He ran around to the sidewalk side of the car where two bodies lay face down, clothing stained crimson and a thick river of red dribbling into the storm drain. Looking over the macabre scene, he saw a figure slowly crawling into the entrance of a small boutique. His initial reaction was to thank God someone had survived whatever had just happened, but after seeing the victim's uniform, he had second thoughts.

A short trail of blood up the sidewalk led to a body clad in S.D.P.O. garb attempting to retreat from the scene, his bloody limbs doing almost no work. Several glistening spots of dark red adorned the navy-blue uniform, creating a crimson trail along the hot, white cement.

Taking pity on the person, Sam ran over and gathered the body in his arms. This poor soul had been so ravaged by deadly force that Sam was unable to tell if it was a man or woman. Blood oozed from his mouth and his breathing appeared to have become more labored. From the state of his tattered uniform, the copious amount of blood, and the faint crackling sound Sam heard with each breath, he surmised the victim suffered from a sucking chest wound, no doubt accompanied by a pneumothorax. He just didn't know what would kill the man first, exsanguination or asphyxiation.

A calm, weeping sound slipped out of the severely disfigured police officer. It wasn't a cry of pain or fear, but a calm, gracious sigh. It was the sound of knowing that the pain would be over in a moment and that he would be leaving this Earth in the arms of a fellow man. Loving, embracing, and selfless. At least he was dying with someone who, even for a moment, held them like they mattered.

The moment didn't last long as the last of the blood coming from the person's marred mouth slowed to nothing. Sam felt the pulse stop. Stunned, horrified, and hope failing, he simply sat there in the small store, holding the mangled body in his arms.

He held the bloodied person in his arms until most of his body had gone numb. He had never felt more tired or beaten down. But he knew he had to find somewhere to hide if he were to gain his strength to continue his search for his family. As he rolled the body off, he heard a muted clink against the concrete. With whatever energy he could summon, he reached around the body along the victim's belt and clasped exactly what he thought it was – a gun.

Struggling to his feet was one of the biggest feats he had ever accomplished by pure will. He exited the boutique and was met by a hot, unsympathetic sun. After stumbling and blindly feeling the seemingly endless store fronts, he finally found a door to a bakery that had, by some grace of God, not been locked. He pushed on it with all his strength and collapsed inside.

Sam immediately passed out, his blood-soaked

clothes cold and his newly-acquired handgun gripped tightly in the palm of his hand.

He woke not long after, lips cracked with thirst and tongue yearning for the taste of water. He blinked several rough sandpaper-like blinks to recall where the hell he was and how he had ended up there. Groaning and wincing, he grabbed the edge of a dusty table and pulled himself to his feet.

Reality hit him hard and he nearly collapsed once more. He had been chasing after his missing wife and children for nearly a week and still he hadn't found them. Horrid scenes of their mangled bodies, like the one he had just stumbled upon, played out in his mind's eye and he withheld a tortured cry.

Shaking from the effort, he collected himself and looked about the store. There were scant crusts of assorted breads, but nothing else. He took several unsteady steps behind the counter, hoping to find something to eat. When it became painfully obvious there was nothing, he let out an audible groan.

It was then he heard a footstep behind him and he froze. He wasn't alone.

CHAPTER THIRTY-FOUR

Day Five: 1645 Hours

Paul and his newly-formed group of six haggard survivors had decided that heading back to the Hunt family house was the best course of action. They agreed unanimously that within the relative peace and quiet of a real home they could buy some time, slow things down, and plot long-term actions. Paul was adamant that should the thugs still be inside, he would single-handedly eliminate the threat.

All members of the new crew upon meeting and saying their cursory introductions, had tacitly agreed that Paul would be their new leader, at least until the house was taken back. Only then would they have a proper meeting of broken minds.

Of course, the most important objective at the moment was remaining undetected. It was bad enough being weaponless, but they were a large and cumbersome group; the bigger the group, the more noise and attraction they were sure to garner.

The going was slow and tedious, but they made it to within half a mile of the Hunt house unhindered. Paul figured, scouring his brain from his years driving the streets as a youngster, that the quickest route was up Park Boulevard. It was a risky plan since the four-lane divided road offered no concealment. To the east of Park

Boulevard was Florida Canyon, a large 150-acre park overrun with brush and native sage smack dab in the middle of the city. Paul knew the area like the back of his hand. His last summer in high school, he had been there every weekend, drinking beers, smoking weed with his friends, exploring the canyon, and getting into all sorts of teenage trouble. To the west was the enormous parking lot for the famous 100-acre San Diego Zoo.

They were tired from the short but painfully slow walk and the sun had begun to set an hour ago. Paul knew dusk was when the walking death machines came out in force, imposing strict quarantine and curfew orders. The group had to find cover – fast.

Paul led the group to John F. Kennedy Middle School, a large, white building with its name inscribed across the top alit from the brilliant full moon overhead. A conspicuous public building such as this was a big risk, but so was roving the streets or trying to break into a random home.

The latch and lock to the metal side door of the school had already been pried open and busted like most buildings they had come across had been. The door made a faint squeal as Paul pushed it ajar. The place was eerily quiet and dark. He let out a faint yet forceful "Hello?" into the echoey blackness. By the long duration of the reverberation, he assumed the room to be pretty large; maybe it was the gym or a large classroom.

He went in alone first, calling again and listening for a report. Nothing. It appeared empty. He didn't want to try their luck too hard and decided if they all slept just inside the door, it would be the best chance they had of not coming across some not-so-favorable types.

He returned to the door, peered out, and described to the group his plan. In their meager tiredness, they agreed unanimously and filed into the encompassing dark. Although traveling as a group, the six divided into their original packs on each side of the doorway, with the exception of Paul, who went to Maggie and the kids.

Upon entering, Donovan and Lindsey went to the right, held each other close in the dark against the wall, slumped to the cold tiled floor, and fell immediately asleep. The same happened with the children after they crept to the left of the doorframe. The two boys nestled into each other and quickly escaped the hellish reality to the desperately-needed release of dreamless sleep.

But not Paul and Mags. They both felt so far past the point of tired, that sleep seemed impossible. But it wasn't just sheer terror that kept them awake. The fact that they were in such close proximity to loved ones – to family – fueled their joy and kept them conscious. For an unknown amount of time, they simply sat in the dark holding each other close like long-lost best friends, Paul's arm over her shoulder, hers around his back.

"I cannot tell you how amazing it was to see you and the kids alive, Mags… I was so sure I was never going to see any of you again. It was truly one of the happiest moments of my life." Paul didn't try to hide the motion of wiping a tear from his eye from his sister-in-law.

"No matter our past, finding you was a gift from God… I mean that," she whispered. He could hear her smiling. Maggie sunk into him and they enjoyed the cherished moment.

Eventually, Paul uttered what they were both thinking. "He's alive."

Maggie's response was immediate and confident. "I know."

"You know I would gladly die getting you and the kids to him." His low voice was the only thing to penetrate the fierce quiet of the dark room.

She let out a soft laugh, catching Paul off-guard. "Sorry… sorry. Not laughing at you." She settled into him. "I know that and we love you for it."

"What the hell you laughing at then?" he hissed.

"Remember the night of Sam's bachelor party and you said you were taking him for a 'quiet night out?'"

He scoffed. "Yeah, barely."

"I knew you two would be getting wrecked; you always did when you went out together."

Paul felt the air grow tense between them, but Maggie continued.

"And when you did, the two of you always got into shit and loved to egg each other on to do the most ridiculous crap."

"Almost to the point of being dangerous," he interjected.

Another small moment of silence took over before Maggie admitted, "I was afraid of that night for a month. When I heard you guys stumbling back to the house at four that morning, I was terrified at what I would hear and see. But to see you two together, stumbling up to the house holding each other up…" She sighed. "He truly loves you."

"Remember when he fell face-first on the lawn? And as I carried him inside, he puked all over me? We laughed our asses off."

Maggie chuckled but when she spoke, her voice was low. "I have *never* hated you, Paul. I was jealous of the relationship you had with him, and it made me lash out at you. I'm sorry for that."

"No please, it was me… I wanted it to be like we were 20 again, and I was pulling him away from you."

"We are grateful you're with us. We feel so much safer. I know you're the only person on Earth Sam would want us to be with in his absence."

He gave her a strong hug that she warmly returned. Maggie was asleep moments later; he soon followed.

A small but sharp slit of early morning light hit Paul's eyelid the next morning, bringing the world back to life. He opened his eyes, fluttering the night away. His back ached fiercely; he had held his sister-in-law while she had cradled the children which had made him the buttressing pillar of their combined weight. It had been another terrible night's sleep for Paul.

Over the years of service, he had trained his body and mind to be on patrol 24-7, making it so every creak and squeak from the environment they were in (of which there were many) sent his adrenal glands pumping and brought him to full consciousness. This had happened so frequently throughout the night, he wondered if he had even got a straight 15 minutes of shut-eye once.

A loud choking snore from Donovan who was lying only five feet from Paul and the girls, woke the entire group.

"How'd we all sleep?" Paul croaked from a painful throat. The response was mainly groaning. "Yeah, me too… Well, let's get ourselves together, find water and food if possible, and try to make it to the house this morning. Sound good?" There was an unexcited chorus of uh-huhs.

"Hey Paul, we appreciate you taking the reins on this, but uh, do we have a plan B if the house is still overrun with reprobates, and we can't uhh… fight them?" Donovan asked, nodding slightly toward Lindsey who was still sitting on the floor.

"We'll figure that out when we get there, I guess, Donny," Paul replied calmly. He had always lived by a saying he had heard from a friend on the SEAL teams years ago: "Panic breeds panic, calm breeds calm." If he was calm, the others would be too.

"Okay, so I'll peek out, make sure it looks clear, then we move, the same we have been – slowly, cautiously, and quietly. If we can make it to the canyon on the other side of the street, there should be plenty of places to hide there."

Once everyone was ready, Paul pushed the door open halfway and disappeared into the fresh morning light. He returned a moment later, motioning the group out.

They had made it a few paces out the door when Paul froze. All the color drained him his face as he gestured for those following him to stop. From the corner of his eye, he saw it. How none of them hadn't heard its loud, metallic steps baffled him. *Fucking fog of war*, he cursed.

Before he could make a move, the armored robot before them announced through its large loudspeakers, "Citizens, you are disobeying lockdown orders."

Paul sensed Maggie and the children wilt behind him. Instinctively, he jumped back and shoved them back into the building, causing them to crash into Donovan and Lindsey who still stood in the open doorway.

Maggie and the children toppled inside along with Donovan and Lindsey as a brilliant, white light erupted around them.

Charred pieces of ash and bone fluttered to the ground outside the door where Paul had been standing. Everything became still, quiet. Maggie stared in horror at the now-empty doorway and the haze hanging in the air.

Although she could not see the murderous bi-pod, she heard it clomp off in another direction, unemotional, unaffected, and cruel. A moment later, machine gunfire broke the quiet of the morning. She shuddered to think of the victims.

For a long while, she and the others sat in the school in shock, slumped on the cold floor in defeat and inconsolable sadness. Just like that, Paul was gone.

CHAPTER THIRTY-FIVE

Day Five: 2230 Hours

Sam stood motionless, his heart thrumming in his ears. He was hyperaware, 100-percent focused on his surroundings. The hair on his arms and neck stood on end. He was certain there was someone else in the store with him – and close.

Shit, he thought. *Does the gun have a round chambered?* He hadn't checked.

But *he* was the one armed, *he* was the one with the ability to take matters into his own hands.

There was a soft shuffling before an unnatural-looking man rounded the corner to show himself.

"Put your fucking hands up! Don't come any closer!" Sam yelled, amazed at his own confidence.

"Friend, take it easy, I don't think we are here at cross purposes," the man replied calmly, endearingly. "We are on the same team. Please lower your gun; I think we can figure this out together."

"No, no. You shut the fuck up. You're one of them. I can tell. Look at what the fuck you're wearing, look at yourself. You look like you're from a fucking alien movie." Sam eyed the unusual smoothness of the man's head and the widened distance between his coal-black eyes. All of the man's proportions were different, foreign. He had a thin torso and hairless, muscular arms. His legs appeared too short for his long body, but were still brimmed with musculature.

The stranger wore slick underwear and a tight-fitting shirt that gleamed metallic in the light filtering through the windows. A network of micro wires spread across the strange garb. The man also had a small, computer-like band around his right forearm.

"Who the fuck are you?" Sam prompted as the man fidgeted. "And what the fuck are you doing here?" He was trying his best to sound domineering and intense, but his words were slurred from exhaustion and his demeanor unintimidating. He tried like hell to keep his newly-acquired weapon trained on the tall man in front of him, but he was fading fast.

Hundreds of simulations and countless hours of drill for this exact scenario inundated his brain, but this was the first time a *real* loaded weapon was pointed at Hax's face. Despite the adrenaline coursing through him, he could only hear one thing. It was a saying his father had once told him – Don't learn how to react, learn how to respond. And *damn* if he wasn't going to try to follow it!

In an honest effort to appear less threatening, Hax took slow, deep breaths to calm himself. He made cautious but purposeful movements to keep from flustering the disheveled man wavering before him. But his captor appeared crazed with thirst and weakness.

"Don't move," the man barked, his voice cracking. "Don't fucking move."

Hax could tell by the way the man handled the weapon that he was proficient; likewise, it was also obvious that this was quite possibly the first time he had pointed it at another human pointblank. That made Hax feel better.

The once-proud military officer obsequiously held his arms high in surrender, surveying the man. Deciding that he needed to test the man's boundaries, Hax took a small step forward. That was all he needed. The man took an anxious and stumbling step backward, the heel of his shoe brushing an empty can. By reflex, the man glanced down.

Hax was on the man before he could look back up. He went for the gun, using disarming techniques he had drilled on a thousand times in his early boot camp days. With ease, he pried the gun from the man's weak grasp and, in the same motion, threw an elbow across his captor's face, connecting squarely with his jaw and subsequently knocking the man unconscious.

Sam opened his eyes, his head throbbing. In fact, his whole body felt as if it were pulsing with the painful rhythm of his heart. His jaw ached fiercely. Groaning, he took in the world around him; his heart sank when he once again remembered the hell that was his reality. He licked his lips, somehow feeling softer flesh on his tongue than he remembered having, and no trace of dried blood.

In the several minutes it took him to regain full consciousness, he came to – *somewhat* – understand two things. Firstly, half a dozen empty water bottles were strewn about where he lay on the dusty floor; secondly, the gun he distinctly remembered pointing at an invader's face was gone. Dread swelled inside him as his focus sharpened. Once more, he found himself stuck in a building with someone he presumed to be malicious and murderous.

Sam got to his feet unsteadily, the profound feeling of dehydration now somehow distant; exhaustion still wreaked havoc on his knees and ankles though. He made it a mere two loud and lumbering steps before he heard the ominous *shleek* of a gun being racked.

Unwilling to remain trapped like what had happened at Dave & Busters, Sam staggered toward the door.

"Stop," a commanding, yet amiable voice said. "Stay right there. Don't do anything stupid or I will shoot."

Sam raised his hands and turned to face the invader. He expected to see that tall hairless thing ready to attack him, face grimaced in revenge. But there was no angry attack, nor a life-or-death confrontation.

The invader appeared from behind what looked to be a giant oven, gun secure in his hand but aimed at the ground.

"What do you want? You know I'm unarmed and don't have shit else," Sam growled.

"I do, and I also know that it's a miracle you didn't piss yourself while you were out with all the water I forced down your throat. Like I told you before, I'm not your enemy. We're on the same side here."

"But you're one of them."

"I am, and I'm not."

"Yeah, all I heard is that you fucking are, and you're the ones that killed my fucking family and destroyed the city and are fucking attacking us!" Sam yelled, his voice cracking. "I should have killed you when I had the goddamn chance."

"Listen. Yes, I came with them, but they betrayed me and tried to kill me the second we landed. I was a commander of a battalion on a mission that I came to fundamentally detest." The man took another step toward Sam, who flinched but held his ground.

"You're full of shit," Sam murmured. "And don't come any fucking closer."

"No. I wish I was."

"Well, get fucking talkin'." Strong words from the guy without the gun. Sam hoped his bravado would convince the invader of – of what? His strength? His willpower?

"Okay, this is going to sound a little crazy to you, but here you go… Where I come from, the world has depleted its store of uranium. So, the U.S. military was given the mission to scour the proximal galaxy for anything we could mine: planets, asteroids, moons, you name it. This is precisely what most Space Force Wings did. But I stupidly volunteered for a crazier faction and this Wing, led by an insane man, had a different plan."

Sam gaped at him, but remained silent.

"Now, bear with me because this is where I will probably lose you; I barely understand it myself. Where I come from, we know how to travel to different universes using extraordinarily powerful magnets and massive atomic detonations. We bring to us the desired universe using these forces." The invader continued, his voice calm and tempered as if he were lecturing Sam. "The other universe is virtually identical to ours with one exception – it's at a different point in time. The longer we hold that magnetic force, the further back in time in the identical universe we could go."

The man must have seen the incredulity and confusion on Sam's face, because he wrapped up his explanation with the following, "Well, we chose this point in your time continuum because we knew in our past this is when the massive store of uranium was found and mined."

"So, you're telling me," Sam began, "you – the United States military – went into the past to steal uranium *from* the United States?"

"Well, not our own uranium per se; yours is a universe precisely like ours, but different and older..." The man thought for a moment and then concluded, "But essentially, yes."

"So why the hell are you blowing up cities and killing Americans if you're the U.S. military?"

"Our orders were to just take-out major causeways and military bases, anything that could thwart counterattacks. Then, right before the invasion, our insane general changed our ROE's. I thought the whole thing was treasonous, horrific even. And for that, they tried to kill me." The man paused. "Since the operation commenced, I guess the others were given shoot-to-kill orders. Meanwhile I was banished and fled."

Sam could tell by the grimness on the man's face that he wasn't lying or exaggerating. He was telling the truth, or at least, telling Sam something he believed. "Okay, so now what? They want everyone, including you, dead? How do you make any difference?"

"I have this." The invader extended his arm to show the com-band screen. "I did everything I could to jam my GPS so they can't track me, but I can still pretty much see everything they are doing – troop movements, new targets, and orders."

Sam observed the man for a long moment before saying, "So, what do you want with me then? It's a fucking free-for-all out there, and your side is flying around and stomping in those walking-things and slaughtering us like goddamn ants."

"Again, I *am* on your side. But while you were passed out, you were talking in your sleep about your family you think is still alive. Is that true, you lost your family?"

Sam couldn't hide his discomfort and the sudden feeling of vulnerability the question brought forth.

The man nodded as if in understanding. "After all we have done, let me at least scrub a bit of this shit off by helping you reunite with them. I never had a family, but in this fucked up shit, I can at least help one."

With that, the man racked the gun again, expelling the round through the ejection port and threw the gun over to Sam, who clumsily caught it. He walked over to Sam and held out his hand in truce. Sam considered him for a long moment before finally taking the invader's hand.

With a smile, the man brought his other hand forward and deposited a fistful of bullets into Sam's palm. For the first time in a week, Sam wasn't alone.

CHAPTER THIRTY-SIX

Day Six: 0430 Hours

The first several hours together was absent of trust or any semblance of friendly communication. Hax thought it wise to let his new counterpart lead the way, and as a proverbial olive branch, be the leader of the two. Although he did mean what he said about wanting to help this man find his family, Hax's primary objective above all else was surviving. If that meant abandoning the man and breaking this short-term pact, he would do so.

Together, they eventually found an older, abandoned home a half mile from where they had met. While resting there, small talk became a little less forced and it wasn't long before the strangers learned a thing or two about each other. Hax discovered that, despite the several hundred years that separated them, he and Sam held many of the same interests and, for the most part and most importantly, the same values.

The conversation started with Sam convivially asking if all the women were as ugly as Hax where he came from. They shared a laugh and then tales of their younger wilder days in the pursuit of sex and adrenaline. The conversation led to other stories of what they did to keep their minds off work and politics, such as hunting, which turned out to be an enduring hobby man could enjoy no matter the forward advancement of his society. Although techniques and weaponry differed, they spent the better part of an hour describing their best hunts.

They talked about their professions and families; Hax

found it fascinating that they shared similar struggles in regards to their parents and friends. Sam eventually confided in Hax his worry for his family and how it was his sole responsibility to find and protect them. "After all," Sam said with a sad smile. "Raising a family is one of the most honorable things a man can do, right?"

Family, county, and God – this was the mantra they agreed upon which best described the hierarchy of values in a man's life. By the time they left their resting place, a new but fragile sense of trust had been fostered between them.

With some disappointment, Sam agreed that they needed to keep moving. He could have sat there for hours learning about this parallel world from which Hax hailed. He was taken aback by how similar everything sounded. Sure, there existed major technological improvements he could barely comprehend, but so much of what Hax explained sounded exactly like Sam's United States.

The two of them were painfully hungry and, above all else, thirsted for a cold beer. After several hours of conversation and getting to know one another, they began laying down a solid plan for how the hell they intended to find Sam's family. They agreed that, for the time being, staying close to the old family house was probably best. Sam had it in his head that it would be the first place his family would go to find him; Hax concurred. The problem now that his parents' house had been taken over by thugs, was whether to hold up in one place and do daily patrols to look for them or to wander the city aimlessly yelling their names. The solution they came up with was essentially to do both.

Most of the walking was still silent, partly out of an abundance of caution for their lives and partly because, although a strong foundation of trust had been built, the two were still, for all intents and purposes, complete strangers from different worlds.

"I just don't get it..." Sam started as they made their way through a back alley behind houses.

"I know, it's unbelievably complex and..."

"No, I don't understand where the hell the military is. Where *my* military is. Why hasn't there been a counterattack? Where is the Air Force? The damned Space Force that was supposed to be the most high-tech branch in the world? How are our leaders just letting this happen and leaving us to fend for ourselves? It just doesn't make any sense."

"I bet they did," Hax offered softly

"Did what?"

"I bet there were massive counteroffensives. I don't think you understand the astonishing firepower and weapon systems our ships have. You've only seen a portion of the assault group."

"What the hell does that mean? There are more of you?"

"Only about half our force comes down as an assault team; the rest, the real battleships, are still about 500 miles over our heads in low-controlled orbit. They have precision magnetic ray cannons, EMP blasts, and pretty standard hypersonic missiles. Those ships overhead, against technology of this century... Shit, it's like a kid with a magnifying glass frying bugs. Except the magnifying glass is actually a super-charged flamethrower. Not even a contest."

"So, you're saying you motherfuckers have most likely repelled all military operations against you without us even knowing?"

"No, I'm saying we most likely destroyed them all before they even scrambled, and whatever jets or missiles *were* in the air, were easily picked off by our weapons…" Hax glanced away squeamishly. Admitting it felt shameful and perfidious.

Sam stopped to glare at him. His body shook with anger and he felt on the edge of tears with frustration and loss.

"*You.* You sick motherfuckers. The fucking U.S. military doing this to its own country. I hope you all burn in hell for what you've done."

"Sam, I am on your side, trust me. I think this is as fucked up as you do."

"Yeah? But you stood idly by as an officer and let it happen, huh? Wow, some brave one you are."

"It's not that simple, it's different there… They would have killed me instantly if I had publicly denounced it."

Sam glowered but kept walking. "They should have."

He felt like a traitor just standing near this guy. But something in him told him that Hax was being forthright. "I know they ousted you for not believing in the mission or whatever. I'm sorry, I know you keep saying we are on the same team. Just… my family…"

"We'll find them, Sam. You have my word, or I will die trying…" And he truly meant that.

There was no handshake, spoken agreement, or barely a nod, but once again they united in resistance. Sam still felt much anger, but for now, Hax was on his side; he needed him.

Around noon, they headed cautiously south down Richmond Street, away from the commercial center. It was at this point that they heard a noise – the distinctly more twenty-first century sound of machine gun fire. It was so incredibly fast that at first it just sounded like the buzz of an airplane propeller. Sam exchanged looks with Hax. That was close.

Although Sam felt anxiety – as any sane person would – it was his duty to go investigate. He realized Hax must have experienced the same thing because they set off together at a jog. Any sign of human activity could mean his family was in danger.

They headed three blocks south as quickly and quietly as they could at a near-run until they reached a field with a tall chain-link fence; school zone signs adorned the perimeter.

Large letters on pale white brick read "John F. Kennedy Middle School." The shooting was coming from there – and so was the screaming.

CHAPTER THIRTY-SEVEN

Day Six: 0615 Hours

They sat in the dark room for nearly an hour with no words spoken, no solace given. Only solemn, unbelieving silence enveloped them. No one dared to look outside or to even speak or move.

Paul had been turned to smoking bits of black charcoal and pieces of him still drifted lazily near the light that filtered through the still-open door. They were hiding indoors, out of sight, but they were far from safe.

Another blast of machine gun fire erupted outside... still frighteningly close.

Maggie held Liam especially close to her bosom. He had been understandably apoplectic directly after his uncle's death; now though, he sat in a daze, his eyes glazed and face empty, staring at the doorway.

Zachary looked at his little brother, troubled by what he saw. He had seen that look before when they had slept in the same room a couple years back. On nights when their parents were out on a date and the disinterested babysitter would let them watch whatever they wanted, they ended up viewing the scariest movie they could find. Of course, Zach would feel guilty afterward seeing the distant and blank look of terror on Liam's innocent little face. Usually, his little brother would go directly to his room and just sit in his bed for hours before collapsing into fits of screams and run around the house as if awoken from a bad bout of night terrors. One time it had been so bad, Liam had ended up running into the street and making it halfway down the block until the babysitter had caught up with him. Zach saw that look now and it made him uneasy.

Zach kept his eyes trained on his little brother, praying an outburst wasn't boiling up inside him. The heavy silence in the small room was interrupted several times with more piercing runs of machine gun fire. The volume was unreal. Every time Liam's face contorted more and he clenched his eyes until it appeared his facial contortions were actually causing him physical pain. Zach was opening his mouth to warn his mom that his little brother didn't look quite right, when Liam jumped from his mom's lap, screamed, and bolted out the door.

Before anyone had the wherewithal to understand what was happening, Liam was out the door, sprinting down Park Boulevard toward the massive expanse of the canyon to the east. Their mom, without a second thought or checking if the coast was clear, took off after her youngest, desperately screaming after him.

In horror, Zach watched from the doorway as she caught up to his brother and tackled him into thick vegetation on the other side of the boulevard. Donovan gripped Zach's shoulders to keep him from also giving chase.

Out of the corner of his eye, Zach saw two people dash after his mother and brother and disappear into the brush alongside them. From somewhere nearby, an electric buzz swelled to a pitch and the heavy clang of metal footsteps on the pavement reverberated. The bipod was back, just 20 yards from the open school door. Its body faced east toward the brush where his brother and mom now hid.

CHAPTER THIRTY-EIGHT

Day Six: 0620 Hours

Creeping along the fence line, they watched one of the armored walkers head north down Park Boulevard behind a row of houses.

"Those things have fucking machine guns on them too?" Sam hissed to Hax.

"Yes. Three main weapons systems, one in each of the upper appendages. A mini gun, a plasma thermal railgun, and a 30mm grenade launcher."

"Jesus Christ."

"Yeah, that's why we avoid them at all costs."

"What were they shooting at? I thought you weren't shooting civilians?" Sam whispered. The grim expression on Hax's face said it all – they were killing indiscriminately, most likely with direct orders to do so.

The silence was broken by a distant, but familiar voice screaming, "Liam!" Sam's heart rose to his throat. That *voice*. Without a word, he bolted after the frantic yells. Hax stayed on his heels.

He made it to the Park Boulevard intersection in seconds, panting and scanning the area like a wild man. Then he saw them, his wife and son scrambling into the thick vegetation along the side of the boulevard. He had found them! By some miracle, by some blessing of God, he had found them!

But he wasn't the only one that had found them. An armored suit had also heard the hysterical calling and come to investigate. Sam darted into the trees and vegetation after his family, uncaring that a murderous bipod still stalked the area.

The world around them melted into a quiet oblivion as Sam ran to his wife and child and hugged her as hard and long as the moment would allow. Sam covered Liam's mouth as the boy tried to scream, "Dad!" He pulled his son into his body and Maggie into his arms as he cried.

The reunion was interrupted as Hax shoved the group to the ground. Liam gasped as he was thrown hard into the dirt. Overcome with emotion, Sam complied with his new comrade and lay atop Maggie.

Hax shushed them as an electrical buzz filled the air and heavy, metal footsteps clanged on the pavement of the boulevard. They were hidden by thick brush and several low-hanging tree limbs, but what they had was concealment, not cover. If the machine decided to open fire – which it undoubtedly would do – they would perish instantaneously.

The four of them lay on the ground, hugging the dirt as low as they could, dust and sand puffing around them with every breath they took. Sam glanced at his son who was closest to the dirt and saw him struggling to breathe. A moment later, his small child coughed. The first cough was thankfully muted, but the next two were full and loud.

The world came down around them. A deafening buzzing like helicopter blades filled the air and the trees around them were sliced off their trunks. Sam shielded Maggie and Liam as heavy limbs came down around them and the earth trembled. The barrage lasted ten seconds but had managed to destroy everything around them, burying them in vegetation, tree limbs, and searing leaves.

The armored suit must have believed it had neutralized whatever it was shooting at, because just after it stopped shooting, it began clomping back down the boulevard. Sam, his family, and Hax remained motionless on the ground, making no noise for several minutes.

When he could no longer hear the plodding of the machine, Sam breathed, "Please tell me Zachary's okay."

"Yes," Maggie wheezed. "He is back in that school along with some others we have been hiding out with…" She gestured to Hax. "Who's this?"

"I'll tell you when we get in there."

Although it was apparent she didn't trust Hax who was studying his com-band and typing on it, Sam didn't care. His priority was now to get them back to the school.

Sam clambered up the steep embankment first and peered over it. The coast was clear for now and that was enough for him. He signaled for them to follow. Taking his wife and child's hand, he ran across the boulevard with Hax a pace behind them. They had made it to the sidewalk, when the armored suit returned.

It must have been waiting, because the machine was sprinting after them at an awkward and unwieldy run.

"Go, go, go!" Sam urged, pushing his wife. He lifted little Liam from the ground, running hard for the open school door. Behind them he saw the machine's appendages directed at them in preparation to fire. Only feet from the school, the world exploded around them, violently hurling the group through the doorway.

Lying wheezing in a darkened room, Sam felt hands on him. Zachary, his oldest, and a man and young woman joined the surviving group, dragging them upright. The air was thick with a rich gray-brown haze. The man, seeing that everyone was alive, hurried to the door and slammed it closed, shrouding the group in total darkness.

Zachary buried himself into his dad's arms, knocking him back to the ground. The much-needed and appreciated reunion of the family that had been separated for an entire week was without a doubt the happiest moment in their entire lives.

Sam sat in the darkness, crying as he held his family. Eventually, he managed to stammer, "How did you guys... Where did you guys go? How did you make it?"

"Jesus, I should ask you the same thing," panted Maggie. "After the explosion on the freeway, we woke up and you were just gone. We tried looking for you, but the things were still flying over the road and we had to find somewhere to hide..." She clutched at him desperately. "When we couldn't find you, we just assumed you would go to your mom's house and... well..." Her sentence faded and her voice trembled. "You... need to know..."

"I know. I went there too. I saw..."

She breathed into his neck, crying. "Sam, I'm so sorry."

"Yeah well, thank God you and the kids made it through this shitty mess. I wonder where the hell Paul is during this. I bet he tried to go to mom's –"

"We were with Paul for a day. He had been traveling with Donovan and Lindsey here... Sam, this morning he was killed by one of them."

Sam did not respond initially; he had become numb to everything macabre. "How, how do you... Do you know for sure?"

"It happened right in front of us... In front of the kids... It was *awful*. I'm so sorry." Maggie hugged him tightly. Although he embraced her in return, his mind was distant with his family's losses. When she kissed his dirty face, he turned and pressed his lips to her forehead, tasting the salt and dirt that had accumulated there.

Suddenly beyond thankful, he grabbed both his kids and yanked them onto his lap. They still needed to figure out where the hell they were and how they were going to escape, but for now, he was content.

CHAPTER THIRTY-NINE

Day Six: 0800 Hours

The group remained in the large room in total darkness, talking only in whispers. They had to figure out where they were, how they were going to escape, and to where they could go. The general consensus was that none of them wanted to split up, but after a short conversation, they decided that they would break off only for a couple minutes in single-person scouting parties to get the layout of the room they were in. Sam would go 20 paces down the left wall, come back, and report. Donovan would do the same down the right. Lindsey would venture just halfway into the center of the room while Maggie stayed with the kids. Hax was to stay by the door and give warning if a killing machine was approaching. They wanted to keep the initial scouting parties close by, in case someone found something or needed a quick response. A moment later, they were off in the dusty dark, creeping along their respective paths.

The two parties missioned with going along the walls were back in a short minute with nothing but empty walls to report. Lindsey was the last to return.

Arms outstretched and groping, Lindsey picked her way through the ruthless black, her heart racing. She took ten paces until she hit something hard with her pelvic bone. She resisted the urge to curse. It was a table. Scooting around it, she counted four plastic chairs. After only another pace and a half, she found another table, this too with chairs around its perimeter. *Cafeteria*, she thought.

She had spent many long hours in cafeterias when she was in school, consequence of a dictator principle who put the kids in detention for the slightest infraction of policy. She had gotten in plenty of trouble while in high school, living in a lower-class neighborhood, only having one parent who was never around to keep her in line. She had spent most of her detention cleaning her school's kitchen. During her time there, she had learned the ins and outs of commercial kitchens, including the fact that, per fire code, all kitchens were to have a means of egress to the outside. *Cafeteria means kitchen, kitchen means exit.*

She returned to the group, clumsily colliding with a few more tables, and reported what she had found. She was positive that if they looked around, they could find the door to the kitchen and a way out. Everyone agreed, but decided that splitting up to "divide and conquer" was just not prudent.

Leading the way, Donovan groped along the wall. He could hear the others behind him doing the same. Why was this cafeteria so dark?

They had made it about a hundred feet and one left turn before Donovan found the threshold for a door. Steeped in anticipation, they lingered by the door, straining to hear beyond it. Although Liam, the youngest, claimed he could hear whispering on the other side, the adults could hear nothing and so overruled him.

Donovan pushed on the door which resisted and made a terribly loud screech. A cacophony of panicked screams erupted from beyond the doorway and a blinding light about 20 feet in front of him blossomed as several high school-age kids escaped through a door leading outside.

"No! No! Don't go out there!" Donovan pleaded, shielding his eyes. "We aren't here to hurt you! Please, stop!" He had expected for the kids to calm and return to the safety of the kitchen; instead, several more who had been hiding behind stoves leapt up and scrambled for the now open external door. "No, wait!"

His cries were drowned out by shrieks of horror as he witnessed in perfect clarity the kids be obliterated, turned to charred dust by a nearby armored suit.

Donovan froze mid-step, his eyes wide and heart thrumming. A sense of dread and horror unlike anything he had before felt filled him.

"Back, get b-b-back," he stuttered, stumbling backward. A barrage of bullets burst through the back door to pepper the interior of the kitchen. A conflagration immediately erupted as several gas pipes feeding the ovens were struck in the hailstorm of depleted uranium shells.

The subsequent blast tossed Donovan and the others in his group into the cafeteria. In the seconds it took for them to find their feet again, thick, billowing smoke had begun to pour through the kitchen door and an eerie light stained the walls.

With years of firefighting experience under his belt, Sam could tell from the quality and quantity of smoke that this thing was already big and burning hot. He calculated that with the fire doubling in size every minute and with a fuel load as large as what the kitchen had, they would be pushed to crawling under the smoke in a matter of minutes.

Sam led the group through the hazy cafeteria back the way they had come. At least now there was enough light to see roughly where they were going. But that didn't last long as the smoke thickened and blotted it out.

The intense barrage of bullets and the resulting explosion had apparently aroused all the squatters in the building as the whole place came alive. People appeared from all over, running in and out of doors at every end of the huge dining hall.

Donovan tried to warn the sporadic groups of panicked, fleeing people, but he knew it was in vain. To the north at the far end of the dining hall was another exit guarded by a heavy metal door. Brilliant sunlight washed over the cafeteria as a couple tried their luck fleeing this smokey hell by forcing open the door and running outside. They couldn't see what happened, but that horrible, electric hum they had come to dread filled their ears.

A massive bombardment of firepower blew through that door, opening a ten-foot section in the wall. The hazy room was illuminated in glorious morning light. Thick, black smoke inched across the ceiling, dropping lower across the cafeteria as the fire grew in intensity and size.

"They're fucking killing us all!" Lindsey screamed, hunkering down by a table.

It appeared to be true. Anyone and everyone who had exited the building was promptly and brutally being killed.

"And we're gonna be burned alive in here," she concluded with a sob.

"No, we are *not!*" replied Sam. "Come on, let's

keep moving." Years of training in dangerous conditions had taught him to keep a cool head in times of high stress or distress. His group needed him more than ever now.

Through the hole in the cafeteria wall, they saw a machine turn to the left and take a few steps out of view. A moment later, another bout of electric radiance swelled followed by a barrage of gunfire. A thousand little beams of light, stretching the entire length of the cafeteria, appeared as the armored suit destroyed the lunchroom.

"They're all fucking here," Hax remarked lowly.

Squatting beside Hax, Sam turned on him. "*You* called them here, you sonofabitch, didn't you?"

This made everyone stop, their eyes on Hax.

"No, you have my word… but they may know I am here."

Sam glared murderously at the man. "What the *fuck* are you talking about?" A nearby wall blew into chunks as another spray of bullets rattled through the dining hall.

"Please, trust me, please. I'm not trying to hurt any of you…" Hax begged.

A tense moment hung around them.

Sam felt his cool slipping; luckily, Maggie stepped in. "You said you trusted him, now come on!" she barked.

Sam held Hax's gaze for a long moment. There was truth in the man's eyes and yet again, he decided to follow his gut. The man wasn't his enemy, at least not right now.

They made their way to the opposite side of the cafeteria and found the opening of a massive hallway which extended 25 yards before disappearing into blackness. They took off at a jog, but the light quickly faded to nothing and their pace was slowed to a walk.

Behind them, yelling continued but everything around them fell still. Smoke had entered the hallway and sat menacingly just above their heads; the air was getting hotter.

Another volley of bullets echoed down the hallway from somewhere far behind them. Either there were several of those things stalking around the school or one had gone on a pathological killing spree, traveling from one side to the other to take out terrified people fleeing for their lives. Either way, if they stayed put, they would undoubtedly soon be dead.

They blindly walked down the hall for what felt like a thousand yards. Sam, being the tallest in the group, started coughing deep, uncontrolled barks as the smoke swirled around his head. Soon they began hunching over just to breath.

They followed the left side of the wall, continuing around a left turn further into the unknown. The smoke crept lower, thicker. Bodies bent in half to remain below the smoke line, they ran. Maggie led the way, followed by Sam and the kids, then Hax. Donovan and Lindsey brought up the rear.

Maggie cursed suddenly when she struck something cold and solid before them. It was a door. Sam fell in beside her, investigating it with frantic hands. The hallway was growing unbearably hot. Maggie gave the door a hard push, but it didn't budge. It was locked.

"Fire doors," Sam responded immediately in the drab monotone of a despondent soul. "They're fire doors. They close and lock automatically to keep fire from spreading. There's no way it's opening."

"Are you sure? How do you know?" Hax pleaded.

'Shit!" Maggie yelled as she found the hands of her two boys and headed back the way they came, bent low. Sam followed. Maybe she was being pulled by her maternal instinct, maybe it was her own will to live, but *she* was leading them.

"Where are we going?" Donovan yelled.

"Anywhere but here!" she screamed.

"We know what the fuck is down there!" Hax interjected.

More gunfire echoed down the hallway.

"Anyone have a better idea?" she yelled, pressing on.

"She's right, come on. We gotta keep moving," Sam called over his shoulder at the others.

Not long after they turned back, they were forced to their knees to scoot along the floor under the toxic air which hung overhead. When that wasn't enough, they were pushed to their bellies to slither along the tiles as the heat swelled around them. Their pace slowed to nothing.

Painful, torturously slow minutes passed as they struggled to find a way out. Then, Maggie felt something on her shoulder, or rather, she felt nothing. A void. The wall she had kept her left shoulder against was gone. She reached out and felt warm metal. It was a door to the outside.

Panting, she rose to her knees and began to search for the handle. She couldn't believe the heat just a few feet above the ground and felt her ears already beginning to burn. She fumbled with the handle, gave it a turn, and then hit the door hard with her shoulder. Nothing. She reared back again and smashed all her weight again into the door; still, it didn't budge.

Her face and neck burned. She became catatonic, the all-consuming sensation of death creeping up to greet her. Her lungs pulsed painfully, begging for oxygen. The thought of her two boys lying dead on the tiled school floor crossed her mind and strength flooded her. With everything she was, she threw herself at the door.

She toppled out hard onto a cement pad four inches

below the threshold, Sam falling on top of her. He reached in, pulled his kids out, and yelled for the rest of the group. They all appeared, crumpling out of the door, coughing, and crawled several feet off the cement landing to the cool dew-covered grass just beyond. All but Hax.

"Where's Hax?" Sam asked, squinting back into the hazy hell.

"Just leave him. This is his damn fault!" Donovan said through coughs.

"Fuck!" Sam drew a deep breath and went back into the black smoke, Maggie crying out after him. The five of them sat panting on the grass, staring at the doorway to hell.

A few seconds later, Sam emerged from the blackness, clothes smoking and skin red, dragging an unconscious Hax behind him. He pulled him out and collapsed on the pavement. Panting at the gloriously rich air, Sam glanced over to see Hax's hand gripping his arm just below his wrist computer; there, through the soot on the screen, a flashing red message read **TRANSMISSION SENT**.

The sunlight was again blinding and the fresh sea air was tainted with the smell of smoke and burning plastics. They had made it out of the inferno alive. Hax, after several seconds, drew a breath and coughed himself to consciousness. Sam looked up at the school. Fifty yards in front of him, the entire roof of what he assumed was the cafeteria was ablaze; heavy, black smoke hung everywhere and flames licked 30 feet into the sky.

Somehow, they had just survived another close run

in with death. Sam crawled to his family and gave them a squeeze. Donovan and Lindsey joined them, taking a moment on the cool, wet grass to just breathe.

A moment later, Sam sat up to study Hax. "How are you doing?" he rasped.

Hax coughed and said one word: "Run."

CHAPTER FORTY

Day Six: 0930 Hours

The grass surrounding the cement landing which they had gathered on was in the middle of a courtyard between four smaller buildings, all part of the John F. Kennedy Middle School campus. There they had temporary protection from the armored suit rampaging on the outskirts of the campus which would undeniably soon fold. The sun, bright and piercing, was eclipsed by the billowing black smoke spilling from the building behind them. They could feel the heat; the inferno was deafening.

"Run, now!" Hax rasped again, barking a deep and painful cough.

"What the hell you talking about?" Sam urged.

"I turned on my com-band. I-I sent a message," Hax explained shakily. "They know where I am and they are going to come down on me with everything they got."

"Holy shit," Donovan breathed. "Why would you do that? What the fuck are you doing?"

"It's the only way you guys can get away. They'll kill us all unless they're focused on something else." Hax looked about the group. "I'll do what I can here to hold them off."

A muted electric hum swelled and two battlecruisers along the horizon came into view.

Hax gestured to them. "Go *now*! Run!"

They turned to run for the other side of the courtyard away from the fire. Only Sam hesitated as he held Hax's gaze.

"If he comes, he'll set this straight. I know he will," said Hax grimly. "He is a good guy... the best."

"Huh? Who?"

"Go, *now!*"

Hax settled back, resting his aching body against the adobe siding to stare into the sky. He was amazed by how he felt in that particular moment. He assumed, as anyone would, that sitting there facing certain death he would be terrified, anxious. But Hax was overcome with a deep stillness, a sense of belonging and duty. He couldn't help but beam with pride of service.

The heavy clomping of the bipedal suits reverberated through the courtyard. Sam gave Hax a slight nod and then sprinted after the others. The south end of the school's campus behind four full sets of tennis courts was fenced off with industrial-height fencing that soared ten feet overhead for the simple reason that the middle school was directly adjacent to the San Diego Zoo. On the other side of the fence was a steep drop that would land them on the walking path of the Elephant Odyssey, the northernmost part of the facility.

Upon reaching the towering fence, the group hesitated for a moment, knowing that a fall from that height could end in broken ankles and feet, but it was their only choice. Scaling the fence in a frantic jumble, the adults helping the two youngsters with their footing, the group escaped the school campus and the brackish air.

Although Donovan twisted his ankle coming down the other side, they proceeded to the white trunk of a massive Ficus tree where they bent over panting under the magnificently dense canopy. Upon hearing the electric approach of a ship, they hugged the trunk. Overhead, a behemoth of a battlecruiser with the number 506 stenciled in white letters on its tail hummed by.

***

Hax remained on the cement landing as he watched the cruiser drift toward him. The message he had sent to his father was short and he prayed to God that it had worked. Hax knew that the moment Trokker got the ping from Hax's com-band, the major general would send everything he had to destroy him. There would be no arrests, for that Hax was certain.

Hax closed his eyes, taking in as much of the crisp, salty air of the coast as he could. It had never tasted so sweet. He let the sun warm his face and body. He thought back to the girl he had been with before departing on this mission from hell.

Deep in his thoughts, Hax saw himself with a life outside the military, maybe married to a woman like her. He pictured several small kids with her eyes and his chin running around the yard, calling to him, full of wonder at how the world worked. He saw himself as a dad like his father: loving but strict, playful yet disciplined. He pictured his kids' first steps, first days of school, bringing home their first girlfriend, and maybe becoming an officer in the military just like their dad and grandpa had been. He saw himself grow old with his hypothetical wife and grandkids out on a beautiful ranch somewhere where the buzz of civilization didn't exist. He pictured himself dying a happy man with his wife and kids by his side.

Eventually, the electric buzz became too loud to

ignore and he opened his eyes, causing the fictitious life to fracture into reality. Five hundred feet overhead a battlecruiser hovered, Trokker undoubtedly at the helm. Hax scanned the courtyard as a dozen armored suits crashed through the middle school to surround him, ray cannons at the ready. He shifted his steady gaze to the azure sky beyond the battlecruiser, hoping in vain to see rescue, a savior. But there was nothing. He was alone.

"Major Packard. You are under arrest for treason against the United States of America," broadcasted a loudspeaker. Hax wasn't sure which of the machines was speaking as the voice echoed horribly through the courtyard, but he was quite familiar with its owner – Dix. "Put your hands in the air."

Hax did nothing for several moments, choosing instead to close his eyes, draw a deep breath, and let the sun touch his skin.

"Major, put your hands in the air, or you will be fired upon."

Hax opened his eyes with a grim sigh and trained his sight on the walker up front whose cockpit was now visible. He could barely make out Dix's face through the plasma shield glass, but he recognized him well. It was destiny – his once-best friend would be there, for better or worse. The weird thing was, Hax didn't blame him; in fact, there were no hard feelings. Although he had been betrayed by him, he still loved the man; Dix was just lost.

"So long, Dix," Hax said, his voice unwavering. The suited armor before him was the only one out of the dozen to lower its weapon.

Hax glanced up at the battlecruiser overhead, certain that Trokker was watching, and then looked at the P-LAVs around him. Slowly, he began to raise his arms in the universal sign of surrender, his heart thrumming in his ears. Only when his arms were fully outstretched did he extend both middle fingers in a final "Fuck you." With a smile, he shifted his gaze once more to the beautiful, blue sky overhead.

CHAPTER FORTY-ONE

Day Six: 0940 Hours

From where they were hiding under the dense tree cover, they couldn't see Hax, but the deafening noise and instantaneous flash of light that came from the courtyard from which they had just escaped meant they didn't have to. An assault akin to a blanket bombing campaign obliterated the school. Sam shielded Maggie as his wife embraced the children and covered their eyes and ears.

There wasn't time for a solemn remembrance or even a word of gratitude for Hax's sacrifice. They had just disturbed a beehive and the area was swarming. Following a main footpath into the zoo, Sam led them to a large, block building with "Elephant Care Center" written over an open garage door. The area was for caring for and cleaning the elephants and appeared remarkably like a scene out of the twentieth-century classic *Jurassic Park*.

The building smelled terrible; they gagged at the mix of rotting animals and a week's worth of elephant shit. But the place looked secure and relatively hidden. As they filed in, Sam looked up, noticing that the ships were dispersing overhead. They all had truly just come for Hax. Whatever he had done on his wrist-thing had worked.

The group was too exhausted to even talk about what to do next, but there was no choice. They had been wandering around the city, surviving by the seat of their pants, and they were all tired of it. They needed a plan to escape this warzone, and they needed it *now*.

Sam spent the first several minutes trying to explain what Hax had told him earlier about how and why the invading United States military was there. No one understood and Sam, trying his best to explain what he had been told, remained pretty confused as well. But what was certain was that Hax had been telling the truth and had sacrificed himself so that they could live.

Donovan and Sam argued about whether to leave. Sam wanted to put this place as far behind him as possible, while Donny preferred to stay put, survive, and wait everything out. He argued that if they were just there for the uranium, they would leave when it was all loaded up. Lindsey took Donovan's side, saying they could wait it out right where they were.

Sam, amazed that he had to remind them of what had just happened an hour before in the school, contended that they had to escape. The invading army would eventually find and kill them, especially if they discovered that they had anything to do with Major Packard.

And so, a rift formed; Donovan and Lindsey chose to hunker down while Sam and his family decided to do what they could to get out of the city. It looked as if there would be no common ground. Just as all accepted their fates – they would be splitting up for good – they heard blasts of a magnitude similar to what they had heard one week prior.

BOOM BOOM BOOM

They all groaned and Lindsey began to sob. There was going to be a round two, a second wave.

Sam and Donovan hurried to the open facility door and peered out. Sam's heart sank and bile rose in the back of his throat. Their worst nightmares were coming true.

In the sky, just barely visible through a hearty deck of clouds, was another flight of ships, identical to the ones that had overrun San Diego – and they were descending.

Sam and Donovan exchanged hopeless looks. Had the ships come to finish the job? Perhaps they were just going to flatten the city for the thrill of it. Sam puzzled through it all. The ships that had been tormenting San Diego for a week were technologically-advanced; they could easily obliterate everything in minutes if they so desired. So why the second wave of troops? Was this a permanent invasion? Were they there to take over the rest of the country? Horrible thoughts flooded Sam's mind.

He shuffled back to his wife and kids.

"What? What is it?" Maggie pleaded, searching his face.

Sam sat down right there on the filthy floor. For the first time in his life, he gave up. He was beaten; *they* were beaten. These invaders were unavoidable. Every person in the city was going to be destroyed.

Maggie joined him and he buried his face in his wife's stomach and cried. He sobbed into her shirt, apologizing for not being able to protect them and keep them safe.

Maggie stroked her husband's dirty hair, too weary to cry. She had cried herself out of tears over the past week. After a moment, she released Sam's grip around her, stood, and approached the garage opening.

She opened her mouth to warn the others who were sulking just inside the facility but was silenced as a series of loud, electric whistles began to swell in decibel. A moment later, a massive explosion shook the building, causing dust to thicken the air.

Maggie staggered back to the others as several more whistles rose into a whine before cracking into explosions that made the earth at their feet tremble. Alarms and sirens began to wail somewhere in the great distance.

Together, the group peered out at the chaos overhead. A battlecruiser, one of the ones that had been tormenting the area for days, now hovered precariously in the air as smoke and fire poured from several openings along its port. Another explosion belched forth from the newcomers and the damaged battlecruiser was blown in half. It crashed violently half a mile away, causing the ground to quake.

Over the next minute, dozens more electric whistles followed by explosions filled the air as ship after ship was blown from the sky and careened out of control to the ground.

Sam ran from the cover to the ten-foot fence they had scaled. He got there in time to see one of the armored suits fleeing from the school down Richmond Street. A strange, yellow-green light shone down on it, rendering it motionless before white, phosphorus sparkles erupted from it. The walker was reduced to a burning pile of smoldering metal.

Sam couldn't help the manic smile that spread across his face. To see their formidable enemies utterly destroyed brought him immense satisfaction. As he watched the new ships lay waste to their own, a thought occurred to Sam, something Hax had said: *If he comes, he will set this straight.*

CHAPTER FORTY-TWO

Day Six: 0940

General Packard sat at the command of the Neptune-Class airship destroyer *Fitzgerald*. He was there with four ships of the same class and size, alongside dozens of transport vessels, smaller frigate-class battleships, and various other landing craft. He had been ordered by the Commander-in-Chief to take the entire Eastern Battle Wing to come to the aid of the United States, an operation that had been initiated by a message he had received just days after Trokker's Battle Wing's departure. No one was quite sure the exact nature and intention of Trokker's mission, but absolutely no one could have ever guessed it was this.

The transmission General Packard had received from his son had been short, but it had contained all the information they needed to ready a force to counter Trokker's rogue outfit. It had read:

ATTN. LT. GEN. PACKARD

I AM SENDING THIS MESSAGE OUT OF PURE NECESSITY AND AS AN S.O.S. YOU WERE RIGHT ABOUT GEN. T. HE ISN'T GOING AS A PEACEFUL CONVOY LOOKING FOR RESOURCES. HIS PLAN IS A FULL INVASION OF SOUTHERN CALIFORNIA.

SO FAR, THE ROE ARE NON-COMBATIVE, BUT I DON'T BELIEVE THIS TO BE TRUE. THE GEN. IS GOING TO WIPE OUT EVERYTHING

IN THE CITY OF SAN DIEGO TO ENSURE THE PAYLOAD.

THE EXACT TIME IN DEEP SLEEP AND COORDINATES ARE
ATTACHED.
I CAN'T HANDLE THIS MYSELF.
DAD, WE NEED YOUR HELP.

He had read the message ten times before bringing it up
the chain of command. He had fought, had put his career on the
line to assure them that his son was to be taken seriously and that
this threat was real.

To launch a counteroffensive of this magnitude was
dangerous and expensive, but he had convinced the higher ups
that, as soldiers of the United States, it was their duty to protect it
from threats both foreign *and* domestic.

The lieutenant general glanced at the two pictures on his
desk that he brought along on every mission. The one of his
beloved wife and the picture of his son and himself at Hax's OCS
graduation.

"General, the ping from Major Packard's com-band
stopped," reported an officer. "The last place it pinged is right in
the middle of that blackened, burning area. I think –"

"Thank you, Captain. I am aware of that..."

It was quiet on the deck as a dozen pairs of eyes looked at
the major general, all knowing the sacrifice his son had made by
pinging his location to the incoming convoy.

The lieutenant general picked up the picture of his son, a
small smile curling the edge of his mouth. He had never been
prouder of Hax, had never been more honored to be his father.
He returned the photo to the console at his post, stood, and
saluted the burning ground where his son had made his final
stand. The rest of the bridge rose as one and saluted in silence to
pay their honors.

Danyel Packard let the tears fall down his cheeks,

unashamed. He was the father of a hero, the father of a man who would forever be remembered as the hero of the Invasion of San Diego.

EPILOGUE

"Maybe you have to know the darkness before you can appreciate the light."

Madeleine L'Engle

THE HUNTS

Sam, Maggie, and the kids – deciding they had had enough death and destruction – left the city in an old, beat-up car they found outside the destruction zone. Heading northeast out of the city, Sam was surprised by how vacant the streets were. He didn't know if it was because the people that would have left were dead or because people were still too petrified to make any big moves.

The family bid farewell to the new friends they had found in Donovan and Lindsey, but didn't promise to keep in touch or visit. This was a part of their lives that they wanted to put behind them.

Travel time through San Diego County was tripled as the family had to take back roads. The interstates and highways were blown to hell and the main thoroughfares were still populated with people searching for loved ones among the rubble. The sheer number of broken and downtrodden faces they passed was staggering.

The long drive home was mostly silent and despondent. Sam's hand didn't leave his wife's knee or hand one time, and his rear-view mirror never left his children. He wasn't going to let them out of his view again.

Zachary and had grown up a decade over that one week, and the usual giddy chortles of playful brothers had silenced to distant, quiet stares. Their innocence was gone.

Pulling into their driveway a day and a half later, the Hunts were met by concerned friends and neighbors who asked countless questions in hushed tones. Sam and Maggie responded vaguely. "We don't know" or "We weren't involved" were their best answers. It was too fresh and painful to talk about. Maybe someday they would reveal how they had survived the attack, but for now, it was easiest to simply say, "We weren't there." They needed peace and quiet. They needed each other.

Each had been affected in their own peculiar way, so all began intensive counseling.

Liam miraculously came out of the whole incident the least affected. Perhaps it was because of his age or the fact that he was a resilient boy, but somehow he remained happy and playful, despite the years of living that had been thrust onto him. He was calmer and seemed to have more appreciation for the things in his life, like his family – especially his family. His night terrors came more frequently, but between the counselling and his loving and supportive big brother, he got through them.

Zachary, on the other hand, was heavily traumatized by the events. What gave him the most significant post-traumatic actress was not the amount of destruction and mayhem he had witnessed, but the heroic act of saving his mom by caving in a man's skull. It felt like every time he closed his eyes, he pictured the blood-soaked rock, the misshapen head with blood and brain matter showing, the look on his mother's terrified face.

He was able to find peace and take his PTSD head-on by writing. He started with small, several-sentence journal entries recalling what had happened. These grew into paragraphs, eventually filling entire notebooks about his experience and how he and his family had survived. It was a better catharsis than any counselor or psychologist could provide, and it helped bring Zachary back from a very dark and scary place.

Sam and Maggie remained deeply scarred by

everything that had happened that week. Sam knew that if it wasn't for the love and support of his wife, he would have crawled back into a bottle, curled up, and died in it. And Maggie, so thankful that she hadn't lost her husband, spent every second she could loving and cherishing him.

Sam went back to work a month later with a new drive and purpose. He treated every call he went on like it was the most important thing he had ever done. He had known what death and loss felt like en masse; he never wanted a fellow American to experience anything like it ever again. He vowed that from then on, if someone was dying in his arms, he would comfort them and cherish them like they were family, like he had that officer who had died in that little Californian store, body riddled with bullets.

Maggie, after taking six months to nurture herself and her children back to as close to normal mental health as they could muster, decided to finish school and become a family counselor. Overwhelmed by a deep sense of service, she endeavored to help families and children struggling with their own mental traumas. She hoped from the hell they survived and witnessed that, God willing, maybe she could do some good and make a difference.

The Hunts grew closer, their survival cementing their familial bonds like never before. Sam and Maggie found a new sense of love, trust, and belonging within each other's arms. The kids feared – understandably – being more than five feet from each other or their parents for quite a long time. Something about believing you've lost everything you've ever loved really makes you appreciate it, hold it close, and never want to let it go.

The Hunt family held their own ceremonies for Paul and Grandmother Hunt. Sam kept in his closet several of Paul's possessions, some he had had since childhood – a small memorial to the brother he loved so much. He hung Paul's most prized possession, an autographed Pat Tillman jersey in a case next to his bed, a small reminder of sacrifice, duty, and family.

Zachary and Liam would always remember their uncle as a selfless hero who had died protecting them. As many with the gift do, Zachary, through his writing, helped Liam deal with the trauma. Aside from his journals, he wrote letters and blurbs to himself and to little Liam with the hope that his younger brother would one day draw strength from them.

Little Brother,

Living through hell can do two things to you it can wreck you or make you.

I know you. I know your constitution; I know how brave and tough you can be. Let the nightmare that we lived through supply you with fuel to take on this world. Let hardship and loss define you and resolve you. Face the future with courage and forthrightness. Appreciate every moment with the people you love. You never know when it could end.

It's okay to put trust in strangers, even when they look different than you. People you meet under uncertain times can become the people you rely on. Don t take them for granted. It is worth everything you have in the world to keep your family together. Fight for it and cherish it.

Never stop fighting.

Sometimes you will feel overwhelmed and won't want to go on. Don't give in. There is so much good and beauty in this world worth fighting for.

This country has its nefarious actors and does things that can challenge trust and sensibilities, but have faith in it. There will always be good Americans willing to risk life and limb and face serious challenges to set the country straight.

Be Brave. Be Honest. Love deeply. Do What's Right.

You have within you the ability to set the world straight. Do it.

Zachary

DONOVAN AND LINDSEY

Donovan and Lindsey stayed in the warzone with the intention to help clean up and rebuild. Saying goodbye to the Hunt family was difficult, despite the fact that they had been with them for such a short amount of time. Somehow, that family had survived it all. Donovan and Lindsey whole-heartedly agreed that they shouldn't be forced to remain in the hellhole of San Diego even one second longer than they had to.

After a couple days at Ground Zero, Donovan became overwhelmed with the amount of death and devastation he continued to encounter and left soon after without a word to Lindsey. After making it back home, the first thing he did was leave his position with IEC. He took what money he had (which was plenty) and moved as far away as he could which, it turned out, was Cambridge. There he spent the rest of his life as a professor at MIT studying new propulsion systems for outer-space travel, staying as far away from uranium mining and weapons research as possible.

It took a long time for Donovan to reach back out to Lindsey. When he finally did, they talked on the phone for hours and promised to do so every week. It was their own kind of catharsis. They remained close friends.

Lindsey wasn't as fortunate as the others after the attack. She also became overcome by the clean-up effort and ended up moving back to Chicago a month in. She had bouts of devastating depression, suicidal thoughts, and a run with drug and alcohol use.

She eventually found herself at the high end of the Chicago Skyway Bridge ready to end it altogether, ready to erase the images that had been clouding her thoughts since the disaster.

By happenstance, Officer Kurt Shirly had just ended his shift shortly after midnight that night and had been crossing the bridge heading home. He had only been on the job a year when he spotted a woman standing on the railing with obvious intentions.

Officer Shirly spent the better part of an hour talking her off the side of that bridge, convincing her to live, convincing her of her worth in God's eyes. In his eyes.

It was at that time that Lindsey finally confided in someone. When she came down, tears flowing down her face, she fell helplessly into the officer's arms, a broken woman. It was the first time she had felt safe in a long time.

Days later, she looked up the officer who had saved her life and contacted him. At first, the invite was just coffee to thank him for saving her life, but by the third date it had sprouted into something much more than that. Two years later, the two were married with a baby on the way. Lindsey had never been happier.

The deadly attack or "The Incident," as the government would classify it after a costly and fruitless investigation, left an indelible mark on everyone unfortunate enough to be involved. Some would argue that they had come out stronger and more appreciative of the things they had in their lives. Many, possessed by intractable fear and anguish and haunted by the memory of it all, were never the same.

As for the Hunt family and Donovan and Lindsey, they survived. As awful as the memories were, they used them to become better and stronger people and to grow closer to those they loved. They thought back on Paul daily in their own ways, knowing that he still protected each and every one of them from where he now eternally rested. They would always remember what Hax, the strange man they had known for two days, had done for them, the sacrifice he made for people he hadn't even known.

They wished they could have learned more about him, that they could have had the chance to meet his father – the one who had come to save them all. But mostly, they just wanted the chance to say, "Thank you."

TROKKER

Trokker's ship was spared from being shot out of the sky by Packard, but he didn't escape justice. He and everyone aboard was awarded the opportunity to live for the trip back home, but that was the only assurance they were given. What happened to them when they got there was out of Packard's hands.

Everyone directly involved in the attack was taken into custody of the United States Military Police for transport to a military tribunal. They were accused of treason against the United States of America, the penalty which, under U.S. Code Title 18, was death. Only 50 people had ever been tried and convicted of treason before that. Now, General Packard was bringing back more than 800 who would have to answer for what they had done.

The court martial trial was short; every officer involved received the same verdict.

The enlisted were jailed for life.

A layer of dust from a warm southeasterly breeze covered Trokker's black and scuffed boots. He stood with dozens of other officers in the red dirt just outside the base that not long ago had been his headquarters. This was the first time in history something of this significance had happened in the United States military; it was the first time this many decorated officers were being put to death.

Packard read off their charges and the punishment, staring directly at Trokker whose hands and ankles were shackled.

Trokker held his chin high in typical defiance until the end.

Pop. Pop. Pop.

They hit the dirt one by one, a gray-red puff of dust whipping up to cover their faces.

Trokker lay dead in the dirt alongside his most trusted officers.

There were no funerals, no processions, no 21-gun salutes. Families of the fallen were told their loved ones were killed in "training exercises." Another massive governmental cover-up. The highest-ranked officers were marked in the annals of history as treasonous tyrants intending to "overthrow the United States government" and buried in nondescript coffins in undisclosed locations.

As soon as the counterattack had begun, Sumpter Dixon had bailed from his P-LAV, shed his military garb, and ran like a coward. He had survived a couple of days, avoiding contact with people and staying in the shadows. But it hadn't taken long for a group of young and very pissed-off San Diegans to find the cowering Dix. They had instantly identified him as one of the invaders, despite his pleading and denouncements. Justice was drawn-out and torturous.

PACKARD

Lieutenant General Packard retired a few months after returning to the southwest base and presiding over the conviction of Tokker and his men. He was promoted after his courageous action to Admiral, one of the highest accolades the Space Force offered, which he accepted honorably but, by no means, happily. The cost of victory was simply too high.

He left the military scared of what the future for the United States would hold. His original mission had been to find resources; he had failed. He knew there were plenty of great leaders and Space Force personnel out there to complete the mission and secure the fate of the country. It just wouldn't be him. Fate took him in a different direction. He was sure the country, the world, would succeed.

Humans always found a way to survive, to thrive. When fossil fuels ran out, humans figured it out. When renewable power failed, humans figured it out. Maybe the uranium age was over, but the age of America's greatness would never end. Humans were amazing that way.

The retired admiral went home to hug his wife, to comfort the mother of her dead son, and to live out the rest of his days by her side in peace.

Charlette Packard was a strong and resilient woman and a prideful mom. She took the news of her son's death as well as she possibly could have. She grieved and suffered, but eventually found solace in the fact that he had died doing what he had loved, what he had been born to do. And he had died a hero.

Admiral Packard and his wife moved to a quaint house

just outside downtown San Diego – the place where their son had made his last stand. They took to sitting on a bench in a small park that had belonged to the San Diego Zoo decades ago. There were no displays of recognition for Hax, no memorials, no plaques. That had happened in a different time, in a different place. But Danyel and Charlette knew.

That's why they came every day to pay respects to their son, bringing their own homemade plaque to read as they sat arm-in-arm on the bench.

Major Hax Packard, Our Dear Son

Not many know the man you were, but we do.
Not many know the selfless soldier that you were, but we do.
Not many know the courage it took for you to stand up and do what is right in the face of adversity, but we do.
Not many know of your sacrifice, but we do.
Not many know you were The Hero of San Diego, but we do.
Not many people loved you,
But we do.

"They shall grow not old, as we that are left grow old:
Age shall not worry them, nor the years condemn.
At the going down of the Sun and in the morning
We will remember them."

Robert Lawrence Binyon

Author's Note

The character Paul was loosely based on my closest friend, Jarrett. He was one of the best people I have ever known; I considered him a brother. He had an intense passion to serve his country, which he did as a police officer. He had a deep, loving side, holding friends and family tightly in his heart. He loved my son dearly and my son loved his uncle Jarrett. He was a patriot, he was charming, he was hilarious, he was passionate. He was Jarrett.

But Jarrett took his life at the young age of 31 shortly after I finished my manuscript. His death was unexpected and incredibly tough on all of us who loved him so dearly.

Hug your family and friends as often as you can, and tell them you love them just as frequently.

RJ Hill

About the Author

RJ began writing as a cathartic hobby during his days off from working at the fire department. After having spent years in the profession and witnessing countless emergencies, he became highly aware of how seriously trauma can affect individuals, especially if they did not implement a healthy outlet for that pent-up stress. Writing soon evolved into a passion that took up much of RJ's free time – and most of his imagination.

The Invasion originated as a dream at which time, RJ – not having any writing experience – put pen to paper and wrote out the basic structure of the story. RJ encourages anyone with a story to tell to pursue the craft of creative writing.

RJ lives in a small mountain town in northern Arizona and spends his free time writing and doting over his wife and two young children whom he adores.

To learn more, visit www.rjhillauthor.com.

In Honor of Jarrett

If you or someone you know is suffering from severe depression or contemplating suicide, help is out there. Please seek it.

"Your story isn't over" - **Project;**
projectsemicolon.com

National Suicide Prevention Lifeline: 1-800-273-TALK (8255)
Or Crisis Text Line: Text HELLO to 741741
Or visit www.Suicidepreventionhotline.org.